the State of US

the State of Us

SHAUN DAVID HUTCHINSON

HARPER TEEN
An Imprint of HarperCollinsPublishers

HarperTeen is an imprint of HarperCollins Publishers.

The State of Us
Copyright © 2020 by HarperCollins Publishers

Library of Congress Cataloging-in-Publication Data

Names: Hutchinson, Shaun David, author.
Title: The state of us / by Shaun David Hutchinson.
Description: First edition. | New York : HarperTeen, [2020] | Audience: Ages 13
    up. | Audience: Grades 10-12. | Summary: "Dean and Dre, the seventeen-year-
    old sons of the Republican and Democratic candidates for president of the United
    States, fall in love on the sidelines of their parents' presidential campaigns"
    — Provided by publisher.
Identifiers: LCCN 2019044941 | ISBN 978-0-06-295031-4 (hardcover)
Subjects: CYAC: Politics, Practical—Fiction. | Presidential candidates—Fiction. |
    Dating (Social customs)—Fiction. | Gays—Fiction. | Friendship—Fiction. |
    Family life—Fiction.
Classification: LCC PZ7.H96183 St 2020 | DDC [Fic]—dc23
LC record available at https://lccn.loc.gov/2019044941

Typography by Corina Lupp
20 21 22 23 24   PC/LSCH   10 9 8 7 6 5 4 3 2 1
❖
First Edition

For Katie
Thank you for always having my back.

"NICE SOCKS."

Nice socks? Smooth is not a word anyone anywhere would ever use to describe me. In fact, in the dictionary, under a picture of me, Andre Rosario, would be a list of words that are the opposite of smooth. Bumpy, lumpy, knobby, stony, rocky, rugged, rutted, pitted. I could go on, but I probably shouldn't. You get the point.

But what else was I supposed to say to Dean Arnault, the son of my father's sworn enemy, and therefore *my* sworn enemy? Okay, fine. "Enemy" is probably me being a little extra, but he's still the son of my dad's political opponent in the presidential race, and the holder of some highly questionable political opinions, and therefore not someone I should've been talking to except that his family and my family were in the same room at the same time and *someone* thought it would be a great photo op, so they kept shoving us together. I had to say something before things got super uncomfortable.

Also, they really were nice socks.

Dean Arnault reached up to brush his hand through his hair, stopped, and dropped his hand to his side like he could hear his mother telling him not to mess up the hard work his stylist had put into making him the perfect picture of a young Republican. Sandy hair with an aggressive side part and not a strand out of place, brown eyes, freckled cheeks, a roman nose, and a chiseled jaw with a tiny dimple in his chin. Not that I thought he was cute. He was wearing loafers, for heaven's sake. Loafers! Like a forty-year-old man on his way to the country club to shoot eighteen holes and discuss long-term investment options.

"Thank you," Dean said after a pause that was too short to be long and too long to be brief. It was like he was on a tape delay so that the censors monitoring him through implants in his brain could bleep out anything scandalous before it had the chance to leave his mouth.

"Could you squeeze in a little more?" the photographer said. "This one's for the history books."

"Yes," Janice Arnault said. "The caption underneath will read 'President Arnault and family with presidential hopeful Tomás Rosario.'"

Everyone, including my parents, laughed like Governor Arnault had told a stunningly hilarious joke instead of insinuating that she was going to win the election, even though she was trailing my father by three points according to FiveThirtyEight.com.

"Or," I said, "it might read—" My mother pinched the back of my arm, and I yelped. She was still smiling, but her eyes told me that this was not the time for my mouth, and that if I didn't shut it, there would be oh-so-much hell to pay when we got home.

"It might read something else," I mumbled, but no one was paying attention to me anymore. Which was probably for the best.

I tried not to make any inappropriate faces while the photographer was snapping pictures, but it was pretty difficult. I'd already made concessions by putting on that ridiculous tan suit, even if I worked it harder than any tan suit had been worked in its life. What I'd really wanted to wear was some kind of fabulous suit-gown hybrid like I'd seen Billy Porter strut the red carpet in multiple times. I'd even conceded to cleaning the polish off my fingernails for the night, though I'd then painted my toes Tangerine Scream in protest. Plus, I'd allowed my mom's stylist to cut three inches off my hair even though I'd liked my hair the way it was. All of those concessions had left me with very little patience for putting up with Janice Arnault and the Von Frat family.

"Dre?" My dad nudged me as the photographer asked for some photos of just the Arnaults. "You're not still upset with me, are you?"

I shrugged, refusing to look at my dad. "Upset? Why would I be upset? It's not like I had plans tonight and that you essentially forced me at gunpoint to abandon my best friend in order to attend *this*."

"I'm sure Mel understands," Dad said. "And there was no gun."

"May as well have been." I had trouble seeing my dad the way other people did. To one half of the country, he was the passionate, handsome, future leader of the country. To the other half, he was a baby-killing, Satan-worshipping foreigner who had no business running anything other than a convenience store. But to me, he was the guy who sang Beyoncé songs with a whisk while making pancakes, was afraid of lizards, forced me to attend ridiculous political events when I had better things to do, and had gone from Dad of the Year to Dad Who? in the span of an election cycle.

"This *will* get easier, Dre."

"You mean when you're president and we have Secret Service agents controlling our every move, and we have to be doubly concerned about the press examining the minute details of our private lives and roasting us for every fumble and fuckup?"

"Language, Dre," my mom said from where she was standing with Jose Calderon, my father's dictatorial campaign manager, pretending not to listen in.

Dad chuckled. "It won't be that bad."

"It's already that bad."

4

"Then at least it can't get much worse." My dad slung his arm around me and pulled me into a hug. I caught Dean watching us, and he quickly turned away like the affection embarrassed him. I figured his parents probably thought there was something unmanly about a father hugging his son. Dean and his dad probably exchanged firm handshakes and the occasional nod.

"Besides," my dad went on. "I might not even win."

"What do you think I wish for every night before I go to sleep?"

"Andre?" Jose was waving for my attention. "The photographer wants a couple with just the children."

"I'm seventeen, so, not a child."

"Do it for me," Dad said.

"Not a chance," I replied, but my dad was already pushing me toward Dean, who was standing in front of a tall American flag.

"I know you hate this, Dre, but it's important to me, okay?"

I shook my head. "Whatever. But you owe me so big. Like, maybe it's finally time to buy me a car big."

Dad clapped me on the shoulder. "Not a chance. Have fun!"

Fun. Sure. I couldn't imagine any world where spending a single second with Dean Arnault would be considered fun, but I trudged toward him anyway because that was the sacrifice I was willing to make to help my father become president of the United States.

5

DEAN

THE PHOTOGRAPHER WAVED at me. "Move in a little closer. I'm sure he won't bite." I threw a glance at my mother, who was clustered off to the side with the Rosarios, laughing at something someone had said, though I couldn't imagine what anyone could possibly find amusing about this situation.

"He's wrong, you know," Andre said quietly as I scooted closer to him. "I do bite."

Andre had huge eyes that were an algae green, framed by long eyelashes. His dark hair was wavy, hung down over his forehead, and it managed to look like he spent a lot of time styling it and also like he rolled out of bed with it looking that way. I admit to being jealous. I'd had the same haircut my entire life, and I doubted Nora, my mom's campaign manager, would have allowed me to change it without first polling potential voters.

6

I threw my arm around Andre's shoulders and put on my most winning smile to prove to him that he couldn't get to me.

"That's it!" the photographer said, and started snapping away.

This wasn't the first time I'd met Andre Rosario. Our parents' campaigns crossed paths more often than people might expect. I also knew him from Dreadful Dressup, the website where he and his partner, Mel, posted photos and videos of monster makeup tutorials. Before Mr. Rosario had won the Democratic Party's nomination, more people had recognized Andre's name than his father's. But this was the first time we'd said more than five words to one another, and I honestly wasn't yet sure whether to treat him as friend or foe.

"I didn't pick them out," I said, trying to make conversation while the photographer moved us into different positions.

"What?"

"The socks." I raised my pant leg to reveal one of the socks, which were gray with bright cartoon bumblebees on them. They didn't really match the suit. "A stylist chose them for me."

"That makes me feel better."

"How so?"

Andre mugged for the camera a few more times before the photographer finally declared we were done. My parents had drifted down the hallway, and I was turning to join them when Andre said, "I'd been telling Mel, she's my best friend, that you usually dress like you're heading to a funeral, which I guess is appropriate tonight since my dad's here to bury your mom, but then I saw the socks and thought I'd misjudged you a tiny bit, only I guess I hadn't."

I could have let it go, but Andre's smug attitude wouldn't let me. "My mother's campaign manager believed a whimsical addition to my outfit would help me appeal to *average* people."

Andre cocked his head to the side. "Did you just call me average?"

"I'm sure I said no such thing."

"Whatever. Why don't you go plug yourself into a wall socket somewhere and recharge?"

"Oh," I said. "Ha, ha. Because I'm a robot—"

"Programmed to do what your mommy tells you."

"Funny," I said. "Except for the part where it wasn't."

Andre stood with his arms folded across his chest. After a moment, he said, "Wait, was that your comeback?" He grimaced. "You obviously got your debating skills from your mom."

"I would destroy you in a real debate."

"Yeah. Okay."

A loud crash ricocheted from down the hall. Someone screamed. Two agents in black suits materialized as if from the walls themselves and were suddenly herding Andre and me into the greenroom they had assigned my mother.

One of the agents, a serious woman with finger-length black hair, poked her head in and said, "Do not leave this room under any circumstances." Her voice was stern and left no room for argument.

"What's going on?" Andre called. "Where're my parents? Is everyone okay—"

But the agent shut the door without answering either question, and when Andre tried to open it, he found that it was locked. He pounded on the door a few times before leaning with his back to it and sliding to the ground.

The whole thing had taken fifteen, maybe twenty seconds, and I wasn't sure *what* had happened, therefore I had no idea whether this was a false alarm and that everything would be all right or if this was a real emergency and that I should be worried.

"Do you have your phone?" I asked.

Before I finished, Andre was digging into his pocket for his cell phone, tapping the screen. I did the same. I tried calling both my parents and Nora, but I couldn't get a signal.

"Damn it!" Andre held his phone like he was about to throw it across the room, which likely wouldn't have helped the situation. "Can't get through."

"Neither can I," I said.

"I'm not surprised with that antique." Andre's voice was shaky. "Isn't that model from like five years ago?"

Heat rose in my cheeks. "I have a tendency to lose things, so my parents see no sense in spending a lot of money on a new phone I'm likely to forget somewhere."

Andre was quiet for a moment, probably doing whatever he could to avoid worrying about what might be happening

9

on the other side of those doors. "It's kind of reassuring to know you're not perfect."

"I never claimed to be perfect, Andre."

"The news sure loves playing it like you are." He looked up at me. "According to them, you're Captain America, volunteering your time to teach underprivileged kids to read and build houses, while I basically murder puppies."

I was scared, which made me want to fire back at Andre, but he was probably scared too. Instead, I grabbed a water from the table and brought it to him. "Here. The first rule of being on the campaign trail is to stay hydrated."

"Thanks." Andre took the water and twisted off the cap but didn't drink. "And it's Dre."

"Pardon?"

"My name," he said. "It's Dre. Only my dad's campaign manager calls me Andre. And my mom, but only if she's really angry, and then she calls me 'Andre Santiago Rosario,' and it's usually followed by some form of 'What did you do?' and a bit of mild profanity."

I smiled in spite of myself. "Good to know. And, hey, I'm certain Secret Service has everything under control. More than likely it's a bomb threat or—"

Dre's eyes popped. "You think there's a bomb?!"

"I did not say that—"

"You know what? How about you don't say anything at all, okay?"

"Sure," I said. "Fine by me."

DRE

I STOOD WITH my ear pressed to the door, trying to hear what was going on in the hallway. It was eerily quiet. The kind of quiet that sent my mind spinning off in a thousand directions, imagining all the different potentially dangerous scenarios that could be playing out.

"Anything?" Dean asked.

"Nope. Not a sound."

"That could be a good sign."

"Or it could mean that some politician-hating dudes with guns are holding everyone hostage, including our parents, in some other wing of the school, and that they're going to start shooting them at any moment."

"I highly doubt that."

"Of course," I said. "Your side practically worships guns,

so I'm sure your parents aren't in any real danger."

The first debate was being held at the University of Miami, which Jose had protested because he claimed it gave Governor Arnault the advantage, but my dad hadn't minded, and it had allowed Jose to ensure the second debate would be held in Nevada. Of course, I bet none of this would've happened if we'd held the debate somewhere boring like North Dakota.

Dean was sitting on a couch with one leg crossed over the other like we were about to enjoy brandy and cigars and engage in casual sexism. He'd been trying to get a signal or log onto the building's Wi-Fi but hadn't had any luck. "How can you be so calm?" I asked.

"Because I trust that the Secret Service details guarding our parents have got everything under control."

"Well, I don't. I haven't been this freaked out since the last time my school went on lockdown for an active shooter." In search of something to eat, I crossed the room to the table where Dean had gotten me the water earlier. There were individual containers of Greek yogurt and bowls of fresh fruit and granola. "Where're the actual snacks?"

"My mother prefers healthy foods."

I ate a handful of granola, but as soon as it hit my stomach, I wished I hadn't. "This isn't food."

"Then why are you stuffing so much of it in your mouth?"

Granola crumbs tumbled down the front of my suit as I rounded on Dean. "Because my parents are out there and I don't know what's happening to them! They could be in a room with a bomb that someone with no experience is going to have to disarm at the last second by cutting the red wire or the blue wire, or there might be a gun-toting psycho roaming the halls looking for someone to kill, and I want to do something—I *have* to do something!—but I can't because I'm locked in this fucking room with you. And the only thing I can do that doesn't involve digging a tunnel out of here is eating food I don't even want! All right? Is that okay with you?"

Ugh. Talking to Dean was like trying to have a meaningful conversation with one of the Secret Service agents.

"I don't actually like guns," Dean said. "My uncle tried to take me hunting when I was eleven, but I couldn't justify killing something I had no intention of eating. Also, when my uncle took down a deer, I cried until I vomited."

"Right, you're a vegetarian. I remember reading that about you." I filled a bowl with strawberries, unsure whether I was going to eat them or throw them at Dean, and resumed pacing around the room while trying not to wonder whether my parents were being held in a room like this or if they were squeezed into a closet along with a dozen other people. "How does your mom feel about having a gun-hating animal lover for a son?"

Dean shrugged. "Just because I don't like guns doesn't mean I don't support the right of others to own them."

I rolled my eyes. Just when I thought we were getting somewhere. "Of course you do."

13

"I suppose you believe we should collect all the guns in the world and shoot them into the sun?"

"It's a lot harder to commit mass murder with a knife." I stopped and flashed Dean a cold look. "Anyway, how can you sit and argue about this shit when our parents' lives might be in danger?!"

Dean held my eyes for a moment before looking away. "Sorry," he said. "I thought if you were fighting with me, you wouldn't worry about your parents as much as I'm worrying about mine."

I opened my mouth to fire the next insult but stopped short. Dean had been trying to help, albeit in a deeply strange way. Goading him into a fight wouldn't have been my preferred method for distracting *him*, but he deserved some credit for the effort.

"Sorry for popping off like that. It's just that I keep imagining all the things that could be happening and every scenario is worse than the next."

"Don't worry about it," Dean said. "It was a bad idea anyway. It's not as if it would have been a fair fight."

I raised an eyebrow at him. "Didn't we already establish this? I'd decimate you."

"Historically, 'decimate' meant to kill one in ten of a group of people, and even in modern usage it doesn't mean to defeat someone or something but rather to destroy a large portion of it."

14

The tiny bit of gratefulness I'd felt toward him before was already evaporating. The last thing I needed from Professor Dean was a vocabulary lesson. "Whatever," I said. "I'd still kick your ass in a fair fight."

Dean was smiling when he finally looked up, and he caught my eye and winked. "If you say so."

"I do!"

"Fine, then."

"Fine!" He was still smiling, so I scowled back and resumed pacing. "I don't know what I did to wind up stuck in a room with you, but I'm sorry for it."

"You're not stuck in here with me," Dean said. "We're stuck in here together, and my mother always says accidents are just opportunities in disguise."

"Your mom also thinks people like me don't deserve the same rights as everyone else, so excuse me if I'm not super keen on anything she has to say on anything."

DEAN

"KNOW YOUR ENEMY" is what my mother would have said. "Be kind to strangers" is what my father would have told me. I didn't know whether Dre was a stranger, my enemy, or both. The only thing I knew for certain was that he hated me, though I wasn't sure what I'd done to deserve his ire. He obviously believed the propaganda about my mother—that she was going to attempt to overturn the Supreme Court decision granting marriage rights to same-sex couples—but he didn't know *me* at all.

"My dad turned down his Secret Service detail." Dre had been pacing around the room eating strawberries for a solid five minutes, acting like I didn't exist.

"I wasn't aware that was something he could do."

Dre nodded. "The only person who can't refuse a Secret

16

Service detail is the sitting president." He paused and set down the now-empty bowl. "He said he didn't want to waste the taxpayers' money."

"That seems like a poor decision."

"'Idiotic' was the word my mom used," he said. "She yelled at him for a solid twenty minutes and told him that if anyone hurt him, they'd better kill him because if they didn't, she would."

Each time Dre wasn't looking directly at me, my eyes darted toward the door. "It sounds like your father might need the Secret Service just to protect him from your mother."

A sharp laugh escaped Dre, and he looked embarrassed by it. "Yeah, he might." His smile faded, and he threw up his hands. "How are you so calm? I mean, I'm freaking out. Why aren't you freaking out?"

"Just because I don't vocalize every fear that scurries through my brain doesn't mean I'm not absolutely terrified that my mother and father are potentially in a life-threatening situation at the moment. The best I can do is pray that everything turns out all right because otherwise I might pound on the door until someone tells me what's going on or my knuckles bleed."

I half expected my tirade would quiet Dre for a while, or at least confuse him into silence, but it seemingly had the opposite effect.

"I was pissed at my dad for making me come here," he said. "Ever since he started campaigning, he doesn't have time to hang out with me unless he needs something from me, like being his prop kid at the debate tonight. Only I had plans with Mel that I had to bail on, and I feel like an asshole for being pissed because he might be hurt and all I can think is that I didn't want to be here in the first place and I was hoping he'd lose so we could go back to our normal lives. I don't want my dad to die thinking I was mad at him."

I wasn't sure if Dre had meant to say all of those things, or what I should respond to. He obviously had some unresolved feelings surrounding his father's run for president, which I could relate to.

"Have you ever told your father what you told me?"

Dre flopped into a chair, finally relaxing a little for the first time since we'd been locked in the greenroom. "He asked me before he ran if I was okay with it."

That came as a surprise, and I couldn't hide my shock. "He did?"

Dre nodded. "Yup. Told me he had a shot, mostly because of the attention he got as the AG working on those immigration cases, but that he'd wait until after I graduated high school if I wanted."

"Why didn't you ask him to wait, then?"

"Because I didn't think he had a chance in hell!" Dre's wild laugh was unsettling. The stress seemed to be getting to him, and I was starting to wonder if I might be safer out in the hall, but we were each dealing with the stressful situation in our own way. "I told him to go for it because I figured he'd flame out during the primaries. Who was gonna vote for my dad, right?"

"Quite a lot of people, as it turns out," I said.

Dre's laughter dissolved; his smile faded. "Yeah. When that little kid died after being separated from his parents at the border, and my dad made that speech, I was like, 'Oh shit. He's got a real chance.'"

"I remember the speech. It was a good one." It had been better than good. The speech had galvanized the Democratic Party behind Rosario and had helped him stand out from the other candidates and secure the nomination.

"After that, I wished I'd asked him to wait," Dre said. "But it's not like I could change my mind without being a total ass."

"Is it the attention that bothers you?" I asked.

Dre shrugged. "Partly. I mean, I know I'm graduating next year and going to college, but I can't do anything without everyone watching and judging and offering snarky commentary."

"You were famous before anyone knew who your father was," I said. "How is this different?"

"The people who knew me from Dreadful Dressup didn't care about *me*. They only cared about whether Mel and I were gonna do some zombie shit for our next video or go in a creepy Cthulhu direction. Now it's like I can't do anything without someone thinking I'm making a statement. People I've never met want to know everything about me. I'm not into changing the world; I just wanna do monster makeup."

19

"Oh." It seemed silly to have that kind of platform and *not* want to help people with it, but I didn't press Dre about it. "What's the other part?"

"What?"

"You said 'partly.' So what's the other part?"

Dre's shoulders slumped. "I know this is gonna sound silly, but I miss my dad. He was, like, my best friend, and now he's never around." There was a moment where it looked like Dre was going to tear up, but then he shook it off. "Anyway, I want my dad to win because he's my dad and he'd be the first Mexican American president *and* I think he'd actually be good at the job, but I kind of want him to lose because I'm selfish and I liked my life the way it was before."

"I get it."

"You do?" Dre's eyebrows were drawn together, and he wore this shocked look like I'd admitted to secretly believing in socialized medicine. "I figured you'd be all about it. Like you've probably got campaign stickers in your locker at school and already know how you're gonna decorate your bedroom in the White House."

I shrugged and nodded. "Those things are true, but sometimes I wonder what it would be like to live a normal life. Before I was the Republican presidential candidate's son, I was the governor's son, and before that I was the war hero's kid. I don't even know what it's like to *not* live under the spotlight. To not have to worry about how I dress or what I say.

"People make fun of me for being so reserved, but it's

better than having them mock me for getting in trouble or embarrassing my family. Not doing either of those things is pretty important to me, though it comes with a price." I'd never admitted any of that before, not even to my friends, but Dre might have been the only person in the world at that moment capable of understanding.

Dre's eyes were wide, somewhere between surprise and pity. "Of all the stuff to have in common, I never figured this would be one."

"You're lucky your dad asked you, though," I said. "My mother never gave me a choice."

TALKING TO DEAN like he was a normal person and not the button-down shirt–wearing antithesis of everything I believed in was weird. I might've once bet Mel that Dean slept hanging upside down in his closet and had underwear labeled for each day of the week, but he was different from what I'd expected, and talking to him was the only thing keeping me from tearing the door off the hinges and forcing the agent outside to tell me what the hell was going on. Even weirder was that talking to Dean was kind of okay.

Maybe I should have been reassured that I hadn't heard anyone yelling outside the door or felt the ground shake from an explosion, but my overactive mind filled in the blanks. I was sure that what I was imagining was worse than the reality, but I couldn't help myself. I don't know what I would've done if Dean hadn't been in the greenroom with me. Talking and arguing with him kept me from fully panicking.

"But you had to know she was gonna run, right?" I said. "Your mom's practically been campaigning since the start of her second term as governor." Whereas my dad's candidacy had felt like a long shot, Governor Arnault's had felt inevitable.

Dean was sitting on the couch, twisting and untwisting the cap on his water bottle. He had the best posture of anyone I'd ever seen, but I wondered if he ever relaxed. Not that this was a relaxing situation.

"Sure," Dean said. "I knew. Everyone knew. It still would have been nice if she had asked me, though."

The longer I spent with Dean, the more I realized he was more complex than I had originally given him credit for. He wasn't quiet because he had nothing to say, he was just more reserved than me. Okay, compared to me, everyone was more reserved. But I was starting to pick up on his tells. The twitch of his lip meant he thought something was funny; he flared his nostrils when he was thinking about something he didn't like; his eyebrows dipped in the middle when he was talking about his mom.

"I would have said yes, of course," he added.

"Of course," I echoed. But the way Dean narrowed his eyes made me wonder if he would have *wanted* to say yes.

Dean cleared his throat. "Either way, it's going to be interesting for whoever winds up in the White House."

"'Interesting' hardly covers it," I said. "Like, am I gonna

23

have any privacy at all? I'll have to move to DC and start a new school for the last five months of senior year. How am I gonna make friends when everyone I meet'll have to be cleared by Secret Service agents? And it's not like I'll be able to sneak out to go to parties."

"You seem like you're pretty good at making friends," Dean said. "I'm sure you'll be okay."

"But what about dating? I've never even had a boyfriend. How am I going to navigate all that?"

Dean shrugged it off. "It's not a big deal."

"Not a big deal?" I knew there were bigger, more important issues than me getting a boyfriend, but sometimes it felt like it was the only thing on my mind. Ever since I'd come out, I'd been dreaming of my first perfect date and my first perfect kiss and my first perfect . . . everything else. It felt like a big deal to me, and I didn't understand how Dean could be so blasé about it. "I suppose it's because you've gone on lots of dates."

"No."

"No girlfriends or boyfriends or anything?"

"Nope."

"And you're not worried you're going to miss the opportunity to find that perfect special someone who's out there waiting for you and without whom you'll wind up alone and lonely for the rest of your life, living with a bunch of shelter dogs and eating cake frosting right out of the container?"

Dean chuckled and rolled his eyes, which for him was the

equivalent of boisterous laughter. "I'm really not. And you shouldn't be either. I mean, first of all, you're assuming that everyone in the world wants to fall in love and that sex is the end-all-be-all of the teenage experience. It's not."

I let out an exasperated sigh. "I know. But I wasn't assuming it about everyone."

"Just me."

"Wait, let me guess. Sex isn't your thing?" I threw it out there as a joke because I had assumed Dean was as obsessed with guns, girls, and glory as the majority of voters expected the seventeen-year-old son of the Republican candidate for president to be.

Dean cocked his head to the side and pursed his lips, pausing a moment before answering. "It's not *not* my thing. Truthfully, I don't know."

The admission caught me off guard, and I had a *million* questions. Was I the only person who knew? Was I the first person he'd ever admitted that to? What, exactly, had he even actually admitted to? Why had he told me? Was it because he knew I was gay? I didn't ask those or any of the million other questions I had. Instead, I said, "Okay?" which Dean seemed to interpret as confusion.

"Asexuality is a spectrum, right?" he said. "I'm somewhere on that spectrum, though I'm not sure where yet. There could be someone out there I might want to have sex with, but I'm honestly not in a hurry to find them."

This was blowing my mind. Hearing Dean Arnault

25

admit he was on the asexual spectrum had totally made me forget that we were having this conversation because we were trapped in a room due to a potential threat to one or all of our parents' lives. Nothing about Dean had made me think for a second that he was like me, and the more I thought about it, the more I wondered what else we might have in common.

"So if there was someone," I said, unable to keep myself from prying, "do you know what they might be like?"

There was that twitch of the lip, that barely there smile. "Not yet. But I believe I'll know them if I find them."

Dean's answer was frustrating but also honest, and I couldn't fault him for it. "Aren't you afraid I might tell someone?"

The easy expression Dean was wearing slipped, and he flared his nostrils. "Are you planning to tell someone?"

"No! I just—"

"Because if you tell anyone, I'll simply deny it. I'll say you made it up, and no one will believe you." Dean looked like he was on the verge of a nuclear meltdown. His face went pale and he looked a bit sick. I don't know if he'd meant to tell me his secret, if it'd slipped out due to the stress of worrying about our parents, or if he'd just needed to tell someone and I was the first person he thought he could remotely trust with the information, but I didn't want him thinking I was going to run off and blab to everyone about him.

"I'm not gonna tell," I said. "I wouldn't do that to you or anyone. Not ever."

"Promise?" Dean asked.

"On my parents' lives." At that moment, I couldn't have made a more serious pledge.

Dean's smile didn't return, but he looked a little less freaked out. "Thank you."

DEAN

BEING TRAPPED IN the greenroom with the son of my mother's chief political rival while not being able to talk to my parents or discover anything about what was going on was terrifying. Neither Dre nor I could get a signal or connect to Wi-Fi, and it felt like we were completely cut off from the world. I was sure my parents would contact me if they could, which was what was worrying me. Something was either blocking cell signals or preventing my parents from using their phones. I hoped it was the former and prayed it wasn't the latter.

I was doing my best to project an exterior of calm because that's what my mother would have expected me to do. She would have told me to lead by example, and I was trying, but it wasn't easy. My fear felt too big for my body, and I wanted to scream it out, but doing so wouldn't have helped my parents, and it would have probably upset Dre even more.

"Are you scared?" Dre asked.

"I used to have nightmares about situations like this when I was younger," I said. "I'd seen protesters outside one of my mother's rallies when she was running for governor, and there were these people screaming and yelling. I don't even remember what they were saying, but I remember the hate in their eyes. It was the first time I realized people actually hated my mother and might want to hurt her, and I couldn't stop being scared for her." I cleared my throat.

Dre was watching me curiously. When he didn't reply immediately, I assumed I'd spooked him by revealing too much. But then he said, "I meant about coming out. Are you scared about what would happen if you came out?"

I felt foolish and lowered my eyes.

"For the record," Dre said. "I'm scared for my parents too."

If I hadn't been locked in that room, I would have made an excuse to leave and fled from the conversation. I was feeling vulnerable and embarrassed for telling Dre that story. But since I couldn't leave, I did what any self-respecting southerner would have done. I pretended it had never happened.

"I don't know if I'm scared about coming out," I said. "You're the first person I've told, and it wasn't so terrible."

"I'm the first person you've told?" Dre stood again and raked his hands through his hair. "This is huge, Dean! I mean, I'm honored, but there should be cake or something."

"Cake?"

"Yes! I think everyone's coming out should involve cake." He stopped pacing and turned to me, wearing this endearingly goofy smile. "Don't you think people would be less anxious about having to do it if they knew there'd be cake at the end?"

"I don't need a cake, and it's not a big deal. I came to terms with being different a while ago, and I figured I'd tell people when necessary." I spread my hands. "Honestly, I've never understood why people feel the need to come out. The only people who really need to know your sexual orientation are your potential sexual or romantic partners."

If I'd learned one thing about Dre in our short time together, it was that he couldn't control his facial expressions. He wore his emotions plainly on the outside. It was kind of sweet, though it would have made it almost too easy for me to beat him in a debate. At the moment, he was looking shocked.

"What?" I asked.

"Nothing," Dre said. "It's just . . . I didn't expect you to be—"

"Anything more than a clone of my mother?"

"Like me."

Dre's answer might have offended me under different circumstances, but there was such an honesty to it that it caught me a bit off guard. Only, before I could come up with a suitable response, the lights flickered and cut out, plunging the room into darkness.

"Dean?!"

"Stay where you are," I said. "The emergency lights will come on in—"

The emergency lights over the door flared to life, bathing the walls in their halogen glow.

"What the hell is going on, Dean?"

I didn't know, and I didn't want to lie to Dre. My heart was pounding faster and my mouth was dry. Keeping him calm was the only thing keeping *me* calm. "Sit," I told him. "You don't want to trip in the dark and break your leg."

Dre marched mechanically to the couch and sat across from me. He tugged at his tie and tried his phone again, his frustration growing. "I can't deal with this!"

"Everything will be fine," I said. "I promise." It would only be a lie if I couldn't keep that promise, but I couldn't bear to see Dre so upset, especially about something over which we had no control.

"Maybe this time, but what about next time? Or the time after that?"

"There's always a bomb scare or a threatening letter or a suspicious package." I was supposed to be trying to make Dre feel better, and I realized I was probably having the opposite effect, so I hurried along. "But in all of the years my mother's been in office, she's never even come close to being in real danger because the people in charge of her security are good at their jobs. And so is the Secret Service."

"I hate this! I hate that every time my dad leaves the house, I'm worried someone with a gun and a twenty-page

31

handwritten manifesto is going to find him and shoot him." He stood and began pacing again despite the dark. "This whole thing is ridiculous. Journalists digging into the most obscure parts of our lives, photographers following us everywhere. What's the upside? What makes this worth the bullshit?"

I tried to come up with an answer that wouldn't sound cheesy, but honesty often carries a whiff of cheese. "The opportunity to make the world a better place. That's the only good reason to do it."

"Is it enough?"

"I hope so."

Dre sat back down, looking slightly more relaxed than before. "Thanks," he said. "I tried talking to Mel about this stuff, but I don't think she gets it."

"I know what you mean."

Dre smiled. "You really do, don't you?"

IF SOMEONE HAD told me that Dean Arnault would be the one who kept me from having a panic attack while my parents' lives were potentially in danger, I would have laughed so hard I might've peed my pants. The idea that we could have anything in common was ludicrous. Yet, there we were, sitting in the dark having a conversation like two people who could've been friends. And the messed-up thing was that there was a small part of me that didn't want the lockdown to end so that I could spend more time alone with Dean.

"So your parents don't know about you, then?" I asked. Dean and I had fallen back into silence, and I needed to keep talking or my brain would spin out scenarios about what was happening on the other side of the doors—like the one where a dude with a bomb strapped to his chest had cornered my parents so he could tell them his hard-luck story and make them feel sympathy for him before blowing them up—and I wanted to avoid that.

"No."

"Is it because your mom would disown you or something?"

Dean's mouth tightened into a frown. "No," he said. "She wouldn't because she's not an awful person. I haven't told her, or anyone, because there's nothing to tell yet. When I know for sure, I'll tell my parents, but until then it's no one's business but mine."

I felt like I'd struck a raw nerve. "What'd I say? I didn't mean to pry."

"It's not that." Dean dry-washed his hands, rubbing them over and over.

"Then what?"

"Before you met me, you'd made these assumptions about me, most of which were probably wrong. And now that you know this one thing about me—a thing that I don't even consider to be a particularly huge part of who I am—you're making an entirely new set of assumptions about me. Most of which are also probably wrong."

"You may not think it's a big part of who you are," I said, "but it's still a big deal. And you can't tell me that your mom running for president isn't affecting your decision to keep it to yourself."

34

Dean opened his mouth, but nothing came out for a second. It was the first time I think I'd stumped him. Finally, he said, "Can we not talk about this anymore?"

I hadn't expected to see Dean look so unsure of himself. I had him on the run, and I could've gone on the attack, really nailed him for being queer and supporting his mom, who definitely didn't support our community, but no matter how Dean had played it off, it'd taken a lot of courage for him to tell me his secret, and I owed him better than jumping on him for it.

I held out my hand. "Gimme your phone."

"Excuse me?"

"Your cell phone?" I said. "Square, flat, probably got some pictures on it you wouldn't want your friends swiping through."

"There are no such pictures."

I couldn't help rolling my eyes. "It was a joke. Now gimme your phone. Unlocked."

Part of me expected Dean to refuse. I'm not sure I would've given up my phone, and if I had, I'm sure Jose would've cussed me out for it. Besides, I was the son of his mother's enemy. But that didn't mean we had to be enemies, did it? Dean and I could be friends, even if our parents weren't.

Dean reached into his coat pocket, unlocked his phone, and handed it to me. The background picture was his mother's campaign logo.

"Mama's boy."

"And proud of it." Dean watched me quietly for a second before saying, "What, exactly, are you doing?"

I held up his phone so he could see. "Downloading Promethean." The app's icon was a stylized flame.

"Okay?"

"And now I'm setting up your account and adding my username to your contacts."

"Why again?"

I sighed the sigh of the weary. Clearly, I had a lot to teach Dean. "Promethean is totally secure. Like, end-to-end encryption that even the company doesn't have the keys to." Dean was still watching me like I was speaking in Klingon. "It's so we can talk? Without anyone knowing? In case you want to. About whatever."

"You want to talk to me?"

"I mean, yeah," I said. "You're not totally horrible, and you're kind of the only other person in the world who gets what this is like."

"I thought people only used this app for sending dick pics and cheating on their significant others."

"Hold up," I said. "I'm having trouble wrapping my brain around hearing you say 'dick pics.'" I shut my eyes and shuddered, though I'd be lying if I said I wouldn't have been into getting a couple of those pics from Dean. He wasn't the type of guy I usually thought was cute, but there was definitely something about his stern-economics-professor-at-a-wealthy-private-school vibe that I liked.

"I'm serious. What are we going to talk about?"

"I don't know. Whatever we want. School, college, how annoying all this presidential stuff is?" I couldn't believe I was having to explain to Dean what two people talked about. He probably didn't have any friends that his mom hadn't vetted and approved.

I handed Dean back his phone. "All set."

Dean immediately tapped the icon to open it. "Prez-MamasBoy?" He glared down his nose at me, and I broke out in a grin, unable to help myself.

"I'm in there as DreOfTheDead. You can change your name if you really hate it."

Dean shook his head, but there was a hint of a smile playing on his lips. "It's fine. The missing possessive apostrophe is killing me, but at least you've come around to correctly assuming my mother's going to win the election."

"Like hell," I said. "Maybe Jackson McMann will surprise everyone and beat both our parents."

"There is an almost zero-percent chance of that happening."

"That's why it'd be a surprise."

Jackson McMann was a billionaire who'd made his fortune starting up and then selling tech companies. He had a reputation for treating his employees like garbage, for thumbing his nose at the law, and for exploiting anyone and everything he could in order to make money. According to my dad, he was an entitled rich dude who'd entered the race as an independent

37

to create chaos and line his own pockets, and because he liked seeing his face on the news. According to my mom, he was an asshole.

"The only way McMann could possibly win is by cheating," Dean said. "And I wouldn't put it past him."

As I nodded my agreement, Dean furrowed his brow and looked at his phone. "Wait, how did you download this if there's no signal?"

Dean was right. I shouldn't have been able to access the app store. "I just—"

The lights came back on, and I stood and rushed toward the door as the agent who'd shut us in peeked her head in and told us the lockdown was over.

"My parents?" I asked.

"Everyone is safe and secure."

Relief flooded through me, and my legs felt like jelly as the adrenaline surge that had been keeping me upright dissolved. I had to hold on to the wall for a second to keep steady.

"See?" Dean said. "I told you everything would be all right."

Moments later, the Arnaults showed up, followed by my parents. My mom and dad wouldn't stop hugging me, even though Dad said there hadn't actually been anything to worry about. A shelf in a janitorial closet had collapsed, spilling chemicals on the floor that might have been dangerous but ultimately weren't. The power going out had been a fluke and had been unconnected to the scare.

"At least you weren't trapped in a room with Jose," my dad was saying as we got ready to leave. "He used the time to force me to go over my schedule for the rest of the week. It was pure torture."

"Sounds like it," I said, but I kept stealing glances at Dean.

From across the room, Governor Arnault said, "I hope you weren't too bored, Dean."

That hint of a smile that I'd come to recognize hit Dean's lips, and he risked looking my way. "Actually, it wasn't terrible."

Not terrible. Dean Arnault thought spending time with me "wasn't terrible." I don't know why that made me so happy, but it kind of really did.

DEAN

I STOOD OVER Tamal, holding my hands under the bar as he breathed in, preparing to lift. Tamal bared his teeth and grunted as he pushed. His arms wobbled and I wasn't sure if he was going to make it, but with one final burst of energy, he powered through. I grabbed the weight, guiding it onto the rack.

Tamal sat up, grinning. "Two-seventy-five, baby!" He grabbed a towel from between his legs and mopped the sweat from his angelic face.

I'd known Tamal since my family had moved to Tallahassee. We were on the baseball team together, and he'd run my campaign for class president. He'd created an app that let students rank issues they thought were the most important. I hadn't thought anyone would bother with it, but Tamal is a heck of a coder and people really love ranking things.

"Good job," I said. "Pretty soon you'll be joining the two-hundred-percent club."

"Doubt it." But Tamal was flexing his arms like he could already see himself lifting 200 percent of his body weight. And maybe he would. Tamal was the kind of guy who usually succeeded through hard work and perseverance. His charming smile and personality helped, but he didn't need them.

The gym was quiet, still in that space between the end of school and the end of work when the only people who were there were students like Tamal and me or adults who weren't stuck in a nine-to-five job. It was a locally owned place, not as big or clean as some of the chains. They taught boxing in the evenings, the owners were nice, and they knew about my mom and made sure no one bothered me, including the press.

"Your turn." Tamal wiped down the bench and helped me change out the weights. I considered myself in good shape, but Tamal seriously outclassed me.

It felt good to push myself, to feel my pectoral muscles stretch and contract as I held the bar steady and drove it upward, defying gravity. I was going to hurt a little when I was done, but it was a good hurt. There was satisfaction in the pain gained from doing something honest and pure. I guess that sounds a little ridiculous, but I felt no shame enjoying a little simplicity in a complicated world.

"You can do better than that," Tamal said between sets. "Gotta make sure you stay in shape until baseball starts or Coach will kick *my* ass."

"Fine. Add another ten pounds, please." The weights clanked as Tamal slid them onto the ends of the bar, and then I quickly grabbed the bar and started the set. An extra ten pounds may not sound like much, but there's a fine line between the exact right amount of weight and too much. Luckily, I had Tamal spotting me.

My arms were jelly after I finished, and I didn't think I could lift so much as a bag of flour, so Tamal and I hit the treadmills. It might have been fall everywhere else in the country, but it was still summer in Florida. Not only was it hot, but there were clouds of gnats everywhere waiting to fly into my mouth. And then there were the mosquitoes. I hated running outside when I didn't have to.

Tamal and I fell into our strides, his heavy-footed and quick, mine light and long. I liked running for the same reason I liked lifting. It was easy to lose myself in the rhythm of it. It was one of the few times when I felt free to let my thoughts and worries fall away and I could exist as the embodiment of physical effort.

But there was one thought I couldn't outrun.

"You know there's a real chance that I won't be playing this season, right?"

"It's your senior year, Dean. We're gonna be co-captains."

42

"I know," I said. "But when my mother wins the election, we'll be moving to Washington, DC. She's already introduced me to the baseball coach at the school I'll be attending and selected my classes, and I've looked into a mentoring program where I can volunteer."

The probability of my mother winning the election had gone up slightly since the debate. Mr. Rosario was magnetic when he was given the space to speak at length, but debates were an area where my mother excelled. Not only did she come armed with facts, but she understood how to deliver them in concise, devastating shots. During her first gubernatorial debate, a newspaper reporter had noted my mother's uncanny ability to slide in a kill shot right before she ran out of time, creating perfect sound bites and viral video clips.

Each side had declared their candidate the winner, and different media sites had provided legitimate analyses of why one candidate had won over the other, and while Mr. Rosario had done well, a week later people were still talking about my mother.

Tamal grunted. "Trying not to think about that, Dean."

"It's difficult for me to not think about it."

"You could stay with me," he said. "You know my folks would go for it. At least so you can finish out senior year."

I didn't bother arguing with Tamal because we both knew it wasn't his parents I'd need to convince. There was no way my mother would let me live with Tamal and miss the opportunity to present the Arnaults as the perfect first family.

"Wait," Tamal said. "Does that mean Astrid's going to be class prez if you go?"

"She's class vice president," I said. "So, yes. She would take over."

"Oh."

"Why?"

"No reason." Tamal glanced at me and stumbled, grabbing the railings to keep from being thrown back against the wall. He cleared his throat when he was running steadily again. "What do you think of her? Astrid, I mean."

I shrugged. "She's a good vice president, editor of the school paper, and she's on the debate team. I think she'll be a good president."

Tamal was avoiding looking at me, which was strange. "I mean, personally."

It took me a moment for the clues to click into place. "You like Astrid?"

Red bloomed across Tamal's cheeks. "Kinda, yeah. She's smart and cute, and I was thinking I might ask her to homecoming."

I held up my hands. "I'm certainly not judging, but homecoming is less than two weeks away. Why have you waited so long?"

"Oh, well, my sister heard Astrid was getting back together with her ex, and I didn't want to get in the middle of all that, but then Nadiya said the ex was toast and I should make my move. Only, you never have a date to these things and we always kind of go as a team, but maybe since you're not gonna be around . . ."

Following Tamal's circuitous explanation took a bit of effort. "I'm going to be here for homecoming."

"But what about after?" he asked. "I know it's not your fault, but I have to start taking care of myself, you know? I won't ask her if you don't want me to, though. We can hit homecoming together, you and me one last time. You might be abandoning me, but you're still my best friend."

I felt like I'd been punched in the gut. My mother hadn't won the election, but Tamal was already making plans like I wasn't going to be in his life. And he was right to do so. Until Election Day, my life was on hold. I couldn't commit to anything too far in the future, and my friends couldn't rely on me. It was one more reason to resent my mother for running, but it was difficult to resent her for doing something she believed in, even if it did complicate my life.

Sometimes we had to make sacrifices for the people we loved. "I think you should ask Astrid to homecoming," I said. "And I think you should do it now."

Tamal was looking at me with big bug eyes. "Like, right now?"

"You have to give the girl time to find a dress."

I watched as Tamal paused the treadmill, got his phone, and called Astrid. He talked to her nearly every day, and yet he kept fumbling over his words now like she was a total stranger.

"She said yes!" Tamal practically squealed, which was endearing. As he started jogging again, a couple of guys nearby threw him a look and shook their heads, but they wisely kept their thoughts to themselves.

"Was there ever any doubt?"

Tamal looked happier than I'd seen him since lunch. He really liked lunch. And dinner. Meals in general.

"Let me hook you up with someone," he said. "Then we can still go together. A double date. You could drive, and we could take the girls to that fancy French place, Chaleur."

I had to put the brakes on Tamal before he planned out the entire night. "I've got to do the whole royal court thing, which will keep me busy, and you know I'm not much of a dancer."

"Unlike me."

"Tamal," I said. "You are my best friend, my brother, my personal computer genius, and you bake a heck of a cake, but you are not a good dancer."

"Says you."

"Says everyone." I ignored Tamal when he rolled his eyes like he couldn't be bothered with the truth about his dancing. "But we can still go as a group. I'll drive and pick you up."

"Like my own private chauffer?"

"No."

"I feel bad you flying solo."

"Don't," I said. "It doesn't bother me."

Tamal's eye caught something on one of the TVs mounted in front of the treadmills. It was me. Well, it was me and my mother and father, and the Rosarios. One of the photos from the debate. We all looked suitably composed and were smiling as if we might have been close friends under different circumstances. Maybe we still could be. Stranger things had happened. Like the unlikely friendship between George W. Bush and Michelle Obama.

"You met the Rosario kid, right?"

"I did."

"And? What's he like?"

Trying to find a way to describe Dre was like trying to describe the feeling of finally scratching an itch in the center of your back that's been bothering you for hours. Amazing, but also weird because scraping at your skin with your nails or a wooden spoon or whatever you can find that will reach the spot shouldn't feel so good. "He was all right," I said. "Excitable and odd, but generally nice."

"Seems like the kind of kid who'd cause a lot of trouble living in the White House."

A smile crept up on me. "He does, doesn't he?"

"What'd you guys talk about while you were holed up in the greenroom?" It had been impossible to hide that there had been a security scare before the debate, especially since it had caused the broadcast to start later than planned, and I'd already told Tamal about it.

"Not much, really. We mostly just talked to keep from worrying about what was going on. We didn't know if there was a bomb or if someone had been shot. I've been through scares like that before—not that it's ever easy—but it was Dre's first time. He held it together surprisingly well. Better than I did my first time."

"Cool," Tamal said. "Hey, you wanna come with me to get a suit? I need something for the dance."

As Tamal started listing his requirements for a suit, none of which I was certain Astrid was going to approve, my phone vibrated. I grabbed it out of the treadmill's cupholder, expecting a text from my mother, or from Nora relaying a question from my mother, but it was a notification from the Promethean app. A message had arrived from DreOfThe-Dead. I checked to make sure Tamal wasn't paying attention and took a peek.

DreOfTheDead: whats a pirates favorite letter

Dre had sent me a joke. And not even a good joke. A bad, bad joke. The kind my father probably would have tried to tell me when I was six. But I didn't want to be a snob, so I responded.

PrezMamasBoy: R?
DreOfTheDead: aye you'd think so but 'tis the C

A sharp laugh busted out of me and I dropped my phone. It smacked the tread and went flying into the wall behind me. I hit the emergency stop and straddled the tread until it slowed enough for me to hop off. My phone's screen was shattered, and I couldn't read anything on it.

"You okay?" Tamal asked. He'd stopped his machine too and was staring at me.

"I am," I said. "My phone is decidedly not."

"What were you laughing about?"

I considered telling Tamal about Dre—I usually told Tamal everything—but something made me want to keep this to myself. "Just something I read."

"It must've been pretty funny."

I smiled impulsively. "Yeah, it was."

DRE

I ROLLED THE twenty-sided die, adding a twist as I threw, and then held my breath as I watched the gold-painted numbers on the emerald-green icosahedron tumble and spin. "Come on, twenty! Come on, twenty!"

The die came to a stop. I blew out the breath and said, "Three. Plus my modifier, which is—"

"Still not good enough," Mel said, wearing an excited grin.

Around the table, the members of my adventuring party groaned.

"You don't have to look so happy about it, Mel," I said.

Mel—Emelda Vincente-Perez—cleared her throat from behind the enormous screen that hid her secret machinations from the rest of us. She rolled her dice. There was nothing

50

more nerve-racking than Mel wearing a shit-eating grin and rolling a whole bunch of dice.

"How many hit points you got, Dre?"

I checked my tablet where I kept my character sheet. "*Lady Poppy Needles* has seventeen hit points left."

"Not anymore," Mel snapped back. "While attempting to pick the lock, the door bursts open. Your delicate fingers slip and you trigger the trap. The chandelier hanging overhead falls and hits you, doing thirteen points of damage. You're dazed. You've got blood streaming down your face and you can't move. But when you look up, you see—"

"The Count of Crows?" I asked hopefully.

Mel's smile grew deeper and more wicked. "The Blood Mistress, flanked by her entourage of impossible children."

More groans from around the table. Adam said, "We are so not making it out of this alive."

"I'll heal Poppy," said Dhonielle. "But it'll cost you. Let me see if you've got anything I want." Her cleric, Father Aurum, was devoted to the god of greed, so she couldn't cast any healing spells without getting paid first.

My phone buzzed in my pocket, and I touched it through my shorts. We were still coming out of one of the hottest Augusts on record—thanks, climate change!—and while it might've been chilly at night, it was still balls-stuck-to-my-leg hot during the day. I had to sneak a peek at my phone under the table because Mel would've smote Lady Poppy Needles on the spot if she'd caught me. It was a notification from the Promethean app.

PrezMamasBoy: Hi, Dre. It's Dean. What are you up to?

Every time. Every time this boy sent me a message, he introduced himself like I didn't know it was him by his screen name. It was like he was writing from the 1950s sometimes, but it was also a little adorable.

DreOfTheDead: playing d&d

PrezMamasBoy: The role-playing game?

DreOfTheDead: no, the drinking game

PrezMamasBoy: I don't drink. I did once, at my cousin's wedding. I snuck some champagne. It didn't agree with all the wedding cake I'd eaten prior to that.

DreOfTheDead: no drinking here either . . . unless you count coffee

PrezMamasBoy: Do you have a vendetta against proper capitalization and punctuation?

DreOfTheDead: nah

DreOfTheDead: just faster without them

PrezMamasBoy: Autocorrect is an option.

DreOfTheDead: turned it off

DreOfTheDead: kept changing my fucks into ducks

PrezMamasBoy: That sounds ducking awful.

DreOfTheDead: was that a joke???

PrezMamasBoy: I have no idea what you're talking about.

DreOfTheDead: i'm onto you arnault

DreOfTheDead: anyway . . . what're you doing

PrezMamasBoy: I'm at a debate tournament.

DreOfTheDead: hopefully you're doing better than your mom did

PrezMamasBoy: My opponent started crying during cross-examination. I think I won, but I don't feel particularly good about it.

DreOfTheDead: what the hell kind of questions were you asking?!

PrezMamasBoy: Good ones, or so I thought.

PrezMamasBoy: The judge is back. I have to go. I will talk to you later. ~Dean

"Dre?" Mel was looking at me like she was waiting for the answer to a question I hadn't heard. "What're you doing?"

"Nothing."

"You're trapped under a chandelier, the Blood Mistress is trying to kill you, your party is in danger, and you're doing nothing?"

I laughed. "Oh. Right. In the game. I guess it's time to show the Blood Mistress how I earned the surname Needles."

Mel, Adam, Dhonielle, Caleb, Julian, Phil, and I made up the sassiest Dungeons & Dragons group that had ever crawled through a dungeon. We were kind of an offshoot of my school's QFA group—that's Queer Friends & Allies—because that's where we all met. Mel, who was a friend and ally, had been the one to suggest we pop by and had forced me to go with her. Dhonielle had heard me and Mel talking about wanting to start a gaming group, and she dragged her BFF, Phil, in. Adam, Caleb, and Julian all followed after. We tried to get together at least twice a month to play on Sundays, but it was tough to work around everyone's schedules. Especially mine.

"Seriously, Dre?"

The others had gone home, and I was helping Mel clean up the dining room. Her house was smaller than mine, but it was homier, and there were never photographers hiding in the bushes, so we usually played there.

"What?"

"It's been two months since we've been able to get you to the table, and you spent half the adventure staring at your phone with that stupid grin devouring your whole face."

"What grin?" I asked, but the second I started thinking about Dean, my lips went and betrayed me.

Mel pointed. "That one!"

I grabbed a slice of cold, congealed pizza from the box on the counter and took a bite. "I've got no idea what you're talking about."

Sometimes I thought Mel had secret mind-reading powers. Like her mom had dropped her on her head when she was a tiny baby and it'd rattled her brain just enough to shake loose a little bit of mental telepathy. It was that or I was super transparent. Yeah, it was probably the second thing.

"Are you seeing someone? Is there a boy? A secret boy? Do you have a secret boyfriend? Why didn't you tell me about your secret boyfriend?! I thought we were best friends, but clearly we're not if you have a secret boyfriend and you didn't tell me. Who is it? Is it Hiro? No, he chews with his mouth open and I know how much you hate that. Oh God, please tell me it's not Caleb. I mean, I know you two flirted with the idea last year, but—"

"It's not Caleb," I said. "It's no one. I don't have a boyfriend, secret or otherwise. I'm starting to think maybe I never will."

Once Mel got going, it could be difficult to reel her back in, but I guess the look on my face reassured her that I wasn't hiding a secret boyfriend from her. The only secret I was keeping was Dean, and I didn't know if we were even secret friends.

"But there is someone?" Mel asked. See? Mind reader.

"No? Maybe. I don't know." I sat down on one of the stools at the counter and threw my half-eaten slice back in the box.

Mel sat on the edge of the table, her feet dangling over the sides. Mel described herself as chubby, I described her as curvy, and the boys in school had been describing her as "Damn, girl!" since she was thirteen. She had a mess of curly hair that always looked like it was on the verge of coming to life, and a scar that cut through her left eyebrow that she'd gotten when she was little and had tripped and hit a coffee table.

"You're obviously talking to someone, right?"

"Yeah."

"Tell me he's not like fifty or offering to pay you for sex or to send you nudes or anything."

My shoulders dropped and I cocked my head to the side, giving her a look like "How gullible do you think I am?"

"So not some old dude?"

"No," I said. "We've met in person. But it's not like that. There's nothing between us, and I don't even know if I'd call us friends. We don't have much in common, though he's definitely more interesting than I expected him to be. But honestly, we're not even from the same planet. He's the opposite of the kind of guy I imagined being with."

"Is he like Chris Grossman?"

"Worse."

"Evan Smith? Please tell me he's not as bad as Evan Smith."

"Worse." I'd been telling Mel everything about everything since the day we met. Our brains had synched up and we'd been inseparable from then on. I'd never kept a secret from her, so it was natural for the truth to slip out. "It's Dean Arnault."

Mel stared at me for a moment, and she had me wishing that mind-reading thing went both ways because I really wanted to know what she was thinking. Then she smiled and started laughing so hard her face turned red and she nearly fell off the table, which would've served her right.

"Good one, Dre. Oh God, could you even imagine? I mean, he's basically the spawn of the devil himself, and his mother's even worse! I bet he takes girls on dates to his mother's campaign rallies, and when he kisses them, thousands of tentacles slide out of his mouth and implant a new alien parasite in the poor girl that replaces her with a clone of his mommy, because of course whatever girl he marries is going to be just like Mommy Dearest."

"He isn't that bad."

"Uh, yes he is," Mel said. "Do you want me to list all of the horrifying things his mother supports?" Before I could stop her, she was ticking them off on her fingers. "For-profit prisons, overturning gay marriage, guns, the continued criminalization of marijuana, tax breaks for big corporations—"

"I get it," I said. "They're awful. And I was kidding, anyway, remember?" It was easier to let her think I'd been joking. Mel could be relentless, and there was no one she hated more at the moment than Janice Arnault, except possibly Jackson McMann, but that asshat had, like, zero chance of being president.

"So who is it really?" Mel asked. "Is it that cutie from the

Apple store? I saw the way he was making eyes at you. No! It's the new guy—what's his name?"

"Malik," I said. "It's not him either. Just, don't worry about it. It's no one and not even worth talking about because nothing is happening."

Mel slid off the table and came around and rested her head on my shoulder. "It'll happen, Dre. You're gonna find someone."

"When?" I asked. "I'm seventeen and I've never even kissed a boy."

"I promise it'll happen. And when it does, it won't be with a gun-loving, sweater vest–wearing hypocrite like Dean Arnault." She shivered and grimaced. "Now come on. Let's go work on our costumes for the con this weekend."

Maybe Mel was right. What was I doing even talking to Dean? We had nothing in common; we didn't live in the same state, so it's not like we could go on dates or do anything normal people did; and his mother was basically evil incarnate. Still, there was something about talking to him that made me feel seen in a way I'd never felt while talking to anyone before, and I didn't want to stop, no matter who his mother was.

DEAN

I STOOD IN front of the mirror and took a picture of myself with my phone, which I'd paid too much to have the busted screen replaced on. Then I deleted it. I took another and deleted that one too.

"Put your tongue behind your teeth when you smile, Dean. Like I taught you." My mother was standing in my doorway. I dropped my phone when I saw her.

"You have got to be more careful with your phone."

"I know. I'm sorry. I don't know why I'm so clumsy lately." Casually, I bent to scoop my phone back up and slid it into my pocket. "I thought you were supposed to be in Wisconsin now."

"Minnesota," she said. "I was. I'm just home long enough to shower and see your father before heading to South

59

Carolina." She sounded exhausted. She looked exhausted. Most people probably didn't see it because my mother was keenly aware of how important it was not to show weakness. As the first Republican woman to gain the party's nomination for president, she had to walk a fine line. She could be strong but not too strong, feminine but not too feminine, funny but not too funny. She could never complain because that would be seen as a weakness. She couldn't be emotional, but she also couldn't be emotionless. And this wasn't new. It had been true going all the way back to her days in the military.

It wasn't fair the way voters and journalists treated her. Every critique of every appearance she made included, somewhere, a section about how she looked: what she was wearing, her hair, her makeup. The same writers never mentioned what Tomás Rosario was wearing, but they were always quick to point out whatever perceived flaws they saw in my mother's outfits.

She had once, after spending two days with no sleep dealing with the aftermath of Hurricane Tiffany, yawned where a television camera could see her. For an entire news cycle there were stories about how Janice Arnault might not have the stamina to be president. All because she'd yawned after staying awake for forty-eight hours. Instead of criticizing her, they should have been applauding her, but they never would.

As a result, my mother took great pains to always present herself as bright-eyed and bushy-tailed. "Smile like you mean it," she often told me. "Especially when you don't." But

I knew my mother, and I recognized the telltale signs of her exhaustion.

"Dressing for an important event?" my mother asked, eyeing my outfit. "I'm not sure about the bow tie."

My cheeks got hot as blood rose into them. "It's for homecoming this weekend."

My mother crossed the room and sat down on my bed. I'd always admired the way she could seem fierce and fragile at the same time without actually being either. And the secret to her success, the secret that her opponents had never figured out even though it was the worst-kept secret in the history of secrets, was that her sincerity was genuine. My mother never *pretended* to care about anything. She found something worth caring about in every issue she tackled. When she gave something her attention, she did so fully and without half measures.

And right then, my mother had turned the entirety of her attention onto me.

"Which lovely lady are you accompanying?" she asked. The promise of a smile touched her lips. "No, let me guess. That darling Sandya on your debate team?"

"No, Mom—"

"Or Laura Jane? Is she still cheerleading? I can't remember seeing her at any of the games this year."

My mother didn't actually have time to attend my high school's football games, but she had them recorded for her so that she could watch them while she was traveling. She felt that it was important to remain loyal to where she lived.

"Laura Jane's still cheerleading," I said, "but—"

"I know. You're taking Mindy Maguire, aren't you? She's a fine young woman. I'll have to say hi when we see her at church."

"Actually, I'm not taking anyone."

My mother's lips twitched. It wasn't quite a frown, but it was the seed of one. "I know you and Tamal enjoy going stag, but aren't you a little old for that?"

"Tamal is taking Astrid."

"Good for him," she said. "Why haven't you found a nice young lady to attend with?"

Standing over my mother was getting awkward, so I grabbed the chair from my desk. "You know I've been hoping to spend more time campaigning with you, and when you win, I'll have to finish my senior year at a new school in DC, so going by myself seemed like the easiest way to avoid leading anyone on."

There was a moment where I didn't know what my mother was thinking. Her reactions were usually telegraphed in ways that I'd grown to recognize, but I was getting nothing from her. "How did I raise such a considerate young man?"

I rolled my eyes playfully. "Oh please. It was all Dad."

My mother laughed and slapped my knee. "That poor man can't raise the blinds without help. But he does look handsome in a suit."

"Mom!"

"Well, if you're not taking anyone, what is with this outfit?"

I resisted the urge to tug the bow tie. It had actually been Dre's suggestion. I'd gone with Tamal to find his suit and had tried a few on myself, just for fun since I had plenty of suits. I'd taken pictures of them in the fitting room and had sent them to Dre. When he'd seen the picture of me in this dark blue plaid suit with the bow tie, he'd gone a bit bananas for it and told me I absolutely had to wear it. It felt a little too daring for me, though.

I couldn't explain any of that to my mother, however. I wasn't sure how she would have reacted to my taking fashion advice from the guy who regularly wore outfits on TV that my mother referred to as "shameful."

"It was an impulsive decision," I said. "I'm still not certain about it. But Nora has been telling me I need to step outside my comfort zone so that my peers will find me more relatable."

My mother's pinched-lipped, squinty-eyed appraisal of me made my skin itch. "I'm not sure this is what Nora meant. I can ask Kiersten for some suggestions. She has the best taste in men's clothes." Kiersten was my mother's stylist, and the one who'd picked out the socks that Dre had mentioned liking at the debate.

"You can ask," I said. "It's not a big deal, though. It's only a dance, and it's tomorrow night, so it's a little late for a costume change."

"She'll be over shortly to help me pack for South Carolina." My mother paused in a way that told me she still had more to say. "But, Dean? When it comes to you, I don't care about any poll. What is it you kids say? You do you?"

"Oh, Mom. Please don't."

"All I'm saying is that I want you to be yourself, no matter who that is."

This was the thing that made people love her. It was why I loved her. Because she was absolutely sincere. There was nothing I could wear, nothing I could become, nothing I could do that would make my mother stop supporting me and loving me. She might not have agreed with all my decisions, but she would never stop loving me for them.

"Is it all right if I haven't figured out who I am yet?"

My mother laughed. "I'd be a little worried if you thought you had it all figured out by seventeen. But that's why it's important to follow the path we've discussed. I want to help you avoid making the same kinds of mistakes I made when I was your age."

The path. The one that would guide me through high school so that I could get into the right college. The one that would lead me to law school and a career in politics like my mother. The one that saw me married by twenty-five and president by forty-five.

"What happens if I don't follow that path?"

My mother's smile turned a little wistful. "You can be anyone you want, and I believe you can do anything you set your mind to doing, Dean. There's no need to worry."

"Thanks, Mom."

My mother stood and yawned, letting her guard down around me. "Well, I had better get moving." She stopped at the door and turned back. "Who were the pictures for?"

"What?"

She motioned at my pocket. "You were taking a selfie when I came in."

I tried not to cringe when my mother said "selfie." She'd actually become a meme at one point, a milestone that she was ridiculously proud of for some reason. I touched my phone through my pocket. "Astrid," I said. "She's helping me decide whether to wear this suit or not."

"Just be careful about the kinds of pictures you send your friends."

"I know," I said. "Never send anyone or post anything online that I wouldn't be comfortable sending to Nana. I won't."

My mother smiled again. "You're a good boy, Dean. Stick to the path, and you'll be fine."

DEAN WAS STANDING in front of a floor-length mirror in his bedroom, wearing the plaid suit that I'd picked out for him. Okay, I hadn't picked it out so much as seen a picture of it that he'd sent me from the dressing room and then bullied and browbeat him into buying it. All that mattered was that he was wearing it. The smile he'd thrown on as an accessory was a bonus. I don't think I'd ever seen him wearing such an unguarded smile before. Not in any of the pictures I'd seen of him. Not that I'd spent hours late into the night googling Dean Arnault. Who would do something like that? Definitely not me.

(Hold on, I gotta go clear my browser history.)

Once I was done admiring Dean in his fancy bow tie, I zoomed in on the picture and peeked around the sides of the mirror to see if I could get an idea of what the secret sanctuary of Dean looked like.

Neat. It looked neat. His bed was made, there was nothing on the floor, the bookshelves were filled with philosophy books and biographies about people I didn't recognize, and I didn't see a TV anywhere. Dean lived in the bedroom of the boy my parents would've killed for me to be.

DreOfTheDead: geek chic never looked so good

PrezMamasBoy: You don't think it's a little too much?

PrezMamasBoy: Wait. Forget I asked. I've seen the way you dress.

DreOfTheDead: jealous much

PrezMamasBoy: Yes. You have found me out. I am so incredibly jealous of your avant-garde sense of fashion.

DreOfTheDead: is that sarcasm i'm sensing

PrezMamasBoy: I'm going to make sure that my mother's first act after she wins the election is an executive order outlawing school dances.

DreOfTheDead: not looking forward to going

PrezMamasBoy: There are many reasons I'm not looking forward to this. Allow me to list them for you.

PrezMamasBoy: They're loud. Music does not need to make your ears bleed to be enjoyed.

PrezMamasBoy: They reinforce the outdated notion that people must pair up in order to lead a fulfilling life.

PrezMamasBoy: One word: dancing.

67

DreOfTheDead: you don't dance?

PrezMamasBoy: Don't be silly. Of course I dance.

PrezMamasBoy: But the only dance I know how to do is, wait for it . . .

PrezMamasBoy: The robot.

DreOfTheDead: you shouldnt make jokes like that

PrezMamasBoy: Why not?

DreOfTheDead: cause its an ace stereotype

DreOfTheDead: you know thats not why i used to make those jokes right???

DreOfTheDead: and i'm sorry about them

PrezMamasBoy: I thought you made those jokes because you were jealous of my impeccable sense of fashion and polysyllabic vocabulary, but your apology is accepted and appreciated.

"What're you laughing at over there, mijo?"

My mom was sitting on the couch with her legs pulled up and a blanket draped over her feet because they were always cold, even during the summer. My mom was beautiful in an old Hollywood glamour sort of way. The one time I dressed in drag, I partially based my look on her, and I was stunning.

"Nothing," I said, which was kind of the truth. I'd been talking to Dean almost nonstop since the debate. When we weren't talking, I was thinking about talking to him. I read back through our conversations over and over, and I imagined what it would be like to see him again. I tried to keep from

68

letting my emotions get away from me, but restraint wasn't one of my strengths.

"Nothing seems to be taking up a lot of your attention lately."

"What?"

Mom pointed at my phone. "You're spending more time than usual staring at that device. Do you need an intervention?"

I dropped my phone on the couch beside me and turned to my mom.

"There's the face of the beautiful boy I gave birth to."

"Ugh, Mom, gross."

"The miracle of life isn't gross."

I shuddered and shook my head. "When's Dad getting home? I'm starving."

My mom checked her watch. "Why don't we order Indian? I don't think we'll see your father tonight."

"Again?"

"It's the campaign," she said. "He didn't do as well in the debate as he'd hoped, and Jackson McMann is causing more trouble than expected."

"Still," I said. "He could at least come home for dinner." Even when Dad was attorney general, he'd made time for us. He had always come home for dinner and had been both willing and eager to help me with Dreadful Dressup. The photos of him made up like a giant zombie bunny had received more comments than any other shoot Mel and I had done. Since he'd started his run for president, I felt like I hardly saw him.

"I know you miss him," my mother said. There was a wistful tone in her voice that said I wasn't the only one who missed Dad. "He still hopes you'll spend some time with him on the campaign trail."

"What about school?"

"You can take a leave of absence from school until after the election."

I threw my hands in the air in celebration. "No more homework!"

My mom glared at me with the exasperated look only a mother could conjure. "I'll speak to your teachers and get your assignments so that you can do them while you're traveling."

It wasn't the first time my parents had made the offer. My dad had suggested it a couple of months earlier, saying it was the kind of opportunity I'd never have again, but I'd turned him down because it was my senior year, which was also an experience I'd never have again. My dad had been disappointed, but he'd understood. He'd done his best to make sure his campaign hadn't disrupted my life more than necessary. But the more dinners my dad missed and the more time he spent away from home, the more I thought about taking him up on the offer just so I could spend time with him.

"I don't know," I said. "I'll think about it."

"Don't think too long," Mom said. "And don't worry about your dad. Everything will settle down again after the election."

Whereas I didn't want my dad to win the election—kind

of—Mom was pretty sure that he *wouldn't* win. All of this stuff was nothing but a weird scenic detour in our lives; we'd return to normal after Dad lost and got this whole trying-to-be-president thing out of his system. That's not to say Mom didn't support him—she did. She campaigned with him, with his running mate, and even on her own, carrying his message all over the country, and she never let on for a second to anyone but me that she didn't think he was going to win. Of course, she hadn't thought he'd win the primary either, and look how that had turned out. My father, the unlikeliest candidate, now had an actual shot at being the most powerful person in the country.

"You spent time with Governor Arnault during the lockdown at the debate, right?"

My mom seemed surprised by the question. She and Dad hadn't talked about the ordeal much. "Yes, why?"

"What'd you think of her? And Mr. Arnault."

"They seemed like perfectly normal people."

"Talk about anything interesting?"

"The weather," Mom said. "What might have caused the lockdown. Mostly we were worried about you and they were worried about their son."

I'd spent so much time concerned about my parents that I hadn't considered how much they'd been scared for me. "But you got along all right?"

My mom smiled. "Did you expect Janice and your father to duel with pistols?"

I laughed. "No, but . . . I guess, do you think it's possible for people who disagree on basically everything to be friends?"

"You know, your father and I don't agree on everything, right?"

"Like what?"

"Education," she said. "I think school, including college, should be free, but your father worries that making college free would devalue it." My mom worked as a librarian in the public school system, so it made sense that she supported free education. "But trying to understand people we disagree with is how we learn and grow."

"So you think you could be friends with people like the Arnaults?"

My mom pursed her lips. "I don't know them well enough to say, but I'd certainly give them a chance. You'll never really know who a person is until you put in the effort to get to know them."

"Hold up," I said, and got my phone.

DreOfTheDead: can I ask a personal question?
DreOfTheDead: i'm gonna do it anyway
DreOfTheDead: so are you like into dating or sex or love or anything?

Mom was looking at me funny when I finished typing my questions to Dean. "What was that about?"

"Just putting in the effort to get to know someone." My stomach growled furiously, and I patted it. "You said something about Indian?"

I knew I was crushing on Dean, but I didn't know if I should. Not like I could control it, but I could at least manage my expectations. Like when I had a crush on Lee Ancrum sophomore year. He was a senior and on the basketball team, and I felt like little cartoon hearts floated around my head every time I looked at him. But he was strictly attracted to girls, so I was able to get over my crush because I knew there was no chance of anything ever happening between us.

With Dean, there were too many uncertainties. He hadn't said he was definitely ace, but that he believed he was on the spectrum, which left open a lot of possibilities, but none that I could count on. If he did like me, there were a million reasons why we'd never work, but it didn't make sense worrying about it if it was a situation that had no chance of happening.

Either way, my mom was right that the only way I'd find out was to ask. I understood how much Dean valued his privacy, and I hoped I hadn't gotten too personal.

I kept my phone with me through dinner, waiting not-so-patiently for the buzz telling me Dean had responded. It finally did while I was cleaning up the dishes. I couldn't just run off and leave them, so I rushed through them as quickly as I could before dashing to my room and shutting the door behind me.

PrezMamasBoy: You can ask. I just hope it's okay if I don't know the answer.

PrezMamasBoy: I'll try to give you one anyway.

PrezMamasBoy: I used to think something was wrong with me. Everyone else talked about sex and attraction in a way that I didn't understand. My friends would see a good-looking girl or guy, and it did something to them that it didn't do to me.

PrezMamasBoy: It took me a while to understand that, for me, attraction isn't about what the person looks like, but about who the person is, and learning who someone is takes a long time.

PrezMamasBoy: Have you ever seen a guy you thought was attractive and developed a crush on him, but when you spent time with him and got to know him, you realized he was awful and that knowledge killed your attraction?

PrezMamasBoy: I'm going to assume the answer is yes. Well, for me, it's basically the opposite of that.

PrezMamasBoy: I hope that makes sense. I'm still trying to understand it myself.

PrezMamasBoy: Sorry, I have to go. Talk to you later, Dre.
~Dean

I smiled, reading what he'd written at least a dozen times. I didn't know what I wanted from Dean, and I didn't know what he wanted from me, but it seemed the possibilities were endless and, for now, that was enough.

DreOfTheDead: it's cool if you don't know the answer . . . i hardly know the answer to anything . . . but i kind of think you explained it perfectly

DEAN

ERIC SHU DODGED the tackle, pivoted, turned, and cranked back his arm. The bleachers shook as everyone rose to their feet. We were down by two touchdowns in the third quarter, and the Spartans had refused to give away a single yard without making our team fight for it. They'd harried Eric all night, forcing as many errors as possible. It looked like they were about to force another. Eric paused. We paused. We prayed. And then he released the ball, throwing it in a tight, high spiral that sailed sixty yards down the field right into the hands of DeMarcus Jackson as he broke away from the cornerback covering him. He put on a burst of speed and crossed into the end zone.

The crowd was so shocked that there was a full second of silence before they realized that our team had scored, and they broke out in a roar of approval. The cheer squad went wild, channeling our enthusiasm into a chant.

Let's go, Lions, let's go!

Let's go, Lions, let's go!

It was infectious, and soon I was chanting with them. Craig ran onto the field to kick the extra point. The ball sailed easily between the posts. I was surrounded by Tamal and Astrid—who kept telling everyone they were keeping things laid-back but whom I caught linking fingers together when they thought no one was paying attention—and Jessi, Fonda, and Shane. I knew them casually, but I'd made it my mission to meet every person in our class and try to know their names. Not because it was good for my image, but because people fascinated me and bewildered me and gave me hope. The more I learned about others, the more I seemed to learn about myself.

My phone vibrated, alerting me that I had three new messages on Promethean. I had to resist the urge to open my phone right then and read them, but the habits my mother had drilled into me were pretty hardwired. *Be present*, she'd often said. When I was with my friends, I should be with them and not be on my phone. Besides, I always had to think of my image. Of what it might look like if I were sitting with my friends staring at my phone and a photographer snapped a photo. Sure, I might look just like every other teenager at the game, but I couldn't afford to look like everyone else. Who I appeared to be reflected on my mother. And there was always a photographer hiding in plain sight in the stands, lurking around a corner, crouching behind a hedge, just waiting for me to do something they could snap a picture of and sell to some gossip blog.

"He thinks we should scrap NASA and let private corporations run all the space missions."

I shook myself out of my reverie, only catching the last bit of what Tamal was saying. "Who?"

"Jackson McMann."

"Oh," I said. "*Him*." The name made me cringe. Before running for president as an independent, McMann had founded a number of startup tech companies, which he had then turned around and sold for obscene amounts of money. He was aggressive and loud. The press loved painting him as a rebellious genius, but everything I knew about him made him seem like a selfish jerk. He'd even written a memoir called *Better than You* that had become a bestseller.

"He's actually pretty brilliant," Tamal said. "He's got a ton of patents, and—"

"That's fine," I said. "But how does that make him worthy of being the US president? He's not even in the race to win. He's just a narcissist trying to drum up attention for his next IPO so that he can get even richer. He doesn't care about anyone or anything but money."

"I'm going for Rosario," Astrid said.

Tamal's eyes opened wide. "Babe!"

Astrid shrugged unapologetically. "What? First Mexican American president *and* he's for free health care? I'm in. I like your mom and all, Dean, but I've got a cousin who's trans, and I can't vote for someone who might make him less safe. And McMann's a joke. Besides, when he was CEO of CaterAid, he wrote a tipping system for the delivery people into the app but kept ninety percent of that money for himself."

I wasn't surprised. McMann said and did things that would have disqualified other candidates easily. He preyed on the fears of voters by casting anyone who wasn't like them as the enemy. It was impossible to know what he believed because it changed based on who he was addressing. He was an opportunist, but the press loved him because he was entertaining. No one wanted to listen to my mother discuss how to battle the opioid crisis when McMann was shouting about Chinese immigrants stealing American jobs and suggesting most of them were probably spies anyway.

"He also thinks we should have facial recognition cameras on every street corner and that we should be using AI to predict crime," Astrid was saying.

"That stuff's messed up!" Tamal said. "They use these predictive algorithms for determining if someone should be paroled, and it's like, should computers really be deciding that stuff? They're as racist as the people who program them."

"See?" I said. "So it doesn't matter how brilliant he is. The man is dangerous."

"Dude, I never said I liked the guy. You know I support your mom. Not that it matters since I won't even be old enough to vote."

"I know. It's just infuriating that he can literally suggest we not worry about solving the drug problem because those overdose deaths are a way of eliminating the weak-minded from society, and people cheer him for it."

"People can be really ignorant," Tamal said.

There didn't seem to be anything left to say about it. Every time someone mentioned McMann, I had to resist the urge to bury them under the mountain of reasons why he was a horrible human being who had no business being president. Aside from being racist, misogynist, homophobic garbage, accusations that he exploited his workers had followed him from one company to the next. He seemed to view people as expendable resources that he could use and then throw away. I knew Astrid and Tamal would never vote for someone like him, but there were plenty of people who would.

"Dean?" Astrid asked, pulling me back from the pit my thoughts were trying to drag me into. "Who're you taking to homecoming?"

"No one."

Tamal motioned at me with his chin. "Waited too long."

"I didn't wait too long," I snapped. "I'm just not going with anyone."

"I was only joking," Tamal said.

The crowd around us rose, roaring as something happened

on the field. Instead of answering Tamal, I stood and turned my attention back to the game, where Reggie Silvers had recovered a fumble and had managed to run it almost to the end zone.

I was still annoyed when I sat back down. It wasn't that Tamal or Astrid had done anything wrong, exactly—it was just that the default settings of the world assumed that I should want to attend homecoming *with* someone, probably of the opposite gender. It was difficult for people to conceive of the possibility that I was perfectly happy going by myself. It would have been easier if I could be honest with my friends, but I wasn't ready to open that can of worms yet. Most of the time, I could handle it, but there were moments when I wanted to stand up and shout at everyone to leave me alone and stop making assumptions.

Tamal clapped me on the back. "Dude, you all right? You seem a little stressed."

"I'm going to use the restroom." Without waiting for a reply, I made my way to the end of the bleachers and down the steps, pausing every few feet to say hi to someone from the debate team or student government or baseball or church. Sometimes it was their parents who stopped me, and even though I wanted nothing more than to find a quiet spot to breathe, I took the time to shake hands and smile and be polite.

Politeness never costs a thing, my mother always said.

When I was finally able to break free of the crowd, I ducked behind the concession stand and pulled out my phone.

DreOfTheDead: can I ask a personal question?

DreOfTheDead: i'm gonna do it anyway

DreOfTheDead: so are you like into dating or sex or love or anything?

I was wondering when he was going to ask. I wasn't embarrassed about it by any means, but he was the only person I could talk to without holding anything back. I could have told my parents, and I didn't doubt that they would have accepted me, but many of my mom's potential voters *wouldn't* understand, and coming out publicly could jeopardize the election. I wasn't worried about my friends rejecting me either, but I couldn't trust them not to accidentally tell someone who might leak it to the press. Dre, however, understood the need for privacy, and the cost of it. I could talk to him about who I really was and trust him to protect my secrets.

The problem was that I didn't know how to explain my sexuality to Dre because I didn't fully understand it myself. I'd believed for at least a year that I fell somewhere on the ace spectrum, but the fact that there was a spectrum instead of a single concrete box I could check complicated my situation even more. I didn't feel the need to define myself by an arbitrary word, but the word that felt like it fit best was "demi."

I typed out and erased my responses to Dre multiple times, once giving him a clinical definition, but finally I embraced my own confusion. I wrote what I felt instead of what I knew and sent it. And then I began to panic. What if I hadn't explained it properly? What if I'd said something offensive? What if I was wrong about Dre and he was playing me and was going to turn around and take what he'd learned to his father? Telling Dre in person had been one thing—if he'd told someone, I could have denied it—but now I'd put it in writing.

My heart was pounding, and I felt dizzy. I'd made a terrible mistake. Now, instead of being able to tell my parents on my own terms, sometime after the election, they were going to learn about it on CNN, and I was going to have to explain it while they looked at me with disappointment in their eyes. I was going to have to live with the knowledge that, if my mother lost the election, it would be because of me.

I needed to return before Tamal wondered where I'd gone. It was too late to take back what I'd written to Dre, so I was just going to have to live with the consequences if he decided to show someone. I barely noticed the people around me as I finished climbing the bleachers and sat down again.

"Feeling better?" Tamal was looking at me with real concern in his eyes.

I couldn't lie to him. I might have been keeping some secrets, but I refused to lie. My phone vibrated, and this time I couldn't resist pulling it out to check. I had a message from Dre.

DreOfTheDead: it's cool if you don't know the answer . . . i hardly know the answer to anything . . . but i kind of think you explained it perfectly

"Dean?" Tamal was still waiting for my answer.

I don't know how Dre knew exactly what to say, but his simple reply eased my fears. I didn't know for certain that he wasn't going to show what I'd written to the world, but I *believed* he wouldn't. I believed he would protect my secret like it was his own. I had no real basis for that belief other than faith, and it was enough. I put my phone away, smiling. "I'm good. Everything is great."

DRE

THE INSIDE OF the convention center was stuffy and hot, and I was having trouble breathing as Mel pulled me through the press of bodies from one booth to the next, talking to comic book artists and writers, buying everything that caught her eye until she ran out of money. Thousands of people dressed like their favorite superhero or comic book villain or Star Wars character wandered and mixed with people in regular clothes. My costume—the Chairman, a villain from the Patient F comics—had been a hit so far, and I'd been stopped a dozen times by fans who wanted a picture, which I happily obliged. However, the paint made my suit heavy and every bit of visible skin was covered in gray makeup, so I was having to drink my body weight in water every hour to keep from passing out. Dean would have approved of my commitment to hydration.

Mel and I slid into the signing line for Ben Fischer, even though it snaked around the outer edge of the convention center and the line managers were clocking it at nearly two hours from our position. Mel and I were both superfans, and I couldn't pass up the opportunity to show off my costume to the guy who'd created the comic that'd inspired it.

"You? Me? Dance after the cosplay contest?" Mel was looking at me expectantly, but I'd been on my phone. "Who're you talking to?"

"My mom," I said. "She's trying to convince me to go to Mass with them on Sunday."

Mel, who was dressed as Princess Bonecrusher, a character from her favorite video game, scrunched her face in confusion. "Since when?"

"You know how it is. They started going again before Dad entered the primary and they want people to see me in church like we're one big happy religious family."

"So you're going to Mass now?"

I shook my head. "I told them if they want me in a church, they gotta find one that doesn't diddle kids, hate gays, or discriminate against women. Like, do they really think I'm gonna find Jesus hanging out with a bunch of folks who keep stones in their pockets so they can be the first to throw them?"

Mel was shaking her head before I'd finished speaking. "You could go and use the opportunity to make a statement. Wear a rainbow suit or something. Hold up a protest sign throughout the service."

"Yeah, I'm not doing that."

"You have an opportunity to speak for people who can't speak for themselves," Mel said. "Don't you think you owe it to them to do it?"

"By embarrassing my dad?" Mel tried to jump in, but I kept going. "I'm not trying to be someone I'm not, and one of the things I'm not gonna do is spend Sunday in church, not even to protest."

"But—"

"Weren't we talking about the dance?" I asked.

Mel was throwing all kinds of judgmental looks my way, and maybe she was right to do so. My dad had used my popularity on Dreadful Dressup to elevate himself when he'd started running. I could've done the same right back to him. Used his platform to call attention to shit most people didn't talk about. But I didn't want to call *more* attention to myself. I just wanted to be left alone to do my thing. Thankfully, Mel didn't push it. This time.

"The theme is Apocalyptic Wasteland."

"Zombies and toxic mutants?" I held up my arms. "I'm not sure I'm dressed for it."

Mel looked down her nose at me appraisingly. "The theme

is only a suggestion." When I didn't reply, she said, "Come on. We're already here, and it's a two-hour drive back home and . . ."

"And what?"

"Nothing," she said. "Forget it."

But it wasn't nothing, and I could tell by the pout she was wearing. "Wait a second." I snapped my fingers as it hit me. "What's his name, and don't give me none of this 'What's whose name?' bullshit. You're meeting someone here!"

Mel's eyes bulged like a Chihuahua's.

"It all makes sense now," I said. "Why you were nervous-singing on the drive over and why you bailed on your demogorgan costume after spending weeks on it in favor of Princess Bonecrusher, which is still pretty amazing but also shows off your—"

"Stop!" Mel said. "Yes! There's a guy." Her shoulders dipped. "Two guys. Maybe."

I snorted and laughed without meaning to. "Two guys? Who're you and what've you done with Emelda?"

Mel flinched when I called out her full name. "It's not like I'm trying to get with both of them at the same time. They're best friends. I met them at the *Magic: The Gathering* tournament last month that you were supposed to go to with me but bailed on like the punk-ass bitch you are."

"I didn't bail," I said. "I was grounded."

"Still a punk-ass bitch," Mel said in a singsong voice.

"Stop stalling and tell me about the guys."

Mel was looking vulnerable in a way I wasn't used to. She was my Amazonian warrior queen. Nothing anyone did could get through the shields she kept up. But there she was looking both guilty and giggly at the same time, like one wrong word could ruin her. It was a weird thing, but I kind of got where she was coming from.

"It's not that complicated," she said. "I met Andy and Tade, and I really hit it off with Andy. We spent two hours talking about everything, and he had an amazing deck."

My eyebrows raised.

"Built around necromancy," Mel said. "Get your mind out of the gutter."

"My mind lives in the gutter. You know that."

"Anyway," Mel said. "Tade was sweet, but he was kind of quiet, and I didn't think much of him. Before we left, we all traded numbers. Getting more than a one-word reply from Andy was harder than completing the tubular level in *Super Mario World*, but Tade started blowing up my phone at all hours of the day and night, making me laugh until I cried."

"So Andy was cool in person, but Tade was good on the phone?"

Mel nodded. "Yeah. And they're both here, and they've both been hinting that they kind of like me, and I like them too, but I don't know which one."

"Which means you want me to go to the dance with you

so I can meet them and tell you which one you should make out with." I sighed dramatically. "I mean, I guess I can fit that in my busy schedule."

"You'll go?"

I had zero interest in going to the comic-con ball and watching a bunch of awkward dudes in Captain America costumes try to work up the nerve to talk to girls in anime costumes. But Mel needed me, and I couldn't say no.

"Sure."

Mel jumped up and down, clapping her hands. "You're going to have the best time! I promise!"

"Yeah," I said. "It'll be a blast."

"What's wrong?"

I did my best to shake off the mood that'd fallen over me. "Nothing."

Mel cocked her head to the side and planted her hands on her hips, giving me that look that told me I was a silly fool for thinking I could pretend nothing was the matter when something clearly was.

"It's just . . . I don't know. It's not fair that you're flirting with two boys and I can't even find one. And it's not fair to you for me to think it's not fair because it's not like you should remain chaste just because I'm a hopeless troll who repels boys, but I can't help feeling sorry for myself because I'm a selfish asshole."

"You're not an asshole."

"Or selfish?"

90

"You're not an asshole."

I slapped Mel's arm. "Thanks a lot."

"If you don't wanna go, I'll tell Andy and Tade we got other plans—"

"No," I said. "We're going. One of us deserves to be happy."

"What about the guy you've been talking to?"

I hadn't heard from Dean since he'd answered my question about being ace. He hadn't seemed upset about it, and his answer had felt so beautifully honest—like he'd peeled away all the artifice he surrounded himself with and showed me a tiny true piece of his soul—but the longer I went without hearing from him, the more worried I got that I'd pushed too hard on something sensitive. I hadn't opened the app since we'd gotten to the convention because I was afraid I'd see \<deleted\> in place of his username.

"I don't know," I said. "There's nothing there."

"It didn't seem like nothing."

"We don't even live in the same zip code, and there's too much shit in the way."

Mel was giving me another look, but I couldn't decipher it. "What?"

"Nothing," she said. "I was just trying to figure out when you became such a sad, scared ball sack."

"Excuse me, what?"

"Aren't you the same Dre who literally crawled through garbage to sneak into a sold-out concert? And aren't you the same Dre who stood up to a guy twice his size for picking on a freshman?"

"Yeah," I said. "But it turned out he wasn't being picked on. They were rehearsing for a play."

"Doesn't matter," Mel said. "You are weird, you are deranged, you are annoying, and you are persistent and fierce as fuck. If you want to make something happen, make it happen. Don't let whatever's hanging you up stand in the way."

I pulled Mel in and kissed the side of her head. "I love you, Mel." And I did. But the problem was that I had no idea what, if anything, was happening between me and Dean, and it wasn't something I could force. If Dean didn't have any romantic feelings for me, I had to respect that, no matter how weird, deranged, annoying, persistent, and fierce Mel thought I was.

DEAN

THIS WAS SUPPOSEDLY the best night of my life. That's what everyone kept saying. Tamal stuck his head out the window and yelled it as I drove us to the dance; Astrid said it from the back seat as we pulled into the parking lot at school. Even Mr. Baxter clapped me on the shoulder and said "Welcome to the best night of your life" as I passed through the metal detectors at the entrance to the gym.

But if they were right, then why was I so bored?

I stood at the edges of the dance floor with my hands in my pockets as a song I didn't like turned into a song I didn't know, and the crowd went a little wild. They were still coming off the high of winning the game the night before, with a touchdown in the final ten seconds, surprising everyone, and we were at that stage of the dance where the homecoming royals had been crowned—Asa Ford and Devi Kapoor—and the need to keep shoes on or worry about hair had passed. The majority of the dancers had given into the Bacchanalian revelry and were, possibly, having the best night of their lives.

I, on the other hand, was not.

It wasn't that I couldn't dance. I had, in fact, proven I knew how to dance with Ellen when she'd had my mother and me on her show. I had actually taken dance lessons. Not to go on the show, of course. My mom had me take them so that I wouldn't embarrass myself if I ever needed to dance at one of her fancy fundraisers or balls. They didn't do the kinds of dancing at school dances that they did at my mom's events, but I still would have enjoyed the opportunity to have semi-rhythmic seizures while surrounded by my friends set to music I probably wouldn't have chosen to listen to if given another option. It was just . . . I don't know. I wanted more than to spend another night pretending.

There was nothing wrong with the concept of a dance; it was the expectations that went along with them that bothered me. If I could have danced without people assuming things about me because of it, I would have. But if I'd wanted to cut loose and dance with Tamal, people probably would have assumed I was gay. If I'd danced with any girl, she might think I was attracted to her and might feel led on when she realized I wasn't. Not to mention that everyone in the gym—students *and* chaperones—had the potential to snap a picture covertly and ruin my life and my mother's campaign. Maybe this could have been one of the best nights of my life if a dance could have been nothing more than a dance, but nothing in my life was that simple.

Nothing except talking to Dre.

I slipped into the restroom and locked myself in the farthest stall from the door. I sat on the toilet and pulled out my phone. Still no new messages from Dre. His reply to my attempted explanation about being ace had been sweet, but it had felt like a period rather than a question mark—a polite smile rather than an invitation to continue talking—and I didn't want to be pushy by initiating another conversation if he wasn't interested.

But there was something about talking to Dre. Explaining my feelings to him about being demi had felt like the day the doctor had removed the cast from my wrist that I'd gotten when I broke it skiing. The moment the cool air hit my hot, itchy skin had been a revelation. I thought I'd never again feel anything so wonderful in my life. And then came Dre.

I didn't want to overshare, though. I could have filled the screen with my feelings, but I'm not sure that would have been fair to him. He had his own friends and his own life, and I didn't know what I would have called us. Secret not-enemies? There were complications to our friendship that we would eventually have to confront if we continued talking. We didn't have to confront them now, though, and I needed someone to talk to about things I couldn't say to anyone else or I might explode, but I was afraid of scaring Dre away.

I slipped my phone back into my pocket and was about to leave the stall when the door banged open. I froze.

"Layla, huh?"

"Seems like it."

"You guys going to Jack's?"

"For the party?"

"No, to sit shiva. Yes, for the party!"

"What's shiva?"

"Forget it. Are you coming to the party?"

"Hell yeah."

"This is the best night of our lives."

I remained motionless, quietly listening to the boys as they peed and talked and *did not* wash their hands. One of the boys was definitely Avi Fleischmann, but I'm not sure who the other was. I couldn't return to the dance this way. I just needed to talk to someone. It might have been a terrible idea, but as soon as the boys left the restroom, I got out my phone, opened Promethean, and began to type.

PrezMamasBoy: Hi, Dre. It's Dean.

PrezMamasBoy: There must be more to being seventeen than this, right? More than discussing who we find attractive and who we want to "get with." More than dances in gymnasiums that still smell like sweaty jockstraps and over-chlorinated water. More than the superficial relationships that we claim mean so much to us but that keep us from really knowing one another.

PrezMamasBoy: More than . . . more than *this*. There must be more than this. Please tell me that there's more than this. That *this* is not the best night of my life.

PrezMamasBoy: ~Dean

I typed furiously, my fingertips tapping against the screen, hitting send after each message. One second later, I began to regret it. I couldn't believe I'd said all of that to Dre. What kind of person was he going to think I was? He was going to think I was a melancholy weirdo who fired off long-winded messages from the stall of a gym restroom instead of having fun with his friends. He was going to read my messages and delete my contact information and never speak to me again. I had to fix it. Or, at least, mitigate the damage.

PrezMamasBoy: Hi, Dre. It's Dean again.

PrezMamasBoy: Forget what I said. I didn't mean it. Okay, that's not true; I did mean it. But you have to believe me when I say that this is no simple case of adolescent ennui.

PrezMamasBoy: Which is, I suppose, how every teenager in the history of teenagers feels. Like their pain is real while everyone else's is phony. Like the isolation they feel is incomparable to the isolation felt by anyone anywhere ever. I think it really is different for us, though.

PrezMamasBoy: We can't do anything without being watched and analyzed.

PrezMamasBoy: Last year, when I had my wisdom teeth

removed, a photographer took a picture of me taking one of the pain pills prescribed to me, and someone ran a story that I was addicted to opioids.

PrezMamasBoy: I'm worried that by the time all this is over, I won't know who I am anymore.

PrezMamasBoy: You are very likely the only person in the world capable of understanding what I mean.

PrezMamasBoy: Other than Sasha and Malia Obama, Chelsea Clinton, or maybe even the Bush twins, but I think there is a difference between remembering how something feels and feeling it in the moment.

PrezMamasBoy: Besides, I doubt the Obamas would take my calls.

PrezMamasBoy: They might take yours. You should try.

I knew I should stop—a voice in the back of my mind was screaming for me to stop—but I couldn't. I just kept typing. Sending the rawness of what I was feeling through my phone to Dre.

PrezMamasBoy: I'm sorry for the barrage of messages. It's just that I'm sitting alone in a toilet stall in the boys' restroom in the gym, which has been decorated in school colors—yellow and blue; go, Lions!—but still has that depressing look of a gymnasium. It reminds me of my great-grandfather's funeral. Even wearing makeup and dressed in his favorite suit, he looked like a corpse.

PrezMamasBoy: I don't know why I'm telling you all of this. You probably have friends to talk to about these feelings. I have friends.

PrezMamasBoy: Okay, I have Tamal. He's a friend. My best friend. But he and I don't talk like this. We talk about baseball and college and I listen to him worry about girls.

PrezMamasBoy: Are *we* friends, Dre?

PrezMamasBoy: I feel like we could be friends, which is a bit surreal if you think about it, but I don't want to assume a friendship where there isn't one.

PrezMamasBoy: I should go before I begin typing out the lyrics of maudlin songs that you would only ridicule me for listening to. I have a serious Troye Sivan addiction.

PrezMamasBoy: Even if all you do is skim these messages, thank you for listening.

I paused with my finger over the button, prepared to sign off, probably for the last time, seeing as I had essentially vomited my feelings all over the screen. It was horrifying, in a way, to see the wall of words on the screen that I couldn't take back. They were like the path of devastation left by a tornado. Tornado Dean. They don't name tornadoes, do they? Hurricane Dean, then. If there was any chance of Dre and I being friends, I'd probably ruined it.

I sat on the edge of the toilet, reading and rereading what

99

I'd written. Everything I'd said to Dre was true, but it was all so embarrassing. There was honesty and then there was what I'd done. The funny thing about honesty is that most people claim to want it until they actually get it. The truth is often ugly and unpleasant. It's why most people, when asked how they are, respond with "Okay" rather than by dumping the truth of how they're feeling on the person who asked. We might all be happier if we answered more honestly. Saying the things I'd said to Dre left me feeling vulnerable and a little sick to my stomach, but I also felt a bit . . . not better, but lighter. No matter how Dre responded, at least I'd told him the truth.

When I turned back to my phone to type my goodbye, I saw three dots indicating that he was typing a reply. I waited, dread sucking a hole in my stomach, for Dre to ask me to stop bothering him, for Dre to tell me I was nothing more to him than the uptight son of his father's political rival.

And then the reply finally came.

DreOfTheDead: of course we're friends
DreOfTheDead: dumbass

FIRST IMPRESSIONS ARE a bitch, and so was I. Especially when it came to my girl Mel. No one was good enough for her.

"What do you think?" Mel had dragged me to a corner of the ballroom that was far enough from the music that I could actually hear her talk. Pulsing colored lights strobed the dance floor as cool costumed freaks danced to music from their favorite movies and TV shows. I kept looking over my shoulder, expecting a photographer or reporter to be lurking somewhere in the shadows, but the nice thing about the convention was that the costumes and sheer number of people afforded me a temporary cloak of anonymity. Tonight, I got to be Dre and not Tomás Rosario's son.

"Honest opinions?"

Mel nodded emphatically.

"Andy's cute. He's got a whole brooding Loki thing going on that I dig, and he's got a sense of humor. Not sure it's a good one, but it's better than nothing. He doesn't seem like the type to hang out with you at a protest; more like he might be willing to give you a ride to one and pick you up after. Overall, he was cool to talk to."

"What about Tade?"

I tapped my chin like I had to think about it. "He's got a sexy John Boyega vibe."

"Star Wars Boyega?"

I shook my head. "*Attack the Block* Boyega."

Mel broke out in a grin. "My favorite Boyega."

"Is there a bad Boyega?"

"Definitely not," we both said at the same time, laughing.

"But," I said, "I couldn't get him to talk about *anything*. Not even *Saga*, and he's dressed like Marko!"

Mel threw up her hands in frustration. "You're not helping, Dre. What am I supposed to do?"

I threw on my best *How are you not seeing the solution to this problem when it's so obviously clear to me and probably everyone else at this silly dance?* look.

"Dre!"

"Hang out with Andy, make out with Tade. Problem solved." I gave Mel a shove toward the dance floor, where the boys were waiting for her. "Begone. Make the pain and suffering I'm enduring by being here worth it."

Mel gave me the finger as she walked away, and I looked on like a proud mama sending her baby bird winging off into the wide world. Of course, I was probably sending her out there to get eaten by a bigger bird, but I couldn't protect her forever.

And then I was bored. I'd been a little bummed that I hadn't even placed in the cosplay contest, but there had been a *lot* of outstanding costumes. And Mel and I had gotten some good exposure for Dreadful Dressup, so it hadn't been a total bust. The ball, on the other hand . . . After fending off yet another girl who'd tried to pull me out to dance, I'd resigned myself to a lonely night waiting for Mel to tire of her boys so we could leave. I *should* have been putting myself out there. Looking for a boy with that twinkle in his eye when I glanced his way, the kind of hidden smile that hinted he might be interested in a dance, but my heart wasn't in it. What I really wanted to do was talk to Dean, which was ridiculous. This little crush of mine was getting out of control and I needed to stop thinking about him. Even if Dean had feelings for me, we couldn't act on them. My father would disown me, and Mel would murder, dismember, and bury me where no one would ever find my body. When it came to politics, I was mostly ambivalent, but Mel was so passionate about her beliefs that she would've seen my growing feelings for Dean as nothing short of a betrayal.

Not that it mattered. I hadn't heard from Dean since the night before. I figured he was embarrassed about sharing being demi with me, and that I probably wouldn't hear from him again. Which sucked. Even if Dean never reciprocated my feelings, whatever my feelings were, I still liked hearing from him.

"Hey! Dreadful Dressup!" A guy in a Pikachu costume, with two friends dressed as Team Rocket, was running down the hall toward me, and before I knew it, I was pressed against the wall with nowhere to go. "Your dad's running for president, right?"

My cloak of invisibility had failed. "Uh, yeah. Look, I was just—"

"Can we get a selfie?"

Pikachu and Team Rocket crowded around me, their phones out snapping pictures. "I love your site. The video where you reimagined all the US presidents as gender-swapped werewolves was genius."

"That was Mel's idea—"

One of the members of Team Rocket got in my face. "Tell your dad he needs to get rid of college tuition. My loans are *killing* me."

"Uh, I'll tell him."

More people were starting to shove in around me, and I was getting claustrophobic. Mel would've rescued me if she'd been there, but I was all alone, and I did the only thing I could think of.

"I have to go to the bathroom!" I shouted, and shoved my way past Pikachu. I ignored the calls for me to come back and shook off the hands that tried to grab me. I would never understand people who felt entitled to touch me without permission. It'd been one thing when Dreadful Dressup had gotten popular and people at the conventions Mel and I went to would stop us for selfies or ask us questions, but everything had changed when Dad had won the nomination. People seemed to think they owned my time and that they could treat me however they wanted. It was bullshit, and I hated it. I wondered if it was the same for Dean.

I wandered the convention hotel, keeping my head down and avoiding crowds, until I found a quiet hallway with a public restroom I could use because, after all that, I actually did have to go. The restroom was the quietest space I'd been in all day, and I stayed for a minute to enjoy the silence. I grabbed my phone and was going to text my parents and let them know I was probably gonna be a little late when I saw I'd accidentally turned it to silent. There were notifications from my mom, a couple from my dad—all just random BS and nothing important—and a deluge from Dean through Promethean. The boy had been blowing up my phone all night and I'd missed it! He probably thought I hated him.

I fired off replies to my parents first, then locked myself in a stall so I could read Dean's messages. They weren't what I was expecting. They were so *real*. And still so very Dean. He'd sent the last one less than a minute earlier, so I typed out a response as quickly as I could, hoping he hadn't put his phone away yet.

DreOfTheDead: of course we're friends

DreOfTheDead: dumbass

DreOfTheDead: whatre you doing

DreOfTheDead: can you go to video???

Dean didn't answer. Of course I'd *just* missed his messages. Welcome to my life. I should've gone out to find Mel, but I read Dean's messages over and over, mining the words for every ounce of meaning. Everything about Dean was so different from me. The words he used, the way he formed his sentences, the creepy corpse metaphor. I never would've used a word like "ennui." Mel would've called me out for a shit if I had, though Dad would've tried to high-five me for using a good SAT word. But for all our differences, I'd never related to something harder than I did to the feelings Dean had described. The isolation. There I was at the con, surrounded by people who were supposedly like me—nerdy like me, outsider like me, freak like me—and I had never felt more lonely. People either ignored me completely or accosted me with questions, treating me like an object rather than a person. Sometimes it felt like even Mel didn't understand me anymore. She always said she'd be there to catch me if I fell, but she was the one who'd grown wings while I was still stuck on the ground.

Then there was Dean, pouring out his soul, and all I wanted right then was to talk to him, but I'd missed my chance. "Damn it!"

My phone buzzed as a Promethean notification popped up asking if I wanted to video-chat with PrezMamasBoy, and I hit that accept button so damn fast.

"Dre? Dre, it's Dean. I can't see you."

Dean sounded like he was in the stall with me, and his face filled the screen. "Shit!" My finger was covering the front camera. I shifted my hold on the phone and held it higher. "Dean!"

"Dre!" Dean's expression reminded me of the way my gramps looked when he tried to video-chat with me, even though he didn't really know what he was doing. "What's wrong with your face?"

"What's wrong with *your* face?" I snapped back.

Dean shook his head and pointed at the screen. "You're gray. Is that makeup? Are you doing a photo shoot?"

Oh yeah. I'd forgotten what I looked like. "I'm at a con." I remembered I was talking to the guy who said "photo shoot" and who introduced himself at the beginning of every text chain, and added, "A comic book convention. There was a cosplay contest. I didn't win, but it's okay. What're you doing?" I peered at the screen. "Are you in the bathroom? Did you call me while you were taking a dump?"

Dean's face went fifty shades of red as he stuttered and stumbled to come up with an answer. "I *am* in a restroom. Public. In a toilet stall, actually. But I am most definitely not 'taking a dump.' I swear. I did come in here to use the facilities, but then I sent you a message, and you responded, and

I was trying to figure out how to request a video chat and accidentally initiated one."

Watching the boy have a mini meltdown was adorable. "If you're not using the toilet, what are you . . . Are you hiding in there?"

Dean cleared his throat. "Yes. I'm hiding in the toilet."

I turned my phone and flashed it around the stall. "Me too."

Dean laughed. A full-throated, no-bullshit laugh that sounded like a hyena gargling hot sand, and it was *glorious*. I'd seen him laugh in clips that I'd found online, and it looked and sounded nothing like this. This was so unguarded and pure.

"You got a nice laugh," I said.

"No, I don't."

I shook my head. "No, you don't. It's pretty ridiculous, but I like it anyway."

It was weird seeing him. Talking to him this way instead of sending messages back and forth, where we could compose the best versions of ourselves. Like Dean's laugh, it was awful, but I liked it.

"Why're *you* hiding?" Dean asked.

"Oh lord. Well, Mel met a couple of guys she likes, and one's kinda cute but chatty and the other one is hot but quiet, and she's been trying to figure out which one she likes best all night. I just couldn't with her anymore."

"Is this what we teenagers call 'drama'?" Yeah. He actually made air quotes when he said it.

"You're like a middle-aged economy professor in a seventeen-year-old's body." I snapped my fingers. "That's what happened, isn't it? You were really a professor at Harvard or something, and one of your professor buddies in the weird physics department figured out how to swap bodies with people, so you killed that dude and stole his invention so you could hijack a younger, hot body. And somewhere out there the real Dean is stuck with wrinkled balls and no idea what the hell happened."

Dean was laughing so hard I thought he was going to drop his phone, and that made me laugh, and I did drop my phone, but thankfully, it landed on the floor and didn't crack the screen because that would have ruined what was turning out to be an okay night.

"Did you call me hot?"

"Relatively speaking," I said, trying to keep my cheeks from turning bright red. "Compared to me, you're a soft six."

"A six?!" Dean held the phone farther away. "But I'm wearing the suit!"

"Which is why you're not a five."

"Wow," Dean said. "I hope this isn't what passes for flirting for you or you might be single forever."

"Who said I was flirting?" Was I flirting? Did Dean *want* me to flirt? Was *he* flirting? Nah, right? I mean . . . no freaking way. That was *not* what was happening. Right?

"Dre?"

I shook off the confusion and threw my grin back on. "Just keeping it real, you know? But I'm sure there are some circles where you're like, maybe a seven or an eight."

"Well, gee whiz. Thanks."

The laughter faded into easy smiles, and the conversation faded into us staring at one another. If we'd been in the same room instead of separated by hundreds of miles, maybe we could've let the silence stand, embraced just hanging out, but it was weird over the phone.

"I liked what you said," I told him. "I get that way too. Lonely."

"You do?"

"Yeah," I said. "All the time. But it's boring. You don't wanna hear about it."

"I do!" he said. "Tell me."

And I believed him. It wasn't something he was just saying because he thought it was what I wanted to hear. He was actually interested. "It's like, all I want in the world is to find one person who gets me for real."

"Your friend—Mel?—she doesn't get you?"

"She does. Kinda. Parts of me, really. But there're always gonna be parts she doesn't get. Like, she thinks I need to take advantage of my dad running for president to raise awareness for stuff, like getting conversion therapy banned and shit. And I've got feelings about all that, but she doesn't understand why I just wanna be me and do my thing. It's not her fault. It's just who she is and who I am and who we are together, you know?"

"I do."

"You really do, don't you?"

"I think so."

"And, like, I'm not so caught up in my own shit to think one person's gotta be responsible for giving me everything I need, but I feel like knowing someone shouldn't be so much work. If it's right, it should be easy. Easier. Easy-ish."

Dean's smile was soft and dreamy. "You're pretty easy."

I snorted. "Bitch, you don't even know me."

"I didn't mean—"

"I'm only playing."

"Oh," he said. "Good. Because I never would have insinuated that you were sexually promiscuous."

I rolled my eyes to hide that I was blushing because Dean was so impossibly cute. I doubted he even knew how adorable he was. "Now tell me why *you're* hiding."

Dean's smile wilted, and he bit his bottom lip. "You'll think I'm being foolish."

"Probably," I said. "Tell me anyway."

"Last year, I danced with Charlotte McBride," he said. "She dragged me out for a song where most of the dancing involved jumping up and down. The next song was a slow one, and Charlotte and I danced to that one too. I love dancing, and Charlotte was nice, so I didn't think anything of it."

"Lemme guess," I said. "She thought something of it?"

Dean nodded. "By school on Monday, she had already

111

told her friends that we were a couple, which was definitely news to me, and I had to break it to her that our dance had been nothing more than a dance, and that I didn't have the types of feelings for her that she had for me. She cried in the middle of the cafeteria. It was mortifying."

"So you're hiding in the toilet to avoid breaking another girl's heart?"

"Something like that."

"Look, you can't be responsible for how other people feel. If you wanna dance, and I really gotta see you dance someday, then get out there and dance. Don't let other people projecting their shit onto you get in the way of you having some fun."

Dean didn't look like he was buying what I was selling. "It's not that easy."

"Jesus," I said. "You need to loosen up."

"You try spending the majority of your life in the public eye and tell me how loose you are."

"Fair point." I pursed my lips, looking at him appraisingly. "But we've got to do something. You're tighter than a drag queen's corset. Why don't you start by undoing your tie."

"Like this?" Dean dipped his finger behind his bow tie and tugged it, giving it a little slack.

"That won't do. Just take it off."

"The tie?"

"Yeah."

Tentatively, Dean pulled one end of his tie until it came undone, the ends hanging around his neck.

"Better," I said. "But you still look a little uptight. It's the side part."

"What's wrong with my hair?"

"Nothing if you're a forty-year-old accountant."

Dean reached up and combed his hand through his hair.

"Nope," I said before he'd even finished. "Mess. It. Up. Dig your fingers in there and really give it a shake."

"Like this?" When Dean was finished, his hair looked like he'd rolled out of bed, which was infinitely better than looking like he'd just rolled out of a business lunch.

"Better." I scrunched my face, squinting and trying to take in the whole picture of Dean. "One more thing I need you to do."

"No matter what you say, I'm keeping my pants on."

I fired off a laugh so loud that it echoed through the restroom. "Damn. You've foiled my plan. How about instead, you walk out of the stall and go to the mirror."

Dean frowned. "Is this necessary?"

"Yes," I said. "You're gonna go gray by graduation if you don't learn to relax."

Dean hesitated, and I thought he was gonna bail, but he finally left the stall and walked to the sinks to stand in front of the mirror. From what I could see of the restroom, it looked weirdly similar to the gym restroom at my school. Dingy, gross. Probably smelled bad too.

"Now what?"

"Now I want you to scream."

"Scream?"

"Scream. Yell. Yowl. Whatever you wanna call it, do it."

"I don't get it."

"You don't have to get it, you just gotta do it." I watched Dean look at himself in the mirror, and I wondered what he saw. His lip quivered like he was about to chicken out. "How about I'll do it with you?"

"I'm not sure—"

I closed my eyes and howled like a wolf, filling the restroom with the unapologetic sound of me.

"Now you!" I said.

"Dre . . ."

"Howl, Dean! Do it or I'm hanging up!"

I let loose another howl, and halfway through I heard Dean's voice join mine. I peeked at the phone, and Dean was howling and laughing and there he was. No walls. Pure Dean. This confident, cute, hilarious guy who was definitely going to crush me like he'd crushed Charlotte McBride.

"Dean?" Another voice came through the speaker, and Dean's howl cut off in the middle. "Uh, everything cool?"

My screen went black, but I could still hear, so Dean must've shoved me in his pocket. "Yes, Mr. Clark. Everything is good. In fact, I think tonight is the best night of my life."

"I thought I heard . . . were you howling?"

"It's a full moon, Mr. Clark," Dean said. "Nothing to worry about. I'll be out in a second."

"Um. Okay. I'll just let you do whatever you were doing."

Dean busted up laughing, and when I could see him again, he had tears running down his face and he could hardly talk. "You should have seen the look on Mr. Clark's face. It was spectacular."

"It's a full moon?" I said.

"I don't know! It was the first response I thought of!"

"That could've gone worse."

Dean glanced off the screen, and I heard another voice but not what they said. "I have to go."

"Yeah, I should probably find Mel before she ditches me."

"Thanks, Dre."

"For what?"

"For helping me feel a little less lonely tonight."

Before I could come up with a smart-ass reply or tell him he'd made me feel less alone too, the screen went dark, and this time Dean was gone for real. I didn't know what had just happened, and I didn't know if Dean was feeling even remotely about me the way I was feeling about him, but I was flying way too high at that moment to care.

HOMECOMING WAS THE last school event I would attend until I either returned to school after the election or began preparing to move to Washington, DC. For the rest of the election, I was given the choice to travel with either my mother or my father so that I could witness the election process in a way few people ever would. I could have traveled with Jeffrey Portman, my mother's running mate, but while he was a perfectly nice man, he was as dull as a butter knife.

But rather than tag along with my parents, I was also given the opportunity to go out on my own. I frequently volunteered with Habitat for Humanity near home, and traveling allowed me to do so outside Florida. Schools often asked me to speak to their students about what it was like being Janice

Arnault's son, and I enjoyed standing on a stage talking to people my age about politics, trying to get them involved in the process that governed their lives. These were things I cared deeply about. I had more autonomy and was more active in the campaign than I think any child of a presidential candidate had ever been, and I loved it. I didn't love the additional attention from the media or how often adults that I met felt empowered to insult me, but that was the price of helping my mother win, and I very much wanted her to win. I also didn't love not getting to see my friends at school. Being able to talk to Dre helped with that.

There was an intimacy to talking to Dre over the Promethean app. An intimacy I didn't feel when I was talking to Astrid or Tamal or any of my other friends. I think part of it was the feeling of privacy created by the app itself. It was as if there was a line from my heart to Dre's phone, and I could pour out my secrets one word at a time to no one but him.

Despite that, I sometimes found myself wishing I could talk to Dre in person. I wanted to see him laugh instead of having to imagine it when he filled the screen with emojis. I wanted to hear the lilting sound of his voice and watch his prominent Adam's apple bob when he spoke. It had only been a couple of weeks since Dre and I were locked in the greenroom at the first debate, and talking to him had become the thing I looked forward to most, which I found surreal, to be honest. Of all the people in the world to share a connection with, Andre Rosario was not the person with whom I would have expected it to happen. That said, I couldn't have imagined not having him in my life, and I found myself wanting more.

"Jackson McMann is a cancer." My mother sneered at her tablet. She and my father were sitting across from me at the breakfast table on Sunday morning before church, enjoying their coffee and trying to read the news. My parents were not, by nature, morning people, but my mother's time in the military had made her one, and we were all on her schedule. I'd already gone for a run before getting to the table.

"He's not going to win, is he?" I asked.

"No one's worried about him winning," my mother said. "But if he splits the vote, keeping me or Rosario from reaching two hundred and seventy electoral votes, then all bets are off."

Without looking up from his iPad, my father reached out and rested his hand atop my mother's. "That's not going to happen, love."

We had learned about this in my US government class when we'd covered the electoral college. "Doesn't it go to Congress? The House votes for the president and the Senate chooses the vice president?"

My mother flared her nostrils. "And do you want to guess how many politicians McMann has in his pocket? I'd like to think our elected representatives aren't foolish enough to throw in with a self-serving maggot like McMann, but a lot of them only care about lining their own pockets."

"You shouldn't get worked up about McMann on an empty stomach." My dad nudged her egg-white omelet toward her. "That's how you wind up with an ulcer."

"I'm not hungry."

"I worked hard making that beautiful breakfast for you, and you're not even going to eat it?"

My mother pursed her lips. "Guilt, Doug? Really? Are you looking to get stabbed?"

"Not this morning." My father covertly moved my mother's fork out of her reach.

"I can never tell when you're fighting or flirting," I said.

"It's a fine line," my mother said, and then she smiled at my father and squeezed his hand.

My parents were weird, though I assumed most children thought that about their parents. But they were also sweet and absolutely perfect for one another. Where my mother could be demanding and ornery, my father was easygoing. My father's lack of ambition made up for my mother's abundance of it. They were a team in every way.

"I still don't understand why McMann is such a big problem," I said. "No independent has ever posed a serious threat before."

My mother had gone back to reading her tablet and spoke without looking up. "Because he's a fear-mongering sociopath."

"I doubt he's a sociopath, dear."

"Like hell," my mother said. "All he cares about is power, and he'll do and say whatever he thinks will win him the election, even if it means tearing the country apart." She shook her head. "He's playing on people's fears. He's got Rosario's voters thinking I'm going to arm toddlers with semiautomatic rifles, and he's got my voters thinking Rosario's going to murder babies and kill God, leaving himself as the only alternative."

I hadn't taken the threat Jackson McMann posed seriously because I didn't believe people would honestly support someone so obviously racist, xenophobic, and misogynistic. I assumed his popularity would flame out quickly and he would become a footnote to the election. But clearly I had been wrong to dismiss him, especially if my mother was concerned.

"How do we fight him?" I asked.

"We don't," my father said. "We ignore him. Eventually, he'll say or do something vile enough to disqualify himself from the race."

I sensed my parents were done discussing McMann, and I needed to go get showered and dressed for church anyway, but an idea had begun to form.

"What if I invited Andre Rosario to join me building houses in Belle Rose on Wednesday?" I blurted out the question before I lost my nerve. It was a bold suggestion, and I wasn't sure how my mother would respond.

My father said "Why?" while my mother silently scrutinized me.

I was already a bit overheated from running, but sweat

beaded immediately under my arms and on my back as I scrambled to explain. "Jackson McMann is divisive, right? He's got voters thinking you and Mr. Rosario can't agree on anything. But if people saw Andre and me working together, it would send the message that you can put aside your differences for the betterment of the country."

"I don't like the idea of you using a volunteer opportunity to score political points," my father said.

"Obviously, we would be there to work," I said. "But not only could we bring some attention to the fact that there are still communities struggling to rebuild after last year's hurricanes, Andre and I working together could show people that, despite their differences, Mom and Mr. Rosario are both invested in making the country better for everyone, while Jackson McMann is only in it for himself."

I folded my hands on the table and waited. I knew I could convince my father that this was a good plan, but convincing my mother was the real test. And I wasn't even concerned that she would dislike my idea; I was worried that she would see through it. That she would see my ulterior motive for inviting Dre. I really did want to help my mother's campaign, and I thought this was a good way to do it, but I mostly wanted to see Dre.

Finally, after staring at me with a stony expression for what felt like an hour, my mother said, "At the very least, it could shift attention away from McMann for an afternoon."

"I think this could be a good thing," I said.

"Maybe." My mother still looked skeptical. "Do you think you can stand spending a whole day with Andre Rosario?"

The thought of spending an entire day hanging out with Dre nearly caused me to smile so big it would have given me away immediately. Thankfully, I was able to suppress it. "If it means helping you, Mom, I'm willing to take one for the team."

DRE

I DIDN'T HAVE to fake being annoyed when Dad woke me up at three thirty in the morning to catch our flight to Louisiana by playing a clip of the kindergarten chorus he'd had to endure listening to the day before. If my aim in the dark had been better, he would've had to explain to reporters how a flying tennis shoe had broken his nose.

You'd think that being the Democratic presidential candidate would mean flying all over the country on private jets, but you'd be wrong. We had to go through security and deal with the TSA getting handsy and crowd around the gate, waiting to get on the plane, even though they were gonna call us by group just like everyone else. The only upside was getting to fly first-class, which I'd never done before. Usually I flew coach and was wedged into a middle seat between people who didn't understand the concept of keeping their elbows to their damn selves. The only reason I'd gotten to ride first was because Jose had traded seats with me so I could spend time with my dad, and both he and my dad told me not to get used to it.

Dad had been surprised when I'd finally taken him up on his offer to spend some time with him on the campaign trail. Happy, but surprised. We'd gone to a rally in Kansas on Monday and a town hall meeting in Minnesota on Tuesday, but it was Baton Rouge on Wednesday that I'd really been waiting for. My parents and Jose had thought the idea of me building houses with Dean for Habitat for Humanity was brilliant, and my dad was already going to be in the state, so all I had to do was reluctantly agree to go so that they wouldn't guess how excited I was.

"Excited" is underselling it. When I wasn't chatting with Dean on Promethean, I was moping around thinking about how far away he was, never imagining that he was scheming a way for us to hang out. Dean was way craftier than I gave him credit for.

My dad was in the aisle seat reading a book about some old dead dude and I was trying to get some sleep in the big, comfy seat when the flight attendant came by to drop off breakfast. I was a little annoyed at being woken up—again—but I was also hungry and the omelet didn't look awful.

"I'm really glad you're here," Dad said.

"On the plane?"

"On the campaign trail." Dad shrugged. "I've missed you, kiddo."

This wasn't a conversation I wanted to have while I was trapped on a plane with nowhere to go. Mostly, I just wanted to eat my mediocre breakfast and crash until we landed in Baton Rouge. "Yeah, me too, Dad."

Dad was eating his own breakfast—yogurt and fruit—and was quiet for a few minutes, but I could tell he wasn't done talking. "I signed us up to take trapeze lessons."

That definitely wasn't what I was expecting. "What?"

"You always said you wanted to join the circus."

"When I was ten."

"It's never too late to chase your dreams."

I sighed at my meal and gave Dad my full attention. "I mean, I'll go, obviously, but what's this about? Are you trying to buy my love? Because a car is the fastest way to my heart."

Dad rolled his eyes, but I was serious about that car. "I know I haven't been around much, and you'll be heading off to college soon. I don't want this election to get in the way of our relationship, Dre."

"Then maybe you should've waited to run." I'd only meant to think it, and as soon as I realized I'd said it out loud, I felt like a dick. But that didn't mean I wasn't being honest.

"I did ask," my dad said.

"Ugh, I know. It's just . . ."

"You can say whatever's on your mind, Dre."

It wasn't fair for me to be bringing all this up. I'd had my chance to tell him I didn't want him running, and I'd told him to go for it. Holding it against him now made me feel like an ass. "It's nothing," I said. "I just miss you is all."

My dad was quiet for a while. Things were weird between us now and they'd never been that way before. My dad had been my best friend, and sometimes it felt like we hardly knew each other anymore. Only, I wasn't sure which of us had changed.

"Skip building houses," Dad said after the flight attendant cleared our trays. "And I'll have Jose cancel my events today. We'll hang out, just the two of us."

He really meant it too. Jose would've flipped out if I'd let Dad torch his schedule to play hooky with me. But I kind of wanted to say yes.

"It'll be like when I used to pick you up early from school and we'd go get ice cream and not tell your mom."

I laughed. "She always knew anyway, though."

"I still don't understand how."

I sighed. "I can't, Dad. And neither can you."

"You don't want to build houses anyway," he said. "Remember the birdhouse?"

"I was nine!"

"They had to condemn that birdhouse, Dre. Three birds almost died."

"Now you're just making shit up."

126

"Are you calling your father, the future president of the United States, a liar? I'm pretty sure it's in the Constitution that you can't do that."

I laughed in spite of myself. "Thanks, Dad, but I can't leave Dean hanging."

"Sure you can," Dad said. "We'll tell the Arnaults you came down with the flu."

It was the kind of thing Dad and I had done all the time before, and I was so tempted to say yes. But as much as I wanted to hang out with my dad, I wanted to see Dean more.

"Maybe next time," I said.

My dad nodded, trying to hide his disappointment at me not bailing on my plans with Dean. "When this election is over, I'll make it up to you."

I felt bad about what I'd said and I didn't want him going back out on the campaign trail feeling guilty and thinking he could be my dad or he could be president but that he couldn't be both. I didn't want him to be president, but I kind of thought he'd do a halfway decent job.

"Make it up to me by winning," I said. "Take down Janice Arnault and Jackson McMann, and win this bitch."

Dad hugged me and kissed the top of my head.

"I'd also take a car."

"Not happening."

"But it could."

"Nope."

127

Dad picked his book back up, though I caught him smirking my way. I rolled my eyes and made sure he could see me. Then I pulled out my phone to see if Dean had written. We'd been talking nonstop, but he hadn't mentioned the trip to Louisiana, and I didn't want to bring it up because I was afraid I'd jinx it. Instead, we talked about everything else. Comic books and movies and college and how he'd gotten to meet Ariana Grande even though he didn't know who she was at the time, and I had never been more jealous in my life. Talking to Dean was the brightest spot in my every day, and I could hardly believe I was going to get to see him in a couple of hours.

At the same time, I was terrified to see him because it wouldn't just be us. There would be reporters and other volunteers present. We'd have to be careful what we said and how we acted toward one another. I was also scared because, as much as I didn't want to admit it, I was seeing Dean as more than a friend, and I didn't know if I could take him not seeing me the same way, even though it was pretty likely that was all he considered me. Maybe I should've told him what was on my mind, but I decided to play it casual instead and see what happened.

My phone buzzed, but instead of a message from Dean, it was one from Mel.

Mel: you get the latex?

Dre: latex . . .

Mel: for the fantasy fish shoot?!?

Mel: i will murder you if you forgot

Dre: i didn't forget

Oh yeah, I'd definitely forgotten. Liquid Dreams, a special effects studio, was holding a Fantasy Fish Photo Challenge. The prize was cash and makeup and the chance to intern for Liquid Dreams, but the exposure was the biggest reward. I'd forgotten, when I'd agreed to build houses with Dean, that I'd already made plans with Mel to work on the challenge.

Shit.

Dre: im in louisiana with my dad today

Mel: Okay.

Dre: capitalized and punctuated?!?

Dre: dont be like that

Mel: i'll see you when youre back

Dre: im sorry

Dre: didnt i suffer through the ball with you so you could choose between your boys

Dre: a choice you still havent made btw

Mel: this is more important than a stupid dance

Mel: forget it

Dre: don't be like that

Dre: mel?

Dre: mel????

My dad was looking over at me when I dropped my phone in my lap with an exasperated sigh. "Everything all right?"

It wasn't fair for Mel to be mad at me. I would've understood if our situations were reversed. And it's not like I was abandoning her just to build houses; I was going to see Dean! It might've helped if she knew that, but she didn't, so I couldn't blame her for it even though I really wanted to. Everything was too damn complicated.

"I don't know," I said. "But I'm probably gonna have to buy Mel a car."

DEAN

DRE WALKED ONTO the site wearing tight jean shorts frayed at the bottoms that showed off a disturbing amount of his extremely hairy legs, and a bright rainbow tank top, making him absolutely impossible to miss. We were about the same height, but he looked so much taller than me. He was long and twiggy, and he walked like he was stomping down a runway in Milan. I admired that about him. He'd known he was going to have to pass through a throng of photographers eager to see the potential first sons together, and he'd deliberately chosen that outfit. It was a bold ensemble that I never would have possessed the courage to wear. And despite Dre not having grown up around the press, they liked him, and he answered their questions with a casual ease I had worked hard to master.

Barriers had been set up to keep the press from disrupting

the worksite, and thankfully, the photographers respected them. They were close enough to take a million pictures of Dre and me together, but not near enough to overhear us if we kept our voices low.

I didn't know why, but I was nervous to see Dre. Our rambling conversations were so perfect that I suppose I was worried spending time together in real life wouldn't be as good. Dre might not have liked me in person or I might not have liked him. We could have wound up actual enemies like most of the public assumed we already were.

"Ah," Dre said as he approached, "I see you're wearing your Wednesday leisure outfit."

I was wearing khaki jeans and a blue campaign polo. "What's wrong with what I'm wearing?"

Dre held up his hands. "Nothing."

"At least I don't look like I'm trying to make a statement."

"You're making a statement all right." He cleared his throat. "Quarterly earnings are down due to market conditions outside of our control."

There was a sharp edge to Dre's joke that drew blood, and I wasn't prepared for it. We'd joked around on Promethean, but those jokes hadn't hurt, and I didn't know what had changed. It was possible I'd overestimated our friendship and had made a mistake inviting him to the build site, but then I wished he would have said something sooner instead of arriving and mocking me in front of the cameras.

A young woman who looked only a couple of years older

than us popped up between Dre and me like she thought she was heading off a fight, even though we were both smiling. "Hiya! I'm Cora! I'm so happy to have you both here. Who's ready to build something?"

I raised my hand. "Is there any work we can do that won't be too tiring? I'm sure Dre's not used to doing manual labor." My annoyance with Dre slipped out, though I should have known better.

Dre rolled his eyes. "Who do you think you're dealing with?"

"Do you know how to put up drywall?"

"No."

"Ductwork?"

"Ducks?"

"Ducts," I said, emphasizing the *T*.

"No to either, but I can't wait for the lecture about it I'm certain you've got prepared, Mr. Arnault." Dre turned to Cora and silently mouthed, *Save me!*

I had no idea what must have been going through Cora's head because I had no idea what was going on, but she finally tossed out a nervous laugh. "I get it," she said to Dre. "You're the funny one."

Dre shook his head. "He's the funny one. I'm the arsonist."

The pitch of Cora's laughter rose an octave, and I imagine she was probably wondering what sin she had committed that her punishment was being saddled with us.

"I'm sorry about him," I said. "It's his first time."

"But not yours?" Cora asked.

"No. I volunteer locally most weekends."

This information seemed to thrill Cora to no end. "Good. I mean, good! Then I think you two should stick together. We actually need painters today, if you don't mind painting."

"*Kiss-ass*," Dre coughed under his breath.

"If you don't know how to paint," I said, "I'm sure we can find you a job rinsing brushes."

"I love to paint," Dre said. "My style is sort of what it'd look like if a cubist was beaten to death by an impressionist."

Cora cut us off. "Splendid. Find Kenny in house three-oh-three down the road, and he'll get you set up with paint and brushes and whatever else you need." Without waiting for us to respond, Cora walked away, muttering to herself, "*This is not worth the extra-credit points.*"

As soon as Cora was out of earshot, I turned to Dre. "Too much coffee this morning?"

"Not enough sleep. Did I take it too far?"

"You were joking?"

Dre's eyes went a little wide. "Weren't you?"

Words spilled out, and I stumbled over them. "You were so mean, and I didn't know what to think."

"I was just playing for the cameras." He hiked his thumb over his shoulder. "And I was scared."

"What were *you* scared of?"

Dre shrugged. "That things wouldn't be like they were on Promethean."

I was relieved but also confused. I didn't know whether I believed Dre was kidding. I wanted it to be true, but even with our conversations on Promethean, I still didn't know him that well. "We should find Kenny." I took off in the direction Cora had pointed.

The worksite was a street of houses; ten in all. The ones farthest from us were mostly built, with the ones nearest little more than a frame. Volunteers scurried over the houses doing the work they were assigned, and the sun was already beating down on me, making me sweat.

Dre walked behind me, and I wished I could think of something to say. This wasn't going the way I had planned, and I wanted the day to be over even though it had hardly begun. My phone vibrated in my pocket. It was a message from Dre.

DreOfTheDead: im sorry
DreOfTheDead: i guess i got carried away
DreOfTheDead: im really glad im here

I stared at the messages for a second and then put my phone away. "I'm glad you're here too," I said loudly enough for him to hear.

Dre caught up to me, and he was beaming when I glanced at him. "I can't believe you pulled this off. I never would've thought of doing something like this. My plan would've involved a large box, packing peanuts, and a lot of stamps."

The thought of Dre shipping himself across the country made me laugh. "That definitely seems like something you would do."

"Right?"

"Did you have any trouble with your parents?" I asked.

Dre shook his head. "They loved the idea of me volunteering but kept asking me if I was sure I could handle spending the whole day with you. I think they were afraid you'd strangle me."

"My parents were also worried I'd strangle you."

"That's fair."

The longer we walked, the more we fell into the rhythm we'd established on Promethean, proving that our conversations *could* translate into the real world. At least for a short while. But there was one thing I still needed to know.

"Do you really think I'm dressed badly or was that part of your plan to throw off the reporters?" I heard myself ask, and hated how pathetic I sounded. Dre didn't need anyone's approval, so why did I?

Dre pulled me to a stop alongside him. He eyed me up and down like he was scrutinizing everything about me. Finally, he said, "You know you're good-looking, but—"

"But?"

"What you wear says a lot about who you are."

"What do my clothes say?"

"My client is not guilty, Your Honor."

"I object!"

"All I'm saying is that it looks like you bought your outfits right off the mannequins at the Gap." Dre made a grab for the bottom of my shirt, but I stopped him. "What are you doing?"

"Relax."

I wasn't worried about him—I was concerned about a reporter snapping a picture at the wrong moment and taking it out of context—but I didn't see anyone around, so I let Dre do what he wanted. He pulled the bottom of my shirt out until it was completely untucked. He stood back to look at what he'd done, then reached up and ruffled my hair, appraising it with one eye until he was satisfied.

"Better?"

"You don't look like your mom dressed you anymore."

"My mom didn't dress me," I said. "I dressed myself."

Dre let out a laugh. "That's even worse."

"I guess," I said. "But if I hadn't, you wouldn't have had anything to fix."

The laughter on Dre's face vanished like it had never been there in the first place. A crease formed between his eyes. "Shit, Dean. I didn't . . . You don't need to be fixed."

I couldn't stop smiling, and I didn't even care.

MY SHOULDERS WERE sore by the end of the first hour, but there was no way I was complaining where Dean could hear, especially since he had the lean muscles of someone who spent his free time lifting weights. He could probably paint all day—and then go run a marathon.

We didn't talk much while we painted, mostly because every time I tried to crack a joke, I screwed something up, and I didn't want to half-ass the paint job in a house someone was gonna be living in. Especially when it was going to be someone who'd lost their house to a hurricane. Those people had been through enough, and they deserved for me to take the job I was doing seriously.

Earlier in the morning, a couple of volunteers popped by

to check on our progress, so they said, but ended up asking if they could take selfies with us. Thankfully, that didn't last long, and other than that, they treated us like we were nothing more than a couple of high school kids working for community service hours. Reporters were allowed into the house at one point so they could take pictures of me and Dean working, and we gave them a couple of good poses, including one of me standing behind Dean with a bucket of paint like I was about to dump it on his head. Eventually, they got bored and left to chase more interesting stories.

The other cool part was just hanging with Dean. Within five minutes of walking into 303, he knew everyone's names and a little something about them, and he was laughing with them like they'd been best friends forever. He drew people to him without even trying. During my first five minutes in the house, I'd leaned against *two* freshly painted doors and stepped in a pan of paint, leaving a single paint shoeprint trailing through the house. Luckily, the floors had been covered with plastic to protect them from fools like me. I might've joked about Dean being uptight, but I admired how natural he was talking to other people. And it didn't seem like an act to me. I think he genuinely enjoyed meeting and talking to everyone. He was also really patient when he was teaching me the best way to paint, and he never got upset when he had to repeat something. It made me wonder if there was anything he wasn't good at.

When lunch rolled around, Dean and I grabbed

sandwiches and wandered off to a park that was still within view of the worksite, and found a bench to sit on.

"Hold up," I said. "Gotta go back. I forgot a drink."

Dean reached into his backpack and handed me a metal water bottle with "Arnault/Portman 2020" and their slogan "For Tomorrow" emblazoned on the side. "I brought this for you. So that you stay hydrated."

"You can't expect me to drink out of that," I said.

"Why not?" he asked. "It's not plastic, so it's good for the environment, right?"

I raised my eyebrows at the bottle. "Jose would kill me if anyone caught me drinking out of a bottle with your mom's slogan on it." I set the bottle to the side, close enough so that I could reach it in case I started choking to death and it was the only option, but far enough away that no one would think it was mine.

Dean's shoulders curved inward and slumped down a little. "I just thought you'd be thirsty," he said. "How do you like volunteering so far?"

I couldn't tell if Dean was upset that I didn't want to drink out of the water bottle he'd brought me. It was sweet, yeah, but Jose really would've considered it a disaster if a picture of me drinking out of it showed up, and he probably never would've let me out on my own again.

"It's all right," I said. "Not as much fun as when I put together a Drag Queens Read event at the library where my mom works."

"Did you dress up?"

I smiled as I unwrapped my sandwich—turkey and Swiss with mayo, boring but not terrible—remembering the event. "Yeah. I made up a queen named Betty Don't."

Dean spread a napkin over his lap before pulling his egg salad out of the wrapper. "Aren't drag queen names supposed to be funny?"

"They don't have to be," I said. "But mine was." I waited a beat for him to get it, but he kept watching me all blank-faced. "Betty Don't?" Still nothing, so I said it slower, sounding out each word. "Bet he don't?"

"I'll take your word for it."

"*Anyway*. The queens were the real stars. They just let me play in their world for a minute, and it was fun as hell. The way the kids lit up when they saw us, and how they couldn't take their eyes off us while we were reading to them. It was magical."

Dean ate his sandwich with polite little bites, dabbing at his mouth with his napkin after each. "Please don't think badly of me, but I don't understand the point of drag queens. Are they making fun of women? Do they want to *be* women?"

"Shit no," I said. "First, don't confuse being trans with being a drag queen. They're definitely not the same. Trans women are women, and trans men are men."

"I thought so," Dean said. "But, so then, explain drag."

This was a bigger conversation than I was expecting over lunch. I figured we'd have a laugh about him getting caught howling at his reflection during the homecoming dance or us both spending that evening hiding in toilet stalls, but I hadn't expected to be giving him a lesson on the meaning of drag. Hell, I wasn't sure I was even the right person to be doing it. I knew some queens, and I'd dressed up once, but that didn't make me an expert.

"You've never met a single drag queen?"

Dean shook his head. "They're not the kind of people who usually vote for my mother."

"I wonder why."

"Forget it," Dean said. "We don't have to—"

"No wait." I was fortunate that my parents were the kind of people who'd encouraged me to meet drag queens and organize a read-along with them, but Dean hadn't grown up with my parents. If he was genuinely interested in learning, and his curiosity did seem sincere, then maybe I could give it a try.

"Look, I can't speak for all drag queens, but I view drag as performance art. Queens create a character that's totally separate from who they are when they're not in drag. Some use it to live out their fantasy of wearing beautiful gowns and jewels, some use it as a way to escape the toxic masculinity that's been forced on them all their lives, and others use it as a way to blur the lines between the masculine and feminine.

"When I was Betty Don't, inspired by my mom and by Olivia Newton-John's leather transformation at the end of *Grease*, I felt powerful in a way that I never felt as Dre Rosario. It's the kind of experience that's tough to explain without cinching your waist and shoving you into a pair of six-inch heels."

Instead of laughing, Dean was watching me with the same rapt attention the kids at the library had been watching me with while I'd read to them from my favorite book, *The Girl Who Drank the Moon*.

"I always thought it was nothing more than a bunch of men in dresses."

"No," I said. "And that's kinda the problem with being so sheltered. It's not even enough for me to explain it to you. What you need is to meet some real queens and get to know them." I snapped my fingers. "You should do an event with me. We can use my mom's library, you can dress up and—"

Dean grimaced. "I doubt that would go over well."

"Because of your mom?"

Dean froze, his shoulders tensed, and he looked away from me, focused intently on his sandwich. "She doesn't hate gay people," he said. "We went on *Ellen*."

I considered dropping it. I'd already put Dean on the defensive, and we'd been having such a fun day that I didn't want to ruin it. But I also heard Mel's voice telling me to stand for something or I was just wasting everyone's time, and anyone who knows Mel will agree that she's damned difficult to ignore. "Going on *Ellen* isn't the same as believing queer people deserve the same rights as everyone else. Didn't your mom support amending the state constitution to keep same-sex couples from marrying?"

"Yes, but I'm not my mother."

"Then what do you believe, Dean?"

Dean seemed to have forgotten his sandwich as he stared across the street at a bunch of empty lots overgrown with weeds. I was sure, after this, he was never gonna want to see me again. But I had to know, and better that I found out now.

"What about conversion therapy?" I asked, pressing Dean harder. "Or abortion rights or gun control?"

"Do you support everything your dad believes?" Dean snapped.

"No, but I don't pretend I do either. He's fine letting people keep guns, but I think we should stick all the guns into a rocket and launch them into the sun, and I'm not afraid to say so, no matter who's listening."

I kept waiting for Dean to go off on me. I'd heard about his vaunted debate skills, but he didn't seem to me like he could argue his way out of detention.

"Look," Dean said, spreading his hands. "I don't believe in all of my mother's political views, but I believe in her."

"Bullshit!" I said.

"How so?"

My cheeks were getting hot as I worked myself up. "Do you think same-sex couples deserve the right to get married?"

"Why does it matter?" he asked, his voice rising. "The courts already decided the issue."

"Answer the question, Dean."

"Fine!" Dean threw up his hands. "Yes, I do."

144

"Then how can you support your mom, knowing she doesn't? How can you let her trot you out onstage, knowing folks assume you believe the same things she does, and never say anything?"

Instead of answering, Dean stood, gathered his trash, and walked toward the swings. He sat in one, not swinging. I grabbed my own garbage and tossed it in the can before sitting in the swing beside him.

"I wish this wasn't personal for me," I said. "But it is. Like, how can I be friends with someone who supports someone who thinks I'm not a person?"

"My mother doesn't think you're not a person."

"Just not deserving of the same rights as her."

Dean gripped the cords holding up the swing and sat with his head bowed, not looking at me. Maybe there was no way for me and Dean to be friends. Maybe we were just way too dissimilar.

"It's different for me than it is for you," Dean said. "From the beginning of the campaign, before your father secured the nomination, you were already out there being you. The first time I saw you on TV, you were with your father at a rally, and you were wearing shorts and pink Converse high-tops, and I remember thinking that Nora would have had a stroke if I'd shown up to a rally in an outfit like that."

Laughter burst out of me, and I nearly fell backward out of the swing.

"What's so funny?"

145

"Everything you just said," I told him. "You think it's easy being the out gay Mexican American son of a presidential candidate?"

"I didn't say it was easy—"

"People say you're a clone of your mom," I said. "But they call me a faggot. Think of an object, any object, and someone on 4chan's made a meme of me being penetrated by it. They tell me to go back where I came from, and they don't mean Nevada. I could've thrown on a pair of jeans and a black T-shirt and faded into the background, but that's not who I am. Being me all the time, especially with the shit people say, is hard, Dean, and don't think for a second it isn't."

I expected Dean to apologize, but he snorted derisively. "I didn't mean to imply being you was easy, but you've been living under this microscope for a few months. I've been doing it for *years*. And, no, I don't like all my mom's views, but I'm not supporting Janice Arnault, Republican candidate for president of the United States; I'm supporting my mom."

"You can support your mom and still be yourself."

"How?"

"The campaign can spin anything. They'll just say it shows how tolerant your mom is that she can still love you even though you disagree." I kicked at Dean until he looked at me. "Do you think my dad's campaign wanted me to be so outspoken? Hell no. But Jose figured if I was gonna do it anyway, they might as well use me to appeal to younger voters."

"They're still using you," Dean said.

146

I nodded. "But it's on my terms."

"She's a good person, you know." When I didn't respond, he added, "My mom. She's a good person and she has a good heart."

"Good people make bad decisions all the time."

"Do you think *I'm* a good person?"

The question caught me off guard, and I fumbled for a moment before saying, "That's what I'm trying to figure out."

"I think you're a good person." Dean smiled, but it wasn't the smile he used with everyone else, the one that said, "I'm Dean Arnault, and I've got a deal for you!" It was softer, subtler. It was in his lips and his cheeks, and it reached all the way to his eyes, where it simply said, "Hey."

And when I looked down, Dean's hand was resting on mine.

DEAN

I FOCUSED MY attention on painting. On rolling the paint onto the walls evenly, on not dripping any onto the floor, on rolling right up to the corner without touching the ceiling. My fingers were sore and stiff from holding the pole, but I didn't relent because I knew that Dre was on the other side of the room hoping I would turn around and talk to him, and I just wasn't confident I could open my mouth and say words that wouldn't make an uncomfortable situation worse.

"That's what I'm trying to figure out," Dre had said.

I remember smiling and telling him I thought *he* was a good person. And it was true. He was one of the most honest, genuine people I'd ever met. I hated that I'd given him reason to doubt me, but I also appreciated that he hadn't written me off because we didn't necessarily believe the same things.

I don't remember reaching out and putting my hand on his. At first, I couldn't figure out why his eyes had widened and bulged like a lemur's. Not until he glanced down, which made me glance down, and then I yanked my hand away and said, "Sorry! I didn't mean to do that!"

Dre looked like he was going to laugh or cry. Perhaps laugh and *then* cry or laugh and cry at the same time. I had no idea what to do, so I stood and said we should return to work and then promptly returned to the house. Dre didn't follow for a few minutes.

Pretending it hadn't happened was probably the wisest course of action, but I got the impression that Dre wasn't the type of person to simply forget something, and I didn't want him to get the wrong idea.

"Once," I said, "I was at my great-uncle's funeral—we all called him Uncle Bob. He was a bit of a black sheep." I looked over my shoulder to see if Dre was paying attention, and when he caught me looking, I coughed and cleared my throat.

"Anyway, I was fourteen, and I hadn't known Uncle Bob particularly well, but the whole family had used the opportunity to have an impromptu reunion, so there were a lot of relatives I'd never met in attendance. I was, however, expected to be the perfect son and shake their hands and smile, which I'd been doing for a while and was therefore quite good at. One of my mom's cousins had cornered me, and I'd finally managed to make an escape, and as I was leaving, I shook her hand and said, 'Love you too.'

"We just stared at each other for a minute while my face turned very, very red, and then I walked away."

"Cool story," Dre said. There was a cautious edge to his voice.

"Right. Well, the point is that sometimes we say or do things we don't mean because . . . well, because we just do. I don't . . . I don't want you to get the wrong idea."

"What idea would that be?"

"Nothing," I said. "It didn't mean anything."

That had gone as well as I had any right to expect. The problem was that I wasn't sure whether I was being honest with Dre *or* with myself. I might have touched his hand because it was something my mother did when she was campaigning and someone was telling her a story—a small gesture that let the other person feel like my mother was listening and that she cared.

And I did care because Dre had given me a lot to consider. I didn't necessarily think he was being fair assuming that I supported every single one of my mother's beliefs because I supported her. There had to be room for me to think she could do a lot of good for the country even if I didn't agree with her on some issues.

My phone vibrated in my pocket, and I grabbed it in case it was my mother or Nora, but it was a notification from Promethean. From Dre. I glanced over my shoulder, but he was still painting.

The first message included a photo of me from the back.

DreOfTheDead: from this angle you might actually be a seven

DreOfTheDead: would it be bad if it meant something to me?

PrezMamasBoy: I don't know.

PrezMamasBoy: I don't think so.

PrezMamasBoy: However, I'm not sure it would mean the same thing to you that it did to me.

Dre leaned his roller against the wall and turned around. "I thought it didn't mean anything."

We were alone in the room but not alone in the house. There were people on the other side of each wall, so I lowered my voice to make sure they couldn't hear me. "You know how I am."

"I know *who* you are, Dean. Maybe better than anyone else. And I'm not sure I'm saying what you think I'm saying."

"What *are* you saying?"

"Just that I like hanging out with you. That's it. Nothing more. More would be bananas, right? You're not into anyone like that, and our parents are sworn enemies."

Dre's hyperbolic nature was a constant source of amusement. He could probably make grocery shopping sound like an adventure at the end of the world. "First of all, our parents are political rivals, not Montagues and Capulets."

"So I brought my dueling sword for nothing?"

"Second," I said, ignoring him. "It's not as if I've never been attracted to anyone before. I have had crushes."

"Oh."

I had thought that knowledge would make Dre feel better, but it seemed to have had the opposite effect. He wore an expression that looked like I'd mugged him for his phone and wallet.

"Fine," Dre said. "Whatever. It's still not like we can hang out like friends or whatever."

"We're hanging out now."

"But this was a one-time thing."

"We are two bright young men," I said. "Surely we can concoct a way to run into one another again. We could arrange a different volunteer opportunity."

Dre picked up his roller and continued working. "How many times do you think we can pull this off? It's not like we're in the same state that often."

"It happens more than you think," I said.

A devious gleam crept into Dre's eyes, and he got out his phone. "Where are you next week? I'm in Iowa on Monday."

I shook my head. "Wisconsin."

"Lucky you. How about Tuesday?"

"Pennsylvania."

Dre's smile began to fade. "California."

"I'm in Georgia on Wednesday and Boston on Thursday."

"Chicago on Wednesday." Dre stopped. "Boston?"

I nodded. "My mother's meeting with a group of women in the tech industry. I'm not sure I'm even going."

"You have to go," Dre said.

"Okay," I said. "Why?"

Dre looked like he was going to begin bouncing off the walls. "Because I'm going to be in Rhode Island checking out RISD. My dad was gonna go with me, but he's gotta be in DC that day. I'll be by myself."

"I still don't see how that helps us."

Dre threw up his hands in exasperation. "You applied to Harvard, right?"

"Obviously."

"Then go to Boston with your mom, but tell her you want to tour the school." Dre kept pausing like he thought I was going to finish his thoughts, but I had no idea where he was going with this.

"So we'll both be touring a school," I said. "Then what."

Dre pressed his lips together and looked at me like I was a shelter dog nobody wanted. "We're not going to do the tours," he said. "Boston is, like, less than an hour by train from Rhode Island. We'll ditch the tours and meet up, and then we'll have the whole day to spend together."

In theory, I saw how it could work, but before Dre had finished explaining his plan, I had already come up with a dozen reasons it wouldn't work. "I don't know. What if someone recognized us?"

"We'll wear disguises."

"What if my mother finds out I didn't go on the tour?"

Dre laughed. "Harvard isn't going to call your mom and rat you out for ditching the tour."

The idea of spending more time with Dre *was* appealing, even if it was also slightly confusing, but using a college tour as a cover was a solid plan. "It's risky."

"If you don't want to, then just say so."

"It's not that!"

"Then let's make this happen!" Dre was so eager it was infectious.

"Okay," I said. "But can we agree to put the politics aside? I want to spend time with my friend Dre, not Andre the son of my mother's enemy."

"I'm not sure it works like that," he said. "But we can try."

"Then I will make the arrangements." I let a cautious smile sneak onto my face. The day hadn't gone as smoothly as I'd hoped. There was a lot we didn't agree on and I was confused about my feelings for Dre, but I still didn't want the day to end. It made me feel better knowing I'd get to see him again in a week.

"Hey," Dre said. "I think you're a good person too, though it might just be that I've been breathing paint fumes all day." He winked at me and turned back to his work.

Next week couldn't arrive quickly enough.

DRE

THE DESIGN MEL and I had settled on for the Fantasy Fish photo shoot was Ursula from the *The Little Mermaid* if she had been imagined by Guillermo del Toro. Mel's skin was a mottled shade of violet with some bioluminescent streaks, and each of her thick tentacles spread open like a flower to reveal layered rows of needle-like teeth.

"You've never looked more lovely," I said, standing back and admiring my work. "Or more terrifying."

"Take the pictures, Dre. This shit is hot."

Mel had seemingly forgiven me, though she wasn't her normal chatty self. When I showed up, she didn't want to gossip. She just wanted to get right to work, which was fine. I was used to Mel's cold fronts, and I deserved it this time. I'd already been taking pictures for twenty minutes, and I'd sent a couple

155

of samples to Dean to show him what I was up to, though he hadn't messaged back, which, whatever, right? I wasn't gonna turn into one of those people who freaked out because the boy I had a crush on and who probably definitely didn't have reciprocal feelings for me wasn't haunting his phone waiting for me to write him so that he could reply immediately.

(You're right. I was already that person. Damn.)

I dipped into my bag and grabbed the water bottle Dean had given me and handed it to Mel. "It's important to stay hydrated."

Mel carefully drank, but she noticed the campaign slogan on the bottle before giving it back. "Switching sides?"

I swiped the bottle from her and tossed it on my bag. "Dean gave it to me when I did the Habitat for Humanity thing."

"And you kept it?"

"No reason to throw away a perfectly good bottle. I'll find a sticker to cover it with or something." I held up the camera. "Ready? Give me underwater soccer mom who's had a little too much rosé."

"Could you take this seriously, please."

"I am."

It could have just been the makeup, but Mel was starting to actually look scary. "Maybe this is a joke to you, but not all of us have the money or connections to go to school wherever the hell we want. Some of us have to save money from our shitty minimum-wage jobs and spend our free time doing work we hope will help us get what you take for granted."

"Clearly you're still mad at me for forgetting the shoot Wednesday."

Mel threw up her tentacles. "Yes! I'm still mad!"

"I'm sorry," I said. "Would you like me to burn my apology into the grass on the football field at school?"

"How about you take these tentacles and see how many of them you can shove up your ass?"

Honestly, I was okay with Mel blowing her top at me. Fights with Mel were like puking—best to get them out and over with quickly.

"I get it," I said. "I'm an asshole, but you were the one always telling me to be more active in this stuff, right?"

Mel laughed, which was scary coming from her eyeless, puckered fish face. "I wanted you to fight for things that matter, but the only reason you do anything is to get attention or piss off your dad. I don't know why you're suddenly all about the campaign, but I'm not buying your patriotic act."

Mel tried to turn around, but one of her tentacles caught on a lamp and sent it toppling over, busting the bulb and pulling down the sheet we'd hung for a backdrop. She stood in the center of the destruction for a moment and then flapped around and yelled, "Just get me out of this thing!"

I helped Mel out of the bodysuit and cleaned up the garage while she removed the makeup. When I was done, I wondered if I should take off, but I hated leaving with Mel so pissed. I found her in her room, sitting on her bed in front of a plate of snickerdoodles her mom had baked. She'd changed into sweats and an oversize *The Disastrous Life of Saiki K.* T-shirt and was totally giving off a "disapproving mom catches son watching porn" vibe.

I leaned against the doorway, unsure whether I was welcome in her room. "You ever choose between Andy and Tade?"

"I chose neither because boys are assholes and I don't need one to be happy."

"What happened?"

Mel shoved a cookie in her mouth. The smell was making my stomach rumble. Normally I would've grabbed one, but I was scared Mel would literally bite my hand off if I tried. "Tade, as it turned out, already had a girlfriend. Two, actually."

"And Andy?"

"Asked how soon was too soon to tell someone he loved them."

"That's not so bad, maybe."

"And was also proud that he'd never read a comic book with a girl main character."

"Fuck that guy."

Mel rolled her eyes. "It's whatever. Between work and Dreadful Dressup and college applications and finishing senior year without my best friend, the last thing I need is boyfriend drama."

I took a chance, dropped my bag on the floor, and moved closer to the bed. When Mel didn't immediately murder me, I sat on the edge, but I steered clear of her cookies. "I've been so wrapped up trying to figure out how to help my dad while still being pissed at him, doing all the campaign stuff, and dealing with my own drama, that I didn't think how this was affecting you."

"I used to be able to depend on you, Dre."

"You still can. Mostly."

Mel's tone was softer, a little warmer. "Just . . . don't promise things you can't deliver. If you say you're gonna be there for me, be there."

"I will," I said. "I promise. Pinkie promise. Find me a knife and I'll make it a blood oath."

Mel pushed the plate of cookies toward me, and I gratefully grabbed one. Mel's mom made the best cookies in the world. There was nothing they couldn't mend.

"So what's *your* drama?" Mel asked while I savored my cookie.

I talked with my mouth full, ignoring Mel's look of disgust. "My dad's freaking out because McMann's gonna be in the next debate. After the last debate, he was excited for a rematch with Arnault, but throwing McMann into the mix has him shook. When he's not at rallies and stuff, he's doing nonstop debate prep. But we're doing this trapeze class tomorrow night and I'm so excited!"

Mel's eyes were a little glazed over. "I meant the other stuff.

What about the guy you were talking to? You ever settle that?"

I shook my head. "There's nothing there. Maybe. I don't know. I was all psyched up to accept that he didn't like me and then there was this moment where I thought he did, but then it was gone and he was acting like it was nothing when I was sure it was something."

"Why won't you tell me who it is?" she asked.

"It's complicated."

Mel's face lit up conspiratorially. "Is he married? Is he older? Like a teacher?"

"No, no, and hell no."

"Okay," Mel said. "But if you don't think he's into you, why are you bent outta shape about him?" Before I could answer, she raised her hand to her mouth. "Oh. You really like him, don't you? You've, like, already planned your wedding and the next twenty years of your lives together."

I tried my best to look indignant. "Have not."

"What're your kids' names?"

"Darius, Kayla, and Jorge, but that's not the point."

Mel's expression shifted quickly to pity. "Don't do this to yourself again, Dre."

"I'm not doing anything."

"Falling for a boy you can't have? That's basically your brand. The more he isn't into you, the more likely you are to be into him. I've seen this show before."

"Just forget it."

"Justin Chen."

160

"Drop it, Mel."

"Luis Cantero."

"Mel!"

"Daniel Grant."

I stood, nearly knocking over the plate of cookies, but Mel rescued them at the last second.

"I don't want you getting hurt, Dre."

"I won't get hurt."

"You always get hurt because you throw your heart out like it's a life preserver when really it's just chum for sharks."

I could've pretended to be offended, but Mel was right. I was setting myself up for heartbreak. "I don't know what to do." I slumped back down on the bed beside her.

Mel wrapped her arm around my shoulders and hugged me. "Are you sure he isn't into you?"

"There's a chance," I said. "It's tiny. Super tiny. But even if he is, and it's likely he's not, we're so different."

"How?" Mel asked. "Like you're a Leo and he's a Pisces or like you enjoy charming British comedies and he's into gore-porn horror movies?"

"Worse." I leaned into Mel.

"Who is this mystery guy?"

"I can't tell you." I got off the bed and went to my bag for water. The cookies had left my mouth a little dry; mostly, though, I was trying to avoid looking Mel in the eye. But as I finished drinking and was closing the lid on the bottle, I noticed Mel staring at me, her eyes bulging. "What?"

"Oh my God."

"Mel?"

"It really *is* Dean Arnault, isn't it?"

"Mel, I—"

Mel covered her mouth with her hand. "You told me and I didn't believe you, but that's it, isn't it? He's the mystery guy?"

I was panicking. I tried to laugh and roll my eyes and play like it was a joke, but I knew I was busted. "You can't tell anyone, Mel. I'm serious."

"It makes sense," she said, still working it out for herself. "You met at the debate and, is that where it started?"

"Kind of," I said. "We've been talking on Promethean."

"Of course!"

Dean was going to kill me. I trusted Mel not to tell anyone, and playing coy at this point would only make her dig deeper and could lead to her unintentionally exposing Dean. "But there's nothing going on."

"So he's gay?"

"I don't know." I felt weird talking about Dean without him around. It wasn't my secret to tell, but Mel had already guessed Dean was the guy I was crushing on, and with the information I'd already given her, she could come to the wrong conclusion if I didn't tell her the truth. All I could do at this point was damage control. "He thinks he's probably demisexual, but he hasn't gotten specific about the type of person he might be romantically interested in."

Mel got on her knees on the bed, leaned over, and slapped

my arm. "That's for keeping it from me." She slapped me again. "And that's for having a crush on Dean Arnault!"

"What the hell, Mel?"

"It doesn't matter if he's into you, Dre! How could you even think of being with a guy whose mom would ban abortion, arm teachers, eliminate protections for trans people, and probably thinks global warming is a hoax?"

"Dean's not like that," I said.

"Does his mom know he's demi?"

I shook my head.

"Because he's Mommy's perfect little robot, and—" She stopped short and threw up her hands. "Fuck! I can't even say that anymore because it's a stereotype that I refuse to perpetuate regardless of what a repulsive asshat I think he is."

"Calling him or anyone names for any reason really isn't a good look," I said. "Not that I'm not guilty of it too."

The face Mel made told me in no uncertain terms that this was *not* the time for a lecture on morality from me. I hadn't seen her this angry in a long time. "Do you know how much good he could do if he came out?"

"Mel, you can't tell anyone—"

Mel glared at me. "Do you even know me? Do you think for a second I'd out someone like that? I might really, really want to, but I never would, and you of all people should know that."

I hung my head, feeling ashamed for thinking Mel would consider outing Dean. Of course she wouldn't. "I'm sorry."

"It doesn't change that I think he's a coward for being on Team Arnault while he's keeping a secret like this."

"If you got to know him—"

Mel groaned in frustration. "This is what I'm talking about, Dre. You could be helping Dean see how important it is to come out and be visible in a world that wants to make you both *invisible*. Instead, you're playing house with teenage Mussolini."

"Don't you think you're overreacting?"

"No," she said. "It's gross, and I honestly expected better from you."

I felt like Mel was throwing punches instead of words and that I had no defense against them. Every attack hit hard and left a bruise. "He's not like his mom," I said, my voice barely louder than a whisper. "He's a good person."

"If he won't stand against her when it matters, how good can he really be?"

As the shock of Mel's attacks wore off, anger began to take its place. My cheeks felt hot and I lashed out. "You don't even know him."

"Neither do you."

I didn't know what else to say, so I turned and left. Mel called after me, but I slammed the door behind me and refused to look back.

EVERY HOTEL ROOM my mother stayed in when she traveled was transformed into campaign headquarters while she was in it. Serious people with titles like Communications Director or Campaign Strategist were always hovering around, tapping out messages or rewriting a speech or briefing my mother on the latest news or poll or scandal that might affect the election.

Observing my mother while she worked felt like sitting inside the eye of a hurricane, watching the mayhem swirl. It was intoxicating; I loved every second of it. This was the room where *ideas* were born. This was the room where policies were drafted. This was where people like my mother and her advisors made decisions that could affect hundreds of millions of people, and there was no one I trusted more than my mother to make those decisions. At the same time, watching my mother made me wonder if this was how I wanted to spend *my* life. I believed if I remained on the path I was following, I could be a good or even a great lawyer, and that I could follow my mother into politics, but I wasn't certain I wanted to. Some of my favorite moments in debate weren't when *I* won; they were when teammates I'd helped and encouraged won. Their successes meant more to me than my own. I loved studying new ideas and strategies and then explaining them to others. I wasn't sure how to explain that to my mother or that she would have even understood.

"What're you daydreaming about over there, Dean?" My mother tossed her tablet aside and sat on the sofa across from me, kicking off her shoes and resting her feet on the coffee table. "Did you forget to take your pills?"

I had the inattentive variant of ADD, therefore, instead of being hyper, my mind had a tendency to wander. Sometimes I could stare into space and lose track of an hour without realizing it. Medication didn't fix the problem, but it got me halfway there. The rest required hard work and diligence, both of which I enjoyed.

"I took them." The lines around my mother's eyes were deeper and the bags under them were darker. "Rough day?"

"Jackson McMann is handing us our asses."

"He's a fad, Mom."

"He *was* a fad. Now he's a contender." My mother's frown betrayed her worry in a way I rarely saw. "The CPD's added him to the next debate."

166

"Seriously? The debate commission really let him in?"

She nodded soberly. "Nora's been fighting it. She even reached out to her counterpart in the Rosario campaign to enlist his help, but McMann's polling over fifteen percent and the commission will not be swayed."

"Could you threaten to pull out?"

"And risk giving Rosario and McMann unchallenged airtime?" She waved me off like it was the silliest suggestion she had ever heard. "There is truly only one solution," she said. "I'm going to have to assassinate him."

"Mom!"

"I'm kidding, Dean," she said. "Mostly."

If my mother hadn't been capable of taking out McMann herself, with or without a gun, I might have laughed, but she had been at least as fierce a soldier as she was a presidential candidate. Though she hadn't been able to serve in a combat role while she'd served in the army, she had been part of a mission that had become stranded in unfriendly territory. Her commanding officer was gravely wounded, so my mother took command and led the survivors to safety, despite being injured herself. She had received the Medal of Honor and had captured the attention of a number of powerful people, many of whom eventually became instrumental in helping her begin her political career.

"You'll have to settle for destroying him during the debate."

My mother nodded, but she looked a bit frustrated by the notion that she couldn't actually murder McMann. "Tell me about Belle Rose," she said, changing the subject. "How did that go?"

This was the first time we'd had more than five minutes to talk since I had volunteered with Dre. Nora had been pleased with how well I'd done, and it had kept the news talking about us rather than Jackson McMann for nearly an entire day.

"It was fine."

"Just fine?"

"We spent most of our time painting, and Dre isn't so bad once you get to know him."

My mother arched an eyebrow at me. "Dre?"

"He prefers it over Andre."

"I see," she said. "What was with that ridiculous outfit he was wearing? Did you forget to tell him he was going to be on TV?"

I suppressed a laugh, but couldn't prevent the smile. "Oh, he knew."

My mother pursed her lips, looking like she'd eaten a lemon. "Well, I'm certainly glad he's not my problem."

"Problem?"

"I'm sure he's a nice boy, but I won the jackpot with you, though you could have kept your shirt tucked in for all of the photos."

"You might like Dre if you got to know him. He's quite talented with monster makeup and photography, and he's funny too. Did you know he organized a group of drag queens to read to children? He even dressed up."

My mother grimaced. Her lip curled. "Grown men dressed as women have got no business being around children."

I tried to ignore the face she'd made, but it was difficult. "Dre made it sound like the kids had fun."

"I'm sure he did," she said.

"And he invited me to go to the next one."

A sharp, dry laugh burst out of my mother like a whip crack. "Over Nora's dead body."

"It could be fun."

My mother leaned forward, fixing me with a serious stare. "Look, Dean, I'm glad you got along with Andre Rosario, but don't go treating him like your new best friend. He's not like us."

"Because he's gay?"

"You know I have nothing against those people," she said. "I went on *Ellen* and took you with me. You danced with her! But I have to lead with my heart, and my heart says they're not like us."

When I heard my mother's argument, almost the same argument I'd made to Dre, thrown back at me, it sounded ridiculous. It sounded hollow and cheap.

"What if I were more like Dre?" I asked.

"You're not."

"But what if I were? Would you keep me hidden? Would you pretend I didn't exist?"

My mother's face turned to stone. She might as well have been carved from the side of a mountain. I'd always known her well enough to read her, even when others couldn't, so my inability to do so in that moment made her all the more frightening.

"You're not like Dre," she said. "You're Dean Arnault, you're on the path to a brilliant future, and you're everything I could have hoped for."

I should have let the matter drop, but I kept hearing Dre's voice asking me what I believed. I *had* believed that my mother would love and support me no matter what, but now I wasn't so sure.

"What about when you told me I could be anyone I wanted?"

"Well, I never expected you would want to be more like Andre Rosario." My mother sat up and hushed me before I could speak again. "Enough of this nonsense. I know you love playing devil's advocate, but he's got enough misguided souls advocating for him without you joining the cause."

"Yes, ma'am."

The words came out automatically, but I didn't want to quit talking because I needed to know that this wasn't how my mother really felt. She was just having a bad day and it had made her cranky. This was not who she was. I wanted to stand up and tell her that when she talked about "those people," she *was* talking about me, whether she realized it or not. I might not be as flamboyant or candid as Dre, and we may be different in different ways, but if my mother was going to include Dre in a category of "not like us," then I belonged in it as well.

Only, I couldn't bring myself to say any of those things because while I wasn't sure if I could still believe in my mother, I couldn't bear the thought of her not believing in me.

DRE

IT WAS AROUND eight, and I was sitting at the kitchen table sketching out an idea I'd had for a photo shoot to keep my mind occupied so I didn't have to think. It was a monster whose monstrous bits were all on the inside. From the outside it looked mostly normal, but that was the lure. As soon as you got close, it split open like a Venus flytrap and revealed the deadly truth. I crumpled the paper up and tossed it onto the table with the others. Mel wasn't talking to me, so it was pointless anyway.

I nearly jumped out of my skin when my phone buzzed.

PrezMamasBoy: Hi, Dre! It's Dean.
PrezMamasBoy: Are you excited for tomorrow? Did you get the train ticket to Boston? It's all set up. I've got a list of

172

things we can do. And a backup list in case you don't like anything on my original list.

DreOfTheDead: you are hilarious

PrezMamasBoy: I like to be prepared.

DreOfTheDead: either way im ready

PrezMamasBoy: May I ask you a question?

DreOfTheDead: duh

DreOfTheDead: and you dont have to ask if you can ask

DreOfTheDead: just ask

PrezMamasBoy: Do you think I'm normal?

DreOfTheDead: no

DreOfTheDead: next question

PrezMamasBoy: I'm being serious.

DreOfTheDead: so am i

DreOfTheDead: you are thoughtful and compassionate and brilliant and like no one ive ever met

DreOfTheDead: its part of why i like you

Shit. I stared at the last line. What if Dean read it like I was saying I liked him as more than a friend instead of as just friend? I needed to clear it up without it seeming like I thought the first thing was even a possibility, which it clearly wasn't, but I didn't know what to say. And the longer I waited, the weirder it was going to get.

The garage door slammed shut, and I quickly closed Promethean and turned my phone facedown as my dad walked in carrying his suitcase. He looked like shit. His skin

173

hung a little loose and he was losing weight. The election was eating away at him like a cancer.

"Hey, Dre."

I flipped to a fresh page in my sketchbook and started working, ignoring my dad.

"Where's your mom?"

Without looking at him, I said, "Mom's in Atlanta. Where you sent her."

"You've been alone here all evening?"

"I wasn't supposed to be. My dad was supposed to take me to our first trapeze lesson tonight, and then we were gonna go to our favorite restaurant, but that deadbeat was a no-show."

My dad swore under his breath. "Dre—"

"There's pizza in the oven." I shut my notebook, grabbed my phone, and stormed to my room, slamming the door behind me like I was thirteen again. I dug my backpack out of my closet and started tossing things in for the trip to Rhode Island. My plane was scheduled to take off at six in the morning, and there was no way I'd be awake enough that early to think about what I should bring.

"Planning on running away again?"

I hadn't heard Dad open my door, but when I turned around, his head was sticking in.

"Again? I never ran away."

Dad eased a little farther in. "When you were seven. You were angry with me then too because I didn't buy you an elephant for your birthday. It was all you wanted. You even had a named picked out."

"Fanty."

"You expected he would fly and that you'd go on adventures."

"I'm not running away," I said. "I'm doing my tour of RISD tomorrow. Don't worry, I didn't expect you to remember that either." I stuffed my tablet and my Switch in my bag, along with a couple of books because I couldn't decide which I might want to read.

"You want ice cream?"

"It's late, and my flight's early."

Dad checked his watch. "It's barely after eight. Come on. We're going for ice cream."

It was pointless trying to argue with him, but that didn't mean we had to talk. Too bad Dad couldn't take the hint. He spent the entire drive telling me about a guy he sat beside on the plane who kept farting and waking himself up and then thinking the awful smell was coming from my dad. I refused to give my dad so much as a smile.

Since Dad's guilt was buying, I got two scoops of coffee and one scoop of chocolate and had them smothered in fudge and caramel and sprinkles. We walked outside into the warm, dry air. It was kind of weird being home after traveling so much. I'd grown up in Carson City, so everything was familiar, but it also wasn't in a way. After a while, all the shops and strip malls began to run together in my brain, making it difficult to tell one place from another. We could've been anywhere in the country.

"I'm sorry, Dre. This debate, and McMann being added—"

"Blah, blah, blah. I've heard all this."

"You don't understand what a real threat he is," Dad said. "He's got people worked up and scared. He's got them blaming anyone and everyone for their problems. If I can't prove during this debate how bad he would be for the country, he might have a real shot at winning."

I didn't spend much time sitting around watching the news, but I knew what a creep McMann was, mostly because Mel had spent hours telling me. There were the reports about shady business practices, money he'd paid to women to settle sexual harassment claims, deals with the government for his facial recognition technology. None of it stuck, though. People didn't have time to digest one story about him before three more popped up. But at the moment, I didn't give a shit about Jackson McMann.

"Whatever. It's fine. Can we go home now?"

"I know I messed up, but—"

"No buts, Dad. You messed up, full stop."

"I did, and I'll make it up to you."

"When?" I asked. Before he could answer, I kept going. "It's not just tonight. Ever since you started campaigning, it's like I lost my dad. You're never around, you flake out on everything, and you only trot me out when Jose thinks you can

176

use me to score popularity points because the press loves your unpredictable queer kid. What flamboyant thing will he wear? What odd things will he say? Who knows? That's what makes it fun! But it's never about me."

Dad was staring at me, dumbfounded. "Is that what you really believe?"

"Yes!" I shouted. My ice cream was melting into the cup. I didn't even want it anymore.

"I thought you liked doing campaign events with me."

"Do you know what a pain those are? I hate the press hovering over me all the time and people criticizing what I wear and you never being around. I hate it. But I missed hanging out with you, so whatever."

Pistachio ice cream dribbled down the side of Dad's cone and over his hand, but he didn't seem to notice. "I'm sorry about the trapeze lessons—"

"It's not about the fucking trapeze!"

"Dre—"

"You used to go with me to the comic-cons—"

"I thought once Mel got her license, you wouldn't want me around."

"And you always had time to help with Dreadful Dressup."

"I still do."

"What about Europe?" I asked. "How long have we been talking about spending the summer in Europe after graduation? Just me and you, the Rosario boys. How're you gonna do that if you win the election?"

With each question, my dad's shoulders slipped a little lower. "We can still travel."

I snorted derisively. "Yeah. It'll be the Rosario boys, a squad of Secret Service agents, and a dozen annoying aides who'll need *just a second* a million times a day." I tossed what was left of my ice cream in the trash and headed back to the car.

It was a few minutes before Dad got in. He started the engine but didn't back out of the lot. "I'll drop out of the race."

"No you won't."

"Yes, I will."

I heard the sincerity in my dad's voice, and I knew without a doubt he'd do it because that's the kind of person he was, regardless of how pissed at him I was at the moment. And if I let him, I'd feel like shit for the rest of my life knowing I'd allowed my dad to give up on something he wanted.

"You're not quitting," I said. "Someone's gotta keep McMann and Arnault from making shit worse."

"Dre—"

"I just miss my dad, all right? And it's making me cranky."

"I miss you too. You and your mom." Dad finally put the car in gear and started back toward home.

Getting all that out had felt good, but it hadn't fixed anything. I'm not sure there was any way *to* fix it. If my dad dropped out of the race, the country would lose. They'd be stuck with a man who cared about no one but himself or a woman who wanted to drag the country back to the 1950s.

But if he stayed in and won, I'd have to keep sharing my dad with the world. I had to find some way to be okay with that, and I wasn't sure I could be.

"If you want, I can go with you on your tour tomorrow."

"No!"

Dad glanced over at me as he drove. "Are you sure? I could use a break from the debate prep anyway."

I had to convince him not to come or he'd ruin everything, and I was already anxious about seeing Dean in person again. "It's just a boring college tour," I said. "Besides, if you go, the press will find out and they'll show up and I wanna keep it low-key."

"I don't know. How'd you convince your mother to let you run off to Rhode Island without a chaperone, anyway?"

"I told her you said it was okay."

"Dre!"

"Kidding." I flashed him a grin. "I'm seventeen, Dad. I'll be eighteen in a few months. I can handle it. Fly in, do the tour, stay the night, run up a massive room service bill, meet Mom in Chicago the next day. Besides, it's Rhode Island. How much trouble can I get into in Rhode Island?"

Dad was still eyeing me skeptically, but it wasn't like he was gonna call off the trip and make me miss touring my potential future school. "Just be safe. I love you so much, Dre."

We drove the rest of the way home in silence, and all I wanted to do was shower and get to bed so that it would hurry up and be tomorrow, though I was pretty sure I was too excited to sleep. Alone again, I checked to see if Dean had written back.

PrezMamasBoy: Thank you, Dre.
PrezMamasBoy: I can't wait to see you tomorrow.
PrezMamasBoy: Sweet dreams.
PrezMamasBoy: ~Dean

I couldn't stop smiling, and then I remembered what Mel had said and I knew she was right. He might not mean to, and he probably wouldn't even realize he'd done it, but Dean was going to break my heart.

DEAN

I CHECKED THE time on my phone again, then logged into the Amtrak app to make sure Dre's train hadn't been delayed. I'd made all the arrangements and had even bought his ticket. It's not that I didn't think Dre was capable of organizing his own travel arrangements, but I hated leaving details to others. It wasn't one of my most admirable qualities. I was the person in group projects who usually did all the work. I didn't care who got credit for it so long as I knew it was done and done well. Learning to trust others was difficult for me, but I was trying. When it came to Dre, however, I wanted to leave nothing to chance.

The plan was for Dre to take the 12:12 p.m. Northeast Regional from Providence to the Back Bay station in Boston. The entire trip was scheduled to take forty-four minutes and had only cost fifteen dollars. It was exactly one o'clock, and Dre's train still hadn't arrived.

I didn't know why I was so nervous, but I'd spent all night staring at the ceiling of the hotel room. At two in the morning, I'd gone to the fitness center and run until I was drenched in sweat and my legs had felt as mushy as clay and heavy as lead, but even that hadn't tired me out enough to sleep well.

Dre and I shouldn't have been friends. If we'd gone to the same school, I doubted he would have wanted to hang out with someone like me. He and his artsy friends likely would have spent their time mocking me for being too reserved and buttoned up. He did monster makeup, I studied philosophy. He went to comic book conventions, I attended political rallies. He played Dungeons & Dragons, I played the piano. Badly. The only thing we had in common was that our parents were both running for president, and I wondered if our friendship would end after the election when we no longer shared that unique experience.

I was sure that Dre also believed we had something in common because he was gay and I was exploring my sexuality, but I had never viewed a person's sexual orientation as a defining characteristic *or* a thing over which two people could bond. Maybe I would have if I'd been out or had gone through the experiences the way Dre had. I didn't fault Dre for feeling the way he did about his sexuality; I just didn't share his enthusiasm. For some people, their personality traits were an extension of their sexuality, but that wasn't true for me. My personality was no more influenced by my sexuality than it was by my right-handedness. It was a part of me, but it did not define me.

If we had sat down and made a list of what Dre and I individually believed, I was certain that we would be at odds on nearly everything. And yet, talking to him—just *thinking* about talking to him—made my skin tingle. It made me smile and look like a fool. Nora had caught me staring into space with a goofy grin spread across my face on the plane ride to Boston. I'd been so flustered that I hadn't been able to think up a good explanation for being happy when she'd asked me. But I was. Happy. Thinking about Dre made me happy. And if you had told me there was a nuclear bomb set to destroy Washington, DC, and that answering why Dre made me happy was the only way to prevent it, I still wouldn't have been able to say.

Dre was improbable and inexplicable and getting off the train wearing tight green and black plaid pants that made his legs look runway-model long, a white shirt, and a denim jacket. His hair was curly and wild, and he was grinning from ear to ear.

"You made it!" I stuck out my hand as Dre reached in for a hug and we stumbled into one another awkwardly. Then I tried to hug him, but he went for the handshake and poked me in the stomach.

"How could I not?" Dre asked when we'd finished assaulting each other. "You planned my trip down to the minute." He held up his phone and showed me the messages I'd sent him that morning. "You even planned my bathroom break."

I hung my head. "Sorry. It's my ADD. Making lists and plans helps me manage things. Sometimes I go a little overboard."

Dre laughed it off. "It's fine. I'm not mad about it."

"It's embarrassing."

"Whatever. We've all got our weird things." Dre nudged my foot with his. "I only pee sitting down because I'm a hundred percent sure if I don't, the stream's gonna split off at a weird angle and I'm gonna wind up with piss all over the front of my pants. I used to have nightmares about it happening in public places and I'd have to hide in a stall until it dried."

The idea of Dre worrying about something so silly was comforting. "Please tell me that you're serious and that that's not something you made up to make me feel better."

"Totally true."

"Now I'm relieved."

"Good."

I didn't know what to say next. I froze. Travelers moving away from trains or toward them flowed around us as we stood there like strangers, unsure where to go.

Dre cleared his throat. "So, where to?"

I pulled out my phone and began to answer, but Dre cut me off. "Wait, you were serious about the lists?"

"I'm always serious about lists."

"So, like, you've got an itinerary planned and every hour of our day scheduled to the minute?"

"Pretty much, yes."

"That's so . . ."

"Weird?"

"Perfect," he said. "Where to first?"

Each activity I'd added to the list had seemed like a good idea at the time, but now that Dre was standing in front of me, they all felt like the worst ideas I could have come up with. Unfortunately, I didn't have anything else.

"Well, since it's nearby, I thought we'd start with the Boston Public Garden."

"I'm in. Let's go!" Dre latched his arm through mine and pulled me toward the exit. His enthusiasm was contagious, and I let him drag me along.

It was cooler outside than it was at home, and the air was filled with a million smells, most of which I probably wouldn't have wanted to identify. I was used to worrying about being recognized, but I felt inconspicuous on the crowded city streets. Chaos was a cloak of invisibility, and I loved it.

"Nice hoodie," Dre said. "And did you do something different with your hair?"

The hoodie was a gray zip-up that I was wearing with khaki-colored jeans. I'd had to slip out of the hotel without my mother seeing or she would have said I looked like a common frat boy. But I was proud of my hair.

"The stylist said she was going to add more texture." I shrugged. "I just asked for something a little different."

"It's good," Dre said.

I felt my ears burning, and I wanted the attention off me, so I said, "You look nice too."

"Do I? I just threw this outfit together. By which I mean that I threw the majority of my wardrobe on the floor while I was trying to find something that wouldn't draw too much attention because we're supposed to be incognito, but that still screamed me." He held open his jacket. The inside was lined with superheroes posing like pinup girls.

"It definitely screams Andre Rosario."

"Good."

"So are you sure you're okay missing your college tour?"

"For RISD?" Dre asked. "It's fine. I mean, who even wants to go to school in Rhode Island?"

I had to check the map on my phone to make sure we were going the right direction, but there were also a lot of tourists around, so we could have simply followed them. "Quite a few people, actually. James Franco received his MFA from there, and Seth MacFarlane earned his BFA."

"Did you research RISD?"

"Maybe." I didn't want to come off like a stalker, so I quickly added, "I just wanted to make sure we would have something to talk about."

Dre laughed. "Please tell me you don't also have a list of conversation topics."

"I don't." I absolutely did.

"Good," he said. "But, really, it's fine. I'm not even sure

I'm going to go to college right after graduation. I might take a year off and see what happens."

"Your parents wouldn't mind?"

Dre shook his head. "I mean, I haven't actually brought it up with them, but college is expensive, and I don't see the point in going and wasting the money if I don't even know what I want to study."

"Wait," I said. "What about makeup and Dreadful Dressup? I've seen your stuff, and you're exceptional."

I might have misinterpreted it, but I could have sworn he blushed. "Thanks, but it's tough, you know? Most of the special effects stuff is done on computers now, and I'm not into that. I just want to make sure whatever I decide to do with the rest of my life is something I actually wanna do."

"I understand."

"You do?"

"Don't sound so surprised," I said.

"I'm not, it's just—"

I pointed at the corner and turned, taking him with me. "You thought that I was a clone of my mother and that I was destined to do everything she did? Join the military, go to college, start a career in politics?"

Dre at least had the decency to look sheepish. "Kind of."

"I'm not cut out for the military," I said. "I doubt I'd find it any easier shooting people than animals."

"Plus, you can't eat people."

187

"There is that." I grinned at him. "I love politics and philosophy. My favorite areas are ethics and epistemology."

Dre scrunched his face. "Epistewho?"

"Epistemology. It's the study of knowledge. Like, what do we know? And how do we know what we know? Can we trust what we know? Can we really ever know anything at all?"

"That last part's how I feel pretty much all the time."

I felt like I was lecturing Dre, and I didn't want to bore him. "Anyway, it's all fascinating stuff and will make a solid foundation for me to go to law school and for my future political career, but I'm not certain that's the life I want."

"What else would you do?"

"You're going to laugh."

"I promise I won't."

"I've always been interested in teaching."

"Like kindergarten?"

"High school."

Dre wasn't exactly laughing, but I could tell he wanted to. "Okay, but why?"

"Forget it."

Dre grabbed my arm and pulled me to a stop. "I'm sorry. Tell me more."

I didn't know if he actually wanted to hear about it, but Tamal was the only other person who knew it was a career path I was even remotely considering. It wasn't that I thought there was anything shameful or ignoble about being a teacher; it was simply that most people assumed I would use my talents for politics and didn't consider I might want to do something else.

"Do you know what I love about debate?"

Dre shrugged. "The thrill of destroying your opponent?"

"Okay," I said. "Maybe a little. But mostly I love taking a complex topic, breaking it down, and explaining it to someone who isn't familiar with it. Winning isn't just about being right, it's about making the judges understand the nuances of my point of view, even if they disagree. I love the moment during a debate when I can see the pieces click into place for the judge. That's when I know I've done my job properly."

"Most of my friends are anxious to get the hell out of high school," Dre said. "You're the only one I know looking to go back."

"Often, adults assume people our age aren't smart enough or engaged enough to make a difference, but I think that's a cop-out. I think they underestimate us, and I think I could be the kind of teacher who wouldn't do that."

I'd expected Dre to look bored, but he seemed to be listening. "So why don't you go to school to be a teacher? Study education and get a couple of graduate degrees? Doctor Arnault's got a nice ring."

I sighed, coming across more melancholy than I meant to. "You know how it is. There are just certain expectations that come along with being the son of Janice Arnault."

Before Dre could ask me more, I grabbed the sleeve of his jacket and pulled him across the street so we didn't miss the light. "Come on, we're there."

DRE

THE ONLY THING more colorful than the fall foliage around the Public Garden was me. Usually. I was a little more subdued because we were incognito. Fine. Even toned down, I was a splash of color on the dull canvas of life. The trees weren't bad either. They were a million shades of orange and yellow and red, the colors bright and bold as if waving a dramatic final farewell to beauty before retreating until winter had reached its end. Ducks swam in the lagoon and Swan Boats glided lazily across the water.

And I was there with Dean. I hadn't known what to do when I'd first seen him. I'd wanted to run from the train and leap into his arms like we were in a movie, but I doubted he would've thought it was as funny as me. I didn't know what to expect from the day. Mel was always complaining how guys often looked at friendship with girls as a shitty consolation prize, and I didn't want to be like that. If Dean never had feelings for me beyond friendship, I wanted him to know his friendship was enough. I wanted it to *be* enough. But at the same time, I couldn't help the bubbly, giggly feeling in my stomach when his arm brushed mine or when he looked at me and held the stare a second longer than was necessary.

"Favorite movie?" I asked.

"*A Quiet Place*."

"You like horror movies?"

Dean cocked his head at me. "That movie wasn't horror. A world where no one can talk or make a sound? Sounds like a utopia to me. Your turn."

"*Hedwig and the Angry Inch*. Book?"

Dean puffed out his lips like a duck when he was thinking and it was adorable, so I had to avoid looking at him.

"And don't say *Catcher in the Rye* or I'm bailing on you and going back to Providence."

"Fiction or nonfiction?"

"Both?"

"*Beyond Good and Evil* for nonfiction, and *The Graveyard Book* for fiction."

I didn't recognize the first book and made a mental note to google it when I had a chance, but I knew the second. "Neil Gaiman?" I asked, and Dean nodded. "Not bad. Mine changes, but I'm basically obsessed with this graphic novel called *Descender* right now. The artist, Dustin Nguyen, works in watercolors, and he's brilliant."

"I haven't read any graphic novels."

"That's gonna cost you ten points."

Dean frowned in my direction. "You're assigning point values to my answers?"

"Obviously."

"How am I doing?"

"Shockingly well," I said. "I expected you to be negative double digits by now, but you're still in the black."

Dean glowed at the compliment, and I did enjoy making that boy smile. "My turn," he said. "How did you know you were gay?" As soon as he got the question out, he looked like he wished he'd kept it to himself. "You don't have to answer if it's too personal."

"Nah," I said. "I don't mind." Which was true. I didn't mind. I also didn't know where to start. "It wasn't any one thing, I guess. It was this gradual awareness during middle school that I wasn't like other boys, but not in the obvious ways. I was obviously not like them because I was a little more glam and a little more everything, but people get it wrong when they figure a boy's gay 'cause they caught him wearing his mom's high heels or whatever."

"What do you mean?" Dean asked.

"Dudes can be burly athlete bros and into race cars or

whatever and be super gay or they can love bubble baths and manicures and be straight. All that masculine and feminine stuff is bullshit."

"I get it," he said. "It's like how you assumed that, because of who my mom is and that I'm quiet and reserved, I wouldn't know how to have fun or that I wouldn't enjoy cutting loose and dancing."

"If you keep bringing up your dancing skills, I'm gonna have to make you prove it."

Dean smiled impishly. "Carry on."

"Mel's better at explaining how limiting the constructs of masculinity and femininity are than I am, but anyway, it seemed like the other boys had started speaking a language I didn't understand. I felt shut out and cut off from them without knowing why. And then one day I was watching *Glee* on Netflix and Kurt was swooning over Blaine, and I was just like, 'Me too,' and fanning myself, and I turned to my dad and told him I thought I was gay."

"Just like that?"

I nodded. "Just like that."

"How did he react?"

"A little shook," I said. "But he recovered quickly. Said it was cool and asked if I had any questions. I think he was terrified I was gonna ask about sex, and I think we were both grateful I didn't."

"My father's sex talk was terrible," Dean said. "He was

sweating while he tried to describe the act in clinical terms. It didn't help that my mother was standing in the doorway listening. She finally couldn't stand it anymore and marched in and told me that if I got a girl pregnant, I had better be ready to marry her and start a family."

I laughed in spite of myself. "Accidental pregnancy's one thing I'm glad I don't have to worry about. It could've been worse. At least you didn't have to tell them you're gay."

"Who says I'm not?"

Did I fall into the water and drown and hallucinate Dean saying he might be gay? That must've been what happened because there's no way it happened in real life. No way, no how. But I heard it. I had to play it cool.

"I thought you were maybe demi?"

"That describes sexual attraction," Dean said. "Not the type of person I'm attracted to." He paused. "Sort of. Being demi, I'm only attracted to people I have an emotional connection with, but those people have mostly been men."

Oh my God. Oh my God. Oh my God. Oh my God.

Inside, I was totally freaking out. The chances of Dean possibly having the same kind of feelings for me that I had for him had gone from virtually impossible to probably improbable. But there was still a better-than-zero chance. Outside, though, I was doing my best to keep my shit together.

"Interesting," I said. "Who was your first crush?"

"Neville Longbottom."

This bark of a laugh burst out of me, and I clapped my

hand over my mouth. "Sorry. Didn't mean—"

"It's fine," Dean said. "It's a little silly. But I felt this deep connection to Neville. We were the same. If he were real, I believed he would have understood me in a way no one else seemed able to."

"So that's the kind of guy you like?" I asked. "Nerdy and cute?"

"Brave and honest. Kind of like you."

That was it. Dean had slayed me. I was dead. My bones had turned to jelly, but I was somehow still standing upright. Kind of like me? What about *exactly* like me? Better yet, what about *me*? I wouldn't have described myself as brave or honest, but if Dean thought I was, I wasn't gonna argue. I had a million questions, but I didn't want to overwhelm him. I didn't want to seem too eager—Mel was always telling me I was too eager—so I played it as cool as I could and let the information sit out there between us while we walked.

No one paid us any attention. For all they knew, we were a couple of kids on a date at the Garden, and for all *I* knew, Dean could've thought it was a date. There was something exciting about being in a city on our own. We were free of our parents and the press and all the expectations. It felt like anything could happen.

"I'm happy we did this," Dean said.

"I was surprised you were up for it."

"Walking around a pond?"

"Skipping out on Harvard," I said. "You're all about

perfect attendance and telling the truth. I just didn't think you had it in you."

Dean shoved his hands his pockets and stopped, standing to stare out over the water. "Why do you do that?" he asked.

The air between us grew tense, but I didn't know why. We'd been having fun and now it seemed Dean was pissed at me. "Do what?"

"Act as though there's something wrong with trying to be a good and thoughtful person who tries to do the right thing. Having fun and following the rules aren't mutually exclusive."

Oh. That was why he was pissed. "I was just playing."

"It didn't feel that way."

"I'm not saying there's anything wrong with following the rules, but you *are* a little high-strung. It's like you're always on, always thinking about who's watching or listening. I don't think I've ever even heard you cuss. And I get it. It's like you said about the expectations of being Janice Arnault's kid. But, I mean, it wouldn't kill you to loosen up a little sometimes."

Even as I said it, I worried I was making shit worse.

"I would've lost it a long time ago," I went on. "Shaved my hair into a mohawk or gotten a giant neck tattoo or burned down the governor's mansion."

Dean's expression hadn't changed, and I couldn't tell what he was feeling. "Dean?" I nudged him with my elbow, but he wouldn't look at me.

"You keep acting like I am who I am because my mother

made me this way. I can't deny the influence she's had on me any more than you can deny the influence your parents have had on who you are, but have you ever considered that I dress the way I do because I feel more comfortable wearing clothes that don't make people stare at me? That I don't cuss because I believe words matter, and I prefer to use words that don't offend others? That I'm quiet not because I'm afraid to speak, but because I'm choosing to listen? I know I'm not fully baked yet, and that I still have a lot to learn about the world and about myself, but I happen to *like* who I am."

"I like who you are too," I said.

Dean snapped around to face me. "Do you? Because I often feel like you don't. Like you're tolerating me until you can make me more like you."

I immediately opened my mouth to tell him he was wrong, but he wasn't and I knew it. "Most of the time when we're talking on Promethean or hanging out like this, you're just Dean, and Dean is awesome. He's sweet and somehow insecure and confident at the same time, he's good with people and he's considerate. But there are times when I think of you as Janice Arnault's son, and it's like I can't separate the two."

"Again, you say that like it's a bad thing. Like it's a curse."

"When you talk about her, you're talking about your mom," I said. "But all I know about her is that she thinks transgender soldiers don't belong in the military and that a god

197

I don't even believe in should have more say over the choices I make than I do."

"But that's not who she is," Dean said.

"Isn't it, though?" I reached out to Dean, but he pulled away. "Look, I'm not trying to trash your mom, but I can't act like I don't think a lot of the things she supports are shitty and cruel."

"You don't know anything about her," he said.

Dean started walking again, and I wasn't sure whether I should even follow. It seemed our plan to not talk about this stuff was a failure. Us hanging out at all might've been a bad idea, but I kept hearing Mel's voice in my head, and I wasn't ready to admit defeat just yet. I caught up to him standing by a bronze duck and a trail of bronze ducklings.

"Why haven't you told your mom you're queer yet?"

"The campaign—"

I cut him off. "I didn't ask why you're not out, I asked why you haven't told *her*. You said your parents wouldn't disown you or anything, so why haven't you told them?"

Dean glared at me, and it hurt. It felt like a slap, but I held my ground.

"I'm not scared, if that's what you're implying."

"Are you sure?"

DEAN

I LEFT DRE standing by the bronze ducks and walked until I found a coffee shop. It was busy but not packed, and I got in line. My thoughts were chaos. Asking Dre to meet me here had been a mistake of epic proportions. For as open-minded as he claimed to be, he was so eager to pick at the scabs of who I was so he could check off a box determining whether I was friend or foe. He didn't want to know *me*; he wanted to know how to categorize me. I could be a mama's boy or I could be like him, but I couldn't exist in between. I couldn't love my mother and believe in her but also find some of Dre's beliefs worthwhile. There was no middle ground with him.

When I'd told Dre that I wasn't scared to show my mother who I was, I hadn't been entirely honest. I *was* scared. Not that my mother would reject me, but that I had begun to doubt my belief that she would accept me without reservation. But where I had always admired my mother's commitment to her ideals, her steadfastness was beginning to look like obstinacy, and I wasn't sure she was capable of accepting me for who I was.

Either way, Dre wanted clear-cut answers that I didn't have yet, and I needed time to sort out my feelings.

When I reached the front of the line, I ordered a hot chocolate.

"And a latte." I'd been so lost in my head that I hadn't realized Dre was behind me. He handed the cashier a card over my shoulder.

"Thank you," I mumbled.

"What's your name?" the cashier asked.

I started to answer, but Dre said "Gustav" before I could.

We stood off to the side to wait for our drinks. I should have expected Dre would follow me. His return train to Rhode Island wasn't scheduled to leave until 7:04 p.m., though it wouldn't have been too difficult to change his ticket to an earlier train.

"Gustav?" I asked.

"You looked like you were about to give them your real name, and we're trying to make sure no one recognizes us, right?"

I hadn't thought of that. "Okay," I said. "But Gustav?"

"It just popped into my brain, so I said it." Dre was looking at his shoes, orange Converse high-tops. "I say a lot of things that pop into my brain, most of which I should probably keep to myself."

I wasn't going to disagree, but I did not want to get into a deep conversation while standing in the middle of a coffee shop waiting for our drinks.

"What do you want to do next?" I asked, though my enthusiasm for the day had waned. "There's Faneuil Hall and Quincy Market. We could walk the Freedom Trail. The Museum of Science is nearby or we could go tour the USS *Constitution*. I've also got the JFK Presidential Library and Museum and the Boston Tea Party Ships and Museum on my list. It's up to you."

Dre shrugged noncommittally. "Whatever is fine."

"Gustav?" the barista behind the counter called. "I have a latte and a hot chocolate for Gustav?"

Dre smiled at the young, preppy guy behind the counter as he grabbed our drinks.

"You don't look like a Gustav," the barista said. "Actually, you know who you look like—"

"Thanks!" He dashed for the door, and I followed after. We stood in front of the café, sipping our drinks. The awkwardness we couldn't seem to get past huddled between us again.

"Where to, Gustav?"

"I told you I got nothing."

"Fine," I said. "I have an idea, then."

"Let me guess, a museum?" Dre was smiling when he said it, and I knew he was poking fun at me, trying to ease the tension, but I wasn't in the mood for it.

"Follow me and find out," I said. "Or don't. It's up to you." I started walking at a leisurely pace, sipping my hot chocolate and taking in the city around me. I'd been to Boston before with the debate team, and we'd managed to fit in a little sightseeing, but this was different. Being on my own was different. Being with Dre was definitely different.

Dre walked alongside me, and I could feel the frustration radiating from him in waves. I wondered if he was wishing he hadn't gotten on the train this morning. If he was thinking he could be touring the Rhode Island School of Design instead of spending the day fighting with me. I wouldn't have blamed him if he had been.

"Why didn't you tell me you were attracted to guys?"

I hadn't expected the question, and it took me a moment to answer. "Because I didn't think it was important."

"Not important?!" he said. "You told me you thought you were ace. Why wouldn't you also tell me you were gay?"

"First," I said. "Mostly attracted to men doesn't mean always, so I'm not sure I'd call myself gay. Second, I don't think it means the same thing to me that it means to you."

"Back up a second. What's that supposed to mean?" Having this conversation while dodging the other pedestrians was difficult, but Dre managed to keep up with me.

This was partly why I hadn't told him. I didn't know how to explain it in a way that would make sense to him. "Are you a dog or a cat person?"

"Dog, obviously."

"Me too," I said. "Except that I'm also allergic to both, so I don't necessarily think of myself as a dog person."

Dre shook his head. "That's a terrible analogy."

"It's imperfect, yes—"

"It's messed up."

"Fine." Now I was the one getting frustrated. "Who someone is is more important to me than what's on the outside. Most of my crushes have been on people who happened to be men, but it's all about who they are for me, so gender is kind of irrelevant."

That answer seemed to give Dre pause because he didn't immediately fire off another question. I kept us walking in the right direction, but I wasn't in any hurry.

"Don't you think it could help people to know the truth about you?" Dre asked. "Even if all they know is that you're questioning? Don't you think it's important?"

"There's a video of your father giving a speech at a church, and you were standing behind him with your mom wearing a shirt that said 'Conversion therapy is torture.'"

Dre chuckled. "Yeah, Jose was *pissed*."

"I remember watching the video and thinking how brave you were to stand up for what you believe in. Being this out and proud gay guy is part of who you are, and I admire that. But I want people to think of me as more. I don't want them to reduce me to my sexual orientation."

"Rude," Dre said, glaring at me. "That's not even how it is."

I looked at Dre skeptically. "Do you honestly believe that?

Can you honestly tell me that people don't think of you as the gay one and me as mini-Janice?"

"I'm pretty sure they think of me as the brown kid before anything else," Dre said. "But fine. You might have a point about being pigeonholed. You could still do a lot of good, though."

"Maybe, but I don't want to spend my whole life talking about my sexuality. Isn't that my right?"

Dre was quiet for a few minutes, and I didn't know if I had upset him. Finally, he said, "Can I tell you a secret?"

I nodded.

"Mel's the political one. I mean, I believe in stuff and I stand up for it and all, but Mel's the one who gets really fired up about that shit. I'm kind of ambivalent about politics. I know it's important, but it just doesn't do anything for me."

"You could have fooled me."

Dre shrugged. "That's the point. If I'm shouting about queer rights or wearing a controversial slogan on my shirt or showing up to a *Teen Vogue* photo shoot in rainbow leggings, no one's really paying attention to *me*. I mean, I think it's important for people to see someone like me out there, but they're not really seeing me. Not all of me anyway."

Dre's confession left me unsure how to feel. "Isn't using your beliefs as a way to shield yourself from scrutiny kind of exploitative?"

"I didn't ask for my dad to run for president," he said defensively. "I was happy doing Dreadful Dressup with Mel and having people's criticisms of me revolve around what a shitty job I'd done with a photo shoot."

"It sounds to me like we're both hiding who we really are from the public."

"But I'm not hiding who I am from my family."

"Dre—"

Dre pulled me against the brick wall of a building, out of the flow of traffic. "Look, you said your parents wouldn't kick you out of the house for coming out, and I believe you. But then why not tell them?"

The defensive part of me that had been dreading this question wanted to push Dre out of my way and keep walking. But I didn't. I didn't want to.

"I've been dodging answering this for a while," I said. "And until recently it's been easy to avoid." I looked up at Dre and caught his eye.

"It's okay," he said.

"I don't want her to be disappointed in me." Saying it out loud, the thing I knew but had never put into words, was like tearing off a Band-Aid, painful but also a relief. "I don't think my mother would throw me out or disown me, but I'm scared she'd think of me as a failure. And no matter what else I did with my life from that point on, this one thing about me would always be the reason I wasn't the son she wanted me to be."

Dre was looking at me with pity, and I couldn't bear it, so I dove back into the stream of pedestrians, assuming he would follow. While there was a certain amount of liberation in admitting my fear, doing so also gave it a front-row seat in my mind. Before, it had been a hypothetical abstract I didn't need to concern myself with. Now, I couldn't stop thinking about how my mother had grimaced when she'd talked about Dre. Now, I couldn't stop thinking of her wearing that same expression when she talked about me. Now, it was an inevitability.

But I didn't have to deal with it today.

Dre caught up to me as we neared Faneuil Hall. It was packed with tourists taking pictures under the autumn trees, and I wished I could have snapped my fingers and made them all disappear. I led us into the market, down the brick street, and past the crowded retail shops that served only to remind me that time marched on whether we wanted it to or not.

"For what it's worth," Dre said. "I don't see how anyone could ever be disappointed in you."

"It's like I said. You don't know my mother." I stopped in front of a store and said, "We're here."

Dre looked confused at first until his eyes caught the sign in the window. "You brought me to a comic book shop?!"

"I thought you might like it."

The smile that bloomed on Dre's face was toothy and brilliant and brightened my whole day. It was the best smile I'd ever seen and was worth the pain and frustration it had taken to get there.

DEAN WASN'T WHO I thought he was, and maybe the problem was that I'd already decided who I thought he was before I'd given him the chance to tell me. So, pretty much, maybe the problem was me. I would've given the finger to anyone who'd tried to tell me they knew who I was, especially since I was still working it out for myself. I felt like an asshole, and I kind of deserved it. I had never been worried what my parents would think when I came out. It was such a non-event for me that it barely registered as anything more than another day. But Dean was marinating in that fear, even if he didn't want to admit it. He wanted to believe his mom was a good person, but he was also scared she wouldn't accept him. That kind of doubt could tear a person apart.

Despite his buttoned-up and polished exterior, Dean was kind of a mess. It made me think back to all the things I'd said to him about being uptight or emotionally closed off or whatever, and I felt like a jerk. I'd had no idea what he'd been going through because I hadn't taken the time to ask.

And it might seem shallow compared to the other stuff we talked about, but Dean had also blown my mind with his revelation that he's had crushes on guys. On guys like me. In the span of an hour, the possibility Dean could be into me the way I was into him had gone from dim and distant to a pretty solid maybe, and I had no clue how to react. The part of me that Mel was worried about wanted to spill my feelings right on the floor of Newbury Comics and rub Dean's face in them, but I didn't because everything was still so raw. He'd built a bridge by bringing me to the closest thing to a church for me, and I was pretty sure shoving my feelings in his face would've caused his head to swell and explode in a cloud of confetti.

But the problem that was really messing me up was wondering if we'd even be good together. I know, I know, I was getting *way* ahead of myself, but it's like in tenth grade when I was totally in love with Wesley Anders. I wrote a million awful poems about him and forced Mel to read every single one. Finally, she was like, "What would you even do if he liked you back? You're a flamboyant extrovert, he's a bully. You practically have a different outfit for every hour of the day, he's been wearing the same pair of corduroy pants since school started. You like comic books, he likes beating up people who like comic books."

I'd fallen hard for Wesley because we'd had English together and he'd been nice to me once, probably because he wanted to copy my homework, but it never would've worked. Dean could be another Wesley situation. It might not matter how Dean felt about me if all we did was fight.

But he'd brought me to a comic book store, and I couldn't pass up the opportunity to shop. I grabbed *Monstress* for me because Mel had been bugging me to read it, and I forced Dean to buy the first volume of *Saga*, though I warned him his mom probably wouldn't be cool if she found it. I was in heaven. After, I let Dean drag me to the USS *Constitution* because I could tell he wanted to go even though he was playing like it was no big deal if we didn't. Then we grabbed a late lunch at a deli and walked the Freedom Trail. We'd sort of silently agreed not to bring up our parents or the election or any of the shit we'd talked about before for a while, and it was the most fun I'd had in a long time.

"How many witches do you think are buried here?" I asked.

It was getting close to the time I had to start back to the station so that I didn't miss my train. The day had begun as a total disaster, but now I didn't want it to end. I wanted to run through the city with Dean until dawn and then do it all over again.

"I don't think witches are real."

"Sure they are."

Dean stopped by a headstone. The name and dates carved into it had been worn away so that I couldn't read them. "Wait, do you mean women accused of witchcraft or actual witches?"

"Sure."

"I assume any woman executed as a witch would not have been allowed a Christian burial, and I'm pretty certain magic isn't real."

"Whatever," I said. "Cemeteries are weird anyway. They're landfills for bodies, but people come to visit them. Would you visit the pizza box you tossed out last week?"

Dean frowned, almost looking embarrassed. "It's not quite the same thing."

"Sure it is."

"No, it's not." Dean looked at the grave marker with a kind of awe. "These were people, and cemeteries give us a place to be with and remember the people whose souls have passed on."

I waved my hands in the air. "Wait, so magic is bullshit, but souls are real?"

Dean shrugged.

"I expected more from a debate champion."

"When it comes to religion, I'm willing to embrace the contradiction."

"Even though a lot of churches are kind of intolerant?"

"Not all," Dean said.

We took up walking through the cemetery again, pausing to check out some of the headstones. "My parents keep trying to get me to go to Mass with them, but I'm not into it. Too much hypocrisy."

Dean tapped the center of my chest with the tip of his finger. "I think finding religion here is more important than finding it in a church, though I also understand that it isn't for everyone."

"But I'm definitely going to hell if I don't believe in God?"

Dean laughed. "I'm pretty sure that you're going whether you believe or not." He playfully shoved me with his shoulder.

As much fun as I was having, there was a question on my mind I wanted to ask—no, that I *needed* to ask—and I'd put it off long enough. If I didn't work up the nerve to do it now, I never would.

"I gotta ask you something," I said.

Dean's laughter faded, and his expression grew more guarded. "I'm listening."

"When you were telling me about your mom maybe being disappointed, you said it'd been easy not to think about it until now."

"Yes."

"So, what's different? Why could you avoid it before but not anymore?"

"You." Dean said it so matter-of-factly that I thought I'd imagined it at first. I thought I'd heard what I wanted to hear instead of the actual words he'd said. But, no. He'd said I was the reason, and he'd blown my mind for like the third time in a day.

"Me?"

Dean leaned against an old, thick tree with most of its leaves still hanging on, though they were all yellow and red and orange. He folded his arms across his chest. He looked so calm, and I didn't know how he could be calm when my heart was beating so fast I thought it was going to explode.

"You know how there are times when you're reading a book and there are some things you like and things you don't and some things that are extremely frustrating, but you're kind of ambivalent about it and you're considering setting it aside?"

I nodded, mostly because I had no clue where Dean was going, but I also didn't want him to stop talking.

"And then you reach a point where something happens and everything clicks into place. You're hooked. You want to stay up all night reading because you can't put it down, and it ends up becoming one of your favorite books of all time?"

Even as I was hearing the words Dean was saying, I didn't believe them. I resisted the urge to pinch myself to make absolutely sure this wasn't a dream or that I wasn't hallucinating. Maybe someone had slipped LSD into my latte and it'd just taken a few hours to kick in.

I caught a tremble running through Dean. He wasn't calm at all. Once I knew what to look for, I could see the tremor in his hands and the way he kept biting the inside of his cheek. Hell, that tree was probably the only thing holding him up.

"What're you saying, Dean?"

He looked away at first, but then changed his mind and

caught my eye. "We still have a lot of story left, Dre, but you're quickly becoming one of my favorite books."

"So this is what having a stroke feels like?"

Dean laughed with confusion. "What?"

I probably should've taken a second to gather my thoughts and put them into some kind of order so that I didn't come off sounding like, well, like me, but time was the one thing we didn't have a lot of.

"Are you saying you like me?" I asked. "As in you like me like you liked Neville Longbottom? If you do, I need to hear you say it, because I have this impossible crush on you that I'd resigned myself to you never returning and I need to make sure I understand that what you're saying is what I think you're saying so I don't do something foolish like tell you how I feel."

Dean smiled. He *smiled*. Not a pity smile or a timid "I don't know what else to do" smile, but a big, toothy, confident smile. And if I'd been living in a tragedy, this would've been the moment a random meteor fell out of the sky and smashed into my head and killed me. But my life wasn't a tragedy. Possibly a comedy, but still beautiful. Just like Dean's smile.

"I don't know," he said. I couldn't control the disappointment that hit my face, and he immediately added, "I think, yes, I'm attracted to you, but this is so different from any crush I've ever had."

"Because I'm a real person and not a character in a book?"

"That, and because no connection I've had has ever felt

this strong. Or this confusing. We wind up fighting as often as anything else, and—"

"I'm frustrating?"

"So frustrating!" Dean said. "But I like that. I like that you challenge me. I like that you make me think about who I am and who I want to be."

"I'm sorry for all the assumptions I made about you."

"Thank you for saying that," Dean said.

I walked toward Dean and stood beside him at the tree. "For the record, *I'm* not confused." I brushed my hand with his and linked our pinkie fingers together.

Dean's hand stiffened as he looked around and only relaxed when he was sure no one was watching us. "We've made this complicated."

"Probably."

"What do we do about our parents?" he asked. "I'm still going to be working on my mother's campaign and supporting her and hoping she wins."

At that moment, I didn't care. It was a problem for a day less perfect than this. "We're not our parents," I said. "We're not their surrogates. Let's just agree not to talk about that shit, okay? We can talk about our parents, but as the adults who annoy us and ground us, and *not* as presidential candidates."

"Do you think that's possible?"

"I think we can try."

Dean's finger tightened around mine. "I can't come out."

"It's fine."

"I'm serious, Dre." Dean paused like he was giving me an opening to butt in, but I didn't have anything to say. "I have a lot to consider—*you've* given me a lot to think about. At some point, I am going to have to tell my mother, but not until after the election. I don't want to be a distraction and I don't want to be the reason she loses."

"I can live with that."

"Are you sure?" Dean asked. "I would understand if you couldn't."

"Look, I'm not about forcing you or anyone to come out until they're ready."

"Thank you."

I couldn't believe I was standing there with Dean, holding his hand, talking about *us*. There was an us! I'd almost ditched him when he'd taken off on me earlier, and I would have missed this if I had! It was so much to wrap my brain around.

"So," I said. "You and me?"

"Seems that way."

"What about the distance?"

Dean shrugged. "We worked *this* out."

"And no matter who wins the election, we're gonna end up living in different states."

"We're both graduating at the end of the year, so that would have been an obstacle regardless."

This was happening. This was really happening! I pulled away from the tree so that I was standing in front of him. I needed to look Dean in the eye again to make sure that this was really real. Dean linked the rest of his fingers through mine, and pulled me a little closer, and then my phone buzzed.

Cock-blocked by my own damn phone. I got it out of my pocket and swore.

"What?"

"Train."

Dean looked at his watch and his eyes went wide. "Dre! We're going to be late!"

"We've got time." I was *not* going to leave things like this. He was going to kiss me, I knew he was, and I didn't know the next time I'd see him again.

But Dean grabbed our bags, and he pulled my sleeve, and the moment was gone.

We practically ran all the way back to the train station. Even though it'd gotten colder as the sun had set, I was sweating and breathing heavy because I was so out of shape, which I hadn't wanted Dean to see. But we got to the station on time. Barely. They'd already started letting people onto the train.

"When am I gonna see you again?"

"We will figure it out," Dean said. "You had better go."

This wasn't fair. I wished we hadn't wasted so much time arguing when I'd gotten there. "Wait! We need a picture." I pulled out my phone and threw my arm around Dean's waist.

I caught Dean looking for people who might be watching, but no one was paying attention to us. We were invisible. Besides, I didn't care. I leaned in as close to Dean as I could, breathing in the spring-fresh scent of his hoodie and the citrusy smell of his hair, and I snapped the pictures.

"I'll send them to you."

"Good," Dean said. "Now go!"

I turned to leave, and Dean grabbed my hand. "Wait." He pulled me toward him and around a corner and he kissed me like I was the only person in the universe. He kissed me like I was going off to war and he would never see me again. He kissed me like he meant it, and I kissed him back.

And then he was pushing me toward the gate, and I was running to the train and I barely made it before the train doors closed and we left the station, but for the whole ride home and the rest of the night I couldn't stop smiling because I'd kissed Dean Arnault and he'd liked it.

DEAN

FOR THE FIRST time in years, I felt like I had no idea what I was doing. After I was diagnosed with ADD, in addition to medication, I began cognitive behavioral therapy to develop coping mechanisms that would help me manage my condition. One thing I learned was that I functioned better with a plan, so before bed each night I wrote out a plan for the following day. I might change or update it as the day went on, but I still had it as my touchstone if I fell off track. Eventually, I started using the plans for long-term goals too. I had a college plan and a senior class president plan. I had a plan for how I was going to spend my day in Boston. I had plans for everything.

Except, I never could have planned for Dre.

No one could have planned for a person like Dre. He waltzed in and blew up my life, leaving me standing in the rubble of everything I'd known, and I had never been happier. Or more terrified. Dre was forcing me to confront things about myself and my family that I wasn't ready to deal with. I didn't know if I would ever be ready to deal with them, but I could feel the inevitability of the moment quickly approaching. Keeping my newfound relationship with Dre a secret was difficult, but I didn't want to distract my mother or the public from the election. Once my mom won and became president, I promised myself I would tell her and my dad the truth about everything.

That was the best plan I could come up with.

"Dean? Could you answer the door?" It was the Saturday before the second debate, and my mother had decided to take a night off from her preparations to throw a casual dinner party. I didn't know who my parents had invited—close friends or influential donors. Normally, I was only expected to make an appearance, shake some hands, show off what a smart son I was, and then vanish, but this time my mother had asked me to stay.

I opened the door and was greeted by a couple my parents' age. The Maguires, friends of my parents from church. Him in a casual suit, her in a beautiful blue dress with an empire waist. "Mr. and Mrs. Maguire, nice to see you." I shook their hands and stood aside to let them in.

"And you remember our daughter, Mindy," Mr. Maguire said.

Mindy stepped out from behind her parents and offered

me her hand and a smile. "Hi, Dean." Mindy was tall like her father, but she had her mother's black hair and expressive brown eyes.

Mindy's presence took me by surprise. It was the first time I could remember my parents inviting someone my age to one of their parties. "Mindy. Hi. I mean, hi! Why don't you all come in? My parents are this way."

In the kitchen, my mother and father were putting the finishing touches on dinner, and hors d'oeuvres had already been plated and laid out on the counters for the guests to enjoy. "Mom? Dad? The Maguires are here."

The doorbell rang again, and I spent the next few minutes running back and forth, showing in the Weirs, the Palmers, the Hansens, the Moskowitzes, and the Canteros. Soon, the adults were drinking wine and chatting, spreading through the dining room into the sitting room, while instrumental music provided acoustic atmosphere. I was passed from one adult to the next like an oddity to be marveled at, fielding questions about the campaign and what I'd learned and being told how fascinating it was and how lucky I was to have the opportunity to witness history being made. For my part, I answered their questions, agreed, or smiled when I had nothing to say, just as I'd been taught. I was comfortable around adults in a way that I wasn't always with my peers.

Eventually, I tried to slip away for a moment so I could see if Dre had replied to me on Promethean. We had been in the middle of a conversation when the guests had begun to arrive, and I was eager to answer the questions Dre had asked. I didn't notice Mindy standing beside me until she spoke. "Hi, Dean."

I didn't know Mindy well. We had been in youth group together, and she'd volunteered locally through the church with me a few times, but she didn't go to my school. From what I remembered of her, she was nice but hadn't made much of an impression. "Are you enjoying yourself?"

Mindy was holding a highball glass filled with ginger ale and ice, but it seemed like she was only holding it to give her hands something to do because it was still as full as it had been when I'd gotten it for her shortly after she'd arrived. "So much fun," she said. "I enjoy the part where adults I hardly know treat me like an anomaly because I know a few words with more than two syllables."

I grimaced. "They probably think all teenagers are brain-dead and sit around huffing dry-erase markers."

"Whatever. I'm just here for the free food."

"Really?"

Mindy rolled her eyes. "No. I'm here because my parents told me that I didn't have a choice. I was supposed to be hanging out with my girlfriend huffing dry-erase markers."

I forced out the laugh I'd practiced for those inevitable times when one of my parents' friends made an awful joke that I still had to pretend to find hilarious. "Funny."

"That's me," Mindy said. "I'm a comedienne or whatever." She tapped the side of her glass with her fingernail. "I'm betting you're not the kind of son who'd know how we could sneak some actual alcohol into my drink, are you?"

"Sorry. I don't drink."

Mindy sighed. "Of course you don't." Her shoulders slumped in defeat. "I don't either, not really, but this party is boring. How much trouble do you think I'd get in if I went into the bathroom and set the house on fire?"

My mouth was still hanging open when my mother walked up. "Mindy Maguire, it's so lovely to see you." She was stunning in a black cap-sleeve peplum dress.

"Thank you for having me, Governor Arnault."

"Janice, please."

Mindy had transformed from whatever she'd been a moment earlier into a demure, fawning sycophant, and her performance was as compelling as it was bizarre. "You have such a beautiful home. Thank you for inviting me."

My mother preened at the compliment. "Why thank you, dear. And thank you for keeping Dean company. I sometimes worry that he doesn't spend enough time around people his own age."

"Dean's been great," Mindy said. "He was just telling me how much he loves working on your campaign and that you're exactly the kind of woman this country needs in the White House." She patted my arm. "You're an inspiration."

"Dean is a remarkable young man," she said. "But I don't want to monopolize your time. I'm sure you two have a lot to talk about." My mother smiled at me. "Dean."

"Mom."

The moment my mother's back was turned, Mindy shoved her drink into my hand. "Ugh, I need to puke. Where's the nearest toilet?"

Again, I didn't know whether Mindy was serious or joking, so I pointed her toward the downstairs bathroom and then took the opportunity to run upstairs so that I could check my messages. Dre had apparently been busy and bored.

DreOfTheDead: where'd you go

DreOfTheDead: dean

DreOfTheDead: dean

DreOfTheDead: dean??!

DreOfTheDead: kidding

DreOfTheDead: i'm just bored

DreOfTheDead: im waiting for my dad to give his speech at the rally

DreOfTheDead: ive heard it SO MANY TIMES

PrezMamasBoy: Hi, Dre. It's Dean.

PrezMamasBoy: Sorry. My parents are having a dinner party, and the Maguires brought their daughter, and I guess they expected me to entertain her.

DreOfTheDead: dean arnault: babysitter

PrezMamasBoy: She's hardly a baby. She's our age.

DreOfTheDead: . . .

DreOfTheDead: did anyone else bring their kids????

PrezMamasBoy: No.

DreOfTheDead: so your mom invited a girl your age to the dinner and you havent figured out shes trying to set you up yet?

PrezMamasBoy: It is not a setup.

PrezMamasBoy: Either way, I only have a minute, so to answer your questions in the order you asked them:

PrezMamasBoy: Star Wars.

PrezMamasBoy: Hufflepuff, obviously.

PrezMamasBoy: Before the party I would have said flight, but now I wouldn't mind invisibility.

PrezMamasBoy: And I guess I don't have a preference. I'd be happy with either or neither. It's all the same to me.

PrezMamasBoy: I'll talk to you soon.

PrezMamasBoy: ~Dean

Thinking about Dre, hoping I'd get to see him again, was the only thing that was going to get me through this party. I plastered my fake smile back on and reentered the fray.

DRE

MY DAD WAS a rock star. He stood on the stage in front of an audience of thousands—it didn't matter what state or city we were in—and he owned them from his first word to his last. But speaking in front of crowds like that hadn't come naturally to him. Anyone who'd followed his career might've thought otherwise because he'd come out of law school as the kind of lawyer all the top firms in the country wanted to hire and had started making a name for himself working with the Nevada attorney general's office. But if someone went way, way back, they'd find a shy high school boy—the son of Mexican immigrants—with acne and a stutter, who wouldn't have been caught dead speaking in front of five people, much less five thousand. Becoming a rock star had taken time.

My dad didn't call himself a rock star when he told the

story. I'm pretty sure he didn't think of himself that way either. Instead, when he told his story, he talked about finding his voice. How he'd become part of a punk rock band in high school, which had helped him confront his fear of performing. How he'd joined the debate team and had learned how to use his voice to fight for the issues he believed in. How he'd been ashamed of his heritage because it had made him different, and how he'd learned to embrace it because our differences are what make us stronger. How he'd come from a family that hadn't been able to afford to send him to college, so he'd worked through his undergraduate degree and then through law school. How, as a lawyer, he'd used his voice to fight for those who couldn't.

I'd heard him give this speech so many times I could've given it myself. But it wasn't me people loved, it was my dad. And I guess I couldn't blame them because I loved him too. He was goofy and embarrassing, and I didn't care how many bands he was in when he was my age, the man couldn't sing, but he was still pretty great. Most of the time.

I sat backstage waiting for the reporter from *Teen Vogue* to show up. They'd asked for an interview and I'd been cool with it, and Dad had okayed it so long as Jose sat in. Probably more to protect the campaign from me than me from the reporter. Jose was standing nearby, talking on his phone, waving his hands like he was swatting flies. The man was stitched together from scraps of anxiety, and I wondered what he would do when the election was over and there was nothing left for him to freak out about. Who was I kidding? Jose was the master of finding problems to freak out about.

I used the downtime to see if Dean had answered my very important questions, and I grinned madly when I saw he had. Kissing Dean had changed me. The world was brighter, the stars were nearer. Dean had been wrong in the cemetery. Magic *was* real. I still didn't know how we'd gone from cussing each other out to kissing, but I wasn't gonna overthink it. Fine, I was *definitely* going to overthink it, but not right then. For at least a little while, I was going to enjoy the high of knowing I'd made out with a Hufflepuff who didn't have a definitive opinion on the exceptionally important question of pie versus cake.

"Andre Rosario?"

I finished typing my last message, fired it off, and closed my phone. The woman standing over me was curvy and bright with a short Afro and this violet shade of lipstick that was kind of everything.

I stood and held out my hand. "Dre."

"Holly Clarke."

"I loved the piece you wrote about internet call-out culture," I said. "I bet you got a lot of shit for trying to show both sides of that."

Holly flashed a wide, genuine smile. "I try never to read the comments." She motioned to the chair by mine. We were close enough to hear and see my dad but were hidden from the audience. "The research was eye-opening, though."

"You ever decide whether the internet mobs are a force for good or evil?"

"It's never one or the other," she said. "Often it's both. The internet gives a voice to marginalized people who are usually ignored when they speak. But the speed at which that shit travels discourages deep reflection and rewards shouting the fastest and loudest."

"Right? You wouldn't believe the trolls I gotta deal with sometimes."

Holly gave me a look like, *Did you really just say that?* and said, "I am a queer black woman writing about stuff most folks don't care to think about. Trust me; I believe." She laughed, and I hoped it was to let me know I hadn't stepped in it too badly.

"Hold on," I said. "I just have to get my foot out of my mouth."

Holly laughed again and held her phone out, setting it on her lap. "All right if I record?"

I didn't care, but I checked with Jose, who'd been half listening since Holly had shown up. He nodded tersely and kept on with his phone call.

"Cool," Holly said. "This is mostly a profile, and I've got to tell you that you've got a lot of fans on staff. I thought a couple were going to give me a shove down the stairs so they could take my place."

This was the part I found weird. I understood why people flocked to my dad, and I was happy that so many people liked the work Mel and I did on Dreadful Dressup, but I didn't get why they were curious about *me*. I was no one. There were so many people who were a hell of a lot more interesting. Shit, there were tons more teens who'd done amazing stuff with their lives and deserved to be profiled than me. But Holly wasn't asking them questions, so I did my best to answer and not look like a fool.

We started off easy, talking about my childhood and school and Dreadful Dressup and what it was like thinking my dad could be the president. Eventually, the talk turned to actual politics.

"Is it safe to say you probably wouldn't vote for Governor Arnault?" Holly asked.

"Pretty safe," I said. "Like, she's nice and all, but I can't see voting for someone who wouldn't protect everyone."

"What do you mean?"

"I mean a president's gotta be willing to protect the rights of *all* people, even the ones they don't like."

"Are you referring to Arnault's stance on LGBTQ issues?"

"Yeah," I said. "We're people, and if she wins, she'd be our president too, but she thinks trans soldiers should be kicked out of the army. How's that fair? How's that being the president of everyone?"

Holly smiled along with my answers and nodded like she was hanging on every word. I'd been in some tedious interviews, but this one wasn't so bad. "How about Jackson McMann?" she asked. "Young people, surprisingly, seem drawn to him. Do you have any thoughts?"

"From what I've seen of him, he's kind of a dick." Jose threw me a warning look, but I ignored him. "You worked on group projects in school, right?"

"I hated them."

"Me too," I said. "So you know how there's always the type-A who's gonna wind up doing most of the work, a couple of people who'll contribute just enough to slide by, and then that one dude who argues with decisions and complains non-stop, but never offers any actual solutions to the problems?"

I could tell by the grimace on Holly's face that she did. "Justin Forsyth. Eleventh-grade chemistry."

"That's how I see McMann," I said. "My dad's out there offering solutions to a lot of problems, and McMann's just sitting around shooting them down without offering any of his own. We're averaging, what? Like a school shooting every twelve days or something like that? And my dad's trying to come up with ways to prevent them, but all McMann wants to do is blame people with mental illnesses, and how's that gonna fix anything? It's not."

"So you think McMann doesn't have any actual policy goals?"

I shook my head. "He's all about making people afraid of anyone who isn't like them, because if we're too busy fighting each other, we won't notice he's a fraud."

"You recently spent some time with Dean Arnault," Holly said. "How was that?"

I froze. My blood ran cold, but I was sweating because she knew. "Did not."

Holly frowned. "Didn't you volunteer for Habitat for Humanity in Belle Rose, Louisiana?"

Relief flooded through me. For a moment, I thought she knew about Boston, and I was wondering if I could pull the fire alarm and flee. But she didn't know because of course she couldn't. No one knew.

"Oh," I said, covering with a laugh. "Yeah, that."

"Must not have been memorable."

"It was fine," I said. "Dean is fine. Nice, I mean. He's nice. We painted." I needed to stop talking before I ruined everything.

Holly cleared her throat and paused for a moment, eyeing me with what I hoped *wasn't* suspicion. Thankfully, Jose hadn't been paying attention. "Are there plans for you and Dean to appear together again? Maybe visit a few high schools to talk to students about the importance of voting? You could even hold your own debates."

"No one wants that," I said. "Do they? Jose?"

Jose leaned toward us. "What?"

"Are there schools that want me and Dean Arnault to visit them together?"

"There have been a few requests."

Holly's half grin said, *See?*

I'd been trying to figure out how Dean and I could keep

231

seeing each other, and so far all I'd come up with was that we'd both be at the next debate. But Holly's suggestion was kind of genius. The only problem was making it happen.

I shrugged and said to Holly, "I don't know. Dean probably wouldn't wanna debate me anyway."

"Why not?" she asked.

"Too scared of being shown up."

Holly laughed, and I smiled like this was all a big joke. "Well, maybe we can get him to change his mind."

"I hope so." I caught Holly throwing me a look of curious confusion, so I quickly added, "So I can kick his ass."

"Of course," Holly said, though I got the feeling she didn't quite believe me. "One last question: As an out, gay Mexican American, do you feel any pressure to be a role model?"

I was sure if Dean had been asked a similar question, he would've come up with something brilliant to say, but I had nothing. "I don't feel like a role model," I said. "I'm just Dre, you know? And I think all any of us can do is just be the best versions of ourselves that we can."

As Holly thanked me for sitting with her and took off, I couldn't help wondering if I *was* being the best version of me. If there were kids out there looking up to me, what message was I sending them by sneaking around with Dean? I didn't have an answer for that, and I wished I did.

DINNER WAS A family-style smorgasbord that I was hardly given a moment to eat any of because Mr. Cantero insisted on hammering me with questions like he was giving me a pop quiz. Mindy appeared to be enduring the same treatment at the other end of the table, though she seemed to be handling it with more grace than I. Truthfully, I was distracted. Ever since I'd kissed Dre in Boston, I couldn't stop thinking about him, and this dinner was torture because it was preventing me from talking to him. Then there was the comment Dre had made about Mindy. My parents had never tried to set me up before, so I doubted that was why they had invited her, but there was a small seed of uncertainty that grew bigger the more I thought about it.

I tried to sneak to my room to talk to Dre between dinner and dessert, but Mindy slipped in before I could close the door.

"So this is the bedroom of Dean Arnault?" she said. "It looks like a hotel room."

"I like things to be neat. It makes them easier to find when I need them."

"Figures." Mindy wandered around my bedroom, touching the books on my bookshelf and my debate awards and picking up the framed photos, most of which contained pictures of my parents and me on trips around the country and the world. It took a supreme amount of effort to refrain from politely asking her not to touch my belongings.

"So, uh, what do you study in school?"

"Same as you, probably."

"What do you *want* to study?"

"The queer agenda, how to dismantle the patriarchy, maybe Victorian literature." Mindy pointed at a photo. "Who's this?"

"My friend Tamal. I bet you'd like him."

Mindy glanced over her shoulder at me. "Probably not." She sat on my bed, giving off the impression that she was settling in. "Who are you waiting for a call from?"

"Excuse me?"

"You keep touching your phone through your pocket, so either that's not your phone and you're just touching yourself inappropriately or you're waiting for a call or a message or whatever from someone important."

234

I pulled my desk chair out and sat across from Mindy. "Just a friend."

"Mm-hmmm."

"I swear!"

"That makes me think it's definitely not 'just a friend.'"

There was something about the probing way Mindy was looking at me that made me want to be anywhere else at the moment. "Maybe we should go back downstairs. My dad made petits fours for dessert. One season of that baking show and now he thinks he's star baker."

If Mindy was interested in going downstairs, she didn't show it. "How do you put up with all this fake shit?"

"Excuse me?"

"These people are awful," she said. "That one guy, the one with the mustache—"

"Mr. Palmer."

Mindy nodded. "Him. He spent ten minutes telling me how it was fine for women to work so long as they didn't neglect their families, because it's what God wants for them. And the whole time he was staring at my tits, which God probably would *not* have approved of."

"I'm sure he wasn't—"

"He was." Mindy regarded me quietly for a moment, and I didn't know what to say to her, so I kept my mouth shut. "You don't like me much, do you?"

The question felt pointed, but also not like an accusation. "That's not true—"

Mindy brushed my attempt to lie aside with a sweep of her hand. "You're not my type either. Do you know why your mother invited me tonight?"

I shook my head, afraid to speak because Mindy was kind of scary.

"Because my parents asked her to," she said. "Apparently they're worried because I've never had a boyfriend, and they absolutely *adore* you. They never shut up about what a perfect specimen you are." Mindy stuck her finger in her mouth and mimed puking. "But, look, I don't need a boyfriend because I'm happy with my girlfriend."

"You were serious about that?"

Mindy made a *Duh!* face at me, and I felt like a fool. "So if we could just hang out up here a little longer and let my parents get the wrong idea about what's happening, that would be great."

"Uh . . . sure."

"And I'd really appreciate you not mentioning this to anyone. My parents are freaks and they'd send me to some pray-the-gay-away camp if they found out."

I had no idea what to do. I'd never felt so awkward in my own room before. In a way, it was a relief to know I wasn't the only person pretending to be someone I wasn't, but it was also a little sad. "I'm sort of seeing someone," I said. "My parents don't know. They wouldn't approve."

For the first time all night, Mindy seemed like she was doing more than merely tolerating me. "No shit?"

"We had our first kiss." The memory of kissing Dre was so strong, I could feel his soft lips and taste the espresso and milk on his tongue like it had just happened. "It was amazing."

Mindy was nodding appreciatively. "Doesn't it piss you off, though?"

"What?"

"Having to hide," she said. "Shouldn't our parents just be happy we've found someone who makes *us* happy?"

"Maybe they *could* be if we gave them the chance."

Mindy snorted derisively. "Keep living in that dream world."

My dad's voice called from downstairs to let us know dessert was ready. Mindy stood and headed for the door. "I'll go down first so they'll think we're trying to pretend we weren't up here together." She paused and tugged at the collar of her dress to make herself appear slightly disheveled.

As soon as Mindy was gone, I got my phone back out.

DreOfTheDead: i can forgive anything except not having an opinion on pie vs cake

DreOfTheDead: we're talking about desserts! this is important

DreOfTheDead: and the only valid answer is pie

DreOfTheDead: lemon meringue

DreOfTheDead: im gonna bake you one and force feed it to you till you agree

DreOfTheDead: also

DreOfTheDead: i cant believe im dating a hufflepuff

DreOfTheDead: shit

DreOfTheDead: didnt mean to suggest were dating

DreOfTheDead: unless we are

DreOfTheDead: we kinda went on a date and im hoping we get to do it again

DreOfTheDead: that counts as dating right???

Watching Dre have a meltdown was adorable. I loved the way his brain worked. The lack of filter or artifice. When it came to Dre, what he put out there was who he really was. It was rare to meet someone so genuine. Most people were like Mindy. They changed based on who they were around. Even after she had admitted she had a girlfriend and that her parents had brought her to the party hoping she and I would connect, I still didn't know if the person she was when we were alone was real. It could have been just another false front created for me. But Dre was always Dre no matter who was around.

I gave his question some thought, but I already knew the answer I wanted to give, so I quickly typed it out.

PrezMamasBoy: I suppose we *are* dating. That is, if you would consent to go on another date with me.

PrezMamasBoy: For the record, this is me formally asking.

PrezMamasBoy: I, Dean Arnault, would like to take you,

Dre Rosario, on a date that I hope will involve kissing at some point.

PrezMamasBoy: Do you accept?

Before I could put my phone away, Dre's response popped up on the screen.

DreOfTheDead: yes yes yes yes yes yes yes yes yes yes yes yes yes yes yes yes yes yes yes yes yes yes yes yes yes yes

PrezMamasBoy: Then, I guess you *are* dating a Hufflepuff.

After all the guests had finally left, I was in the kitchen helping my mother with the dishes. It was late, and I would have left them for the morning, but my mother was incapable of leaving a mess sitting out overnight. She was the type of person who, when we moved, couldn't sleep in the new house until every box had been unpacked.

"The party was a success," I said.

My mother looked over her shoulder and smiled. She tossed me a dish towel and motioned at the dishes she'd hand-washed. I began drying them and putting them away.

"I hope the debate on Monday will be equally successful."

"You've got this, Mom."

My mom smiled in my direction. "You and Mindy seemed to have quite a lot to talk about."

"She's . . . interesting," I said. "Not at all who I expected her to be."

"I'm glad you two hit it off," she said. "I've invited her to sit with you and your father at the debate on Monday."

The statement nearly flew over my head because it was the last thing I expected to hear, and it took me a moment to process it. "Why?"

"I thought you might enjoy spending time with someone your own age."

"And?" If Dre hadn't mentioned it and Mindy hadn't explained her parents' reasons for wanting her at the party, I might not have questioned my mother's motives, but now I couldn't help wonder.

My mother dried her hands on her apron before turning to me. "It'll be good for reporters to see you with a nice girl."

"Mindy is nice," I said. "But I'm not interested in her like that."

"It's about optics, Dean," she said sweetly. "Officially, she will be there as a guest of the family. What conclusions journalists choose to draw is up to them."

I wanted to press her on the issue. I wanted to ask her why this was so important to her now when it hadn't been before. She didn't care that I wasn't interested in Mindy romantically, only that others believed I was. I wanted to tell her that I had met someone who made me happy—he also made me confused in a good way and exasperated frequently. I wanted to tell the entire world about Dre so that they could share my happiness. But the world wouldn't have been happy for me. My mother wouldn't have celebrated with cake or pie or any type of dessert. The truth was that I couldn't predict how she would react, and I was scared to find out. So I remained quiet and kept drying dishes until we were done, and then I went to bed.

DEAN AND DRE.

Dre and Dean.

D&D? Nah. Too corny.

Still, Dean and I were a thing. I wasn't sure what kind of thing. A casual thing? A serious thing? A thing we had to keep secret from the world? None of those things? All of them? It was exciting and confusing and a little exhausting. But we had a relationship, and I could barely stop grinning. I wondered if dating someone who was demi was different from dating someone who wasn't. I'd never dated anyone before, and neither had Dean, so it wasn't like either of us had a frame of reference. We'd just have to muddle through it the best we could.

I hadn't told Dean about the *Teen Vogue* interview because I thought it might work better if his reaction to being challenged was authentic. I was proud that I'd come up with the idea on the fly, and I hoped Dean felt the same. I hoped it even worked. Dating was already complicated; dating someone in secret who didn't live in the same state was like doing calculus without a graphing calculator. Still totally worth it.

Mom and Dad were at church, so I left them a note and took off to Mel's for Dungeons & Dragons. We hadn't talked since our blowup when I'd admitted I had a thing for Dean, but D&D was a solid way to work through our issues. She might not like that I was actually dating Dean now, but she'd send some monsters to murder me, I'd fight them off, we'd have a laugh, and everything would go back to normal. That was kind of the way we were.

The first thing that clued me in that something was wrong was the lack of cars in Mel's driveway. Julian and Dhonielle both had their own cars, and at least one of them always drove. I wasn't early, so someone should have been there.

The second clue was Mel answering the door in her Snorlax pajamas, looking at me like I'd shaken her out of a deep sleep she desperately needed.

"What're you doing here, Dre?"

I held up my dice bag. "It's Sunday. Game day?"

Mel's eyes fluttered like she was going to roll them but couldn't quite gather the energy for it. "We play on Saturdays."

"Since when?"

"Since yesterday," Mel said. "It's easier for the rest of us, and with you not around, I made the decision to change the day."

I'd walked to Mel's on big fluffy clouds built from the happiness I felt about Dean, and Mel had just pissed all over them. "Are you serious?"

Instead of replying, Mel walked into the house. She'd left the door open, so I followed her in and into the kitchen, where she poured us each a mug of coffee.

"Like, I know you're mad at me, but how're you gonna play without Poppy Needles? How're you gonna play without *me*?"

Mel drank her coffee black, in gulps that should've burned her esophagus all the way down. "It was easy, actually."

"Fuck off."

"Feel free to leave anytime, Dre."

I couldn't stand anymore. I slumped onto the stool at the kitchen counter. Really, I should've walked out the door since Mel obviously didn't want me there, but I couldn't. The others were cool and I liked hanging out with them, but I didn't need them the way I needed Mel, and I needed Mel like I needed to breathe. I'd thought she needed me too, but I was obviously wrong.

"The world doesn't stop because you're busy."

"You think I'm mad because you changed gaming days and, okay, I am, but I'm more mad that you didn't tell me."

"I didn't think you'd even show up," she said. "It's not like you show up for anything else these days."

"That's not fair."

"It is and you know it."

"Whatever," I said. "You're right." The truth was that I didn't want to fight anymore, and I hoped by giving in, we could maybe skip over a few steps and start getting back to normal. I had so much I wanted to tell her, mostly about Dean. "Since we're not gaming, do you wanna do a dressup? I've got this idea for a gruesome unicorn—"

Mel looked away from me. "I can't. I have plans."

"What?" I asked. "I'm not doing anything. I could tag along. Unless it's a date. Is it a date?"

Mel still wasn't looking at me, and I knew it wasn't a date before she replied. "Me and Dhonielle and Lev are driving to Sacramento."

"Okay?"

"Jackson McMann is having a rally," Mel said. "We're going to protest."

"I could go. What're we protesting?" There was a lot to choose from. McMann had suggested during an interview with *Rolling Stone* magazine that all Muslims were terrorists. He'd gone on record with the *Washington Post* as saying that he supported the death penalty and believed states should execute *more* people and speed up the process by eliminating appeals. And during a segment on *The View*, he'd actually had the nerve to tell Whoopi that if women wanted to be paid as much as men, then they should take better care of their bodies and dress for the pay raises they wanted. All of which barely scratched the surface of awful things Jackson McMann had said and done.

Mel scoffed. "Yeah, as if your dad or Jose would let you be caught dead at a McMann rally, even just to protest."

"Obviously, I wouldn't tell them." I definitely would've gotten reamed if cameras caught me at the rally, but it was a price I was willing to pay.

"Why? This isn't even your thing. You wouldn't care about politics if your dad wasn't running."

I wanted to tell her that wasn't true, but it was. So I told her something that *was* true. "I just want to hang out with my best friend. And if that means carrying signs with catchy slogans on them and chanting, then I'm ready."

"What if I don't want to hang out with you?"

"Mel . . ."

"Still crushing on the son of Governor Satan?" Mel asked.

"We're dating, actually," I said, like that was a good comeback when I knew it wasn't. "And I thought we agreed to stop with the name-calling?"

Mel's eyes widened in surprise. "You're dating him? His mom thinks women who're raped and have abortions should be put in prison, but you're lecturing me on calling him names?"

"Dean and I decided not to talk about that stuff."

"How fucking convenient for you," Mel said, her voice rising. "It must be nice to be able to ignore everything so long as it doesn't affect you and your chances of getting a piece of ass."

"It's not like that, Mel." None of this was going the way I thought it would. Blood was burning my ears, and I felt like

I was going to burst. "I just wanted to play D and D and then tell my best friend that I'd had my first kiss. I thought you were that person, but it looks like I was wrong."

I got up and left, slamming the door behind me. Mel didn't even try to follow, which I knew because I stopped as soon as I'd turned the corner at the end of her street and waited to see if she would. I gave up after five minutes and walked the rest of the way home.

Mel was being so unfair! I knew she didn't agree with everything my dad did, and she stayed my best friend, but *I* was an asshole because I wasn't going to hold Dean responsible for all the shit his mom did. She was so willing to give everyone the benefit of the doubt except for Dean. She wouldn't even do it for me, and I was supposedly her best friend.

Whatever. Fine. If that's what Mel wanted, then we were done.

I slammed the garage door when I got home, still pissed, and I didn't notice my parents standing in the kitchen like they were waiting for me. They were still in their church clothes, but they did *not* look like they were filled with God's love.

"Weird," I said. "Both of you in the same room at the same time. Haven't seen that in a while." I was trying to make a joke, but it just came out mean.

"So," Mom said. "How was Boston?"

My fight with Mel had left me battered and bruised, and Mom's question was the punch that knocked me out.

"I don't know—"

"Your mother asked you a question, Andre."

I was scrambling, and I couldn't come up with a lie fast enough.

My mom held up a printout that I couldn't read from where I was standing. "We've got eight seventy-three at Bottomless Cup, eighty-nine fourteen at Newbury Comics." Mom stopped and stared at me over the paper. "Really, Dre? Ninety dollars on comic books?"

"We gave you that card for emergencies," my dad said. "Did you think we just paid it and never looked at it?"

"I didn't think—"

"Clearly," Dad said. I couldn't remember the last time he'd looked at me like that, and it gutted me.

Mom set the paper down. "You snuck off to Boston without telling us. Did you even tour the school in Rhode Island?"

"I walked around campus."

"Why?" Dad asked. "What was in Boston?"

I couldn't tell them about Dean. Telling Mel had been one thing, and I was regretting that, but if I told my mom and dad I'd met Dean there, they might tell Dean's mom and then we'd have to explain why we were there, and I couldn't do that to Dean.

"I don't know."

"That's not good enough," Mom said.

"Is that why you didn't want me going with you when I offered?" Dad asked, though I was sure he knew the answer.

Unable to speak, I just hung my head and let them yell. They called me irresponsible, and Mom lectured me about how dangerous it was and how there were people out there who might have recognized me and kidnapped me. Mostly, Dad just glared at me with a look that bore all the disappointment in me he felt, and that was the worst thing of all.

"Obviously, you're grounded," Dad finally said when my parents had run out of other things to say. "It's clear you aren't mature enough for this. You'll go back to school. No more events, no more traveling, and no more phone."

No more Dean. That's all I heard. "Dad, you can't—"

"Enough," he said. "Give me your phone and go to your room. I can't look at you right now."

This couldn't be happening, but it was. I'd messed up and I was never going to get to see Dean again. I could feel the tears coming, and I threw my phone on the counter and ran out of the room before letting my parents see me cry.

DAD KEPT PACE beside me easily as we jogged through the neighborhood. He waved at the neighbors out working in their yards, taking advantage of the slightly cooler early evening, and kept up a conversation with me that let me know this was nothing for him. My father competed in triathlons, only giving them up recently when his travel schedule made it too difficult for him to train. But he still enjoyed showing off in front of me, especially since we were only on our fourth mile and I was already getting winded.

"We leave for Las Vegas tomorrow," my father said. "Are you ready?"

I was crawling out of my skin to see Dre, though I hadn't heard from him since the day before, which was slightly strange. But I assumed he was helping his father with debate prep and hadn't found time to write me. My mother had been holed up with her advisors, preparing every free second she had.

"Did you know Mom invited Mindy Maguire to the debate?"

"She mentioned something about it."

"Do you know why?"

"A favor to the Maguires, I think," he said.

Ever since my conversation with my mother in the kitchen, I hadn't been able to stop wondering how she would react if she knew about my feelings for Dre. She had always said she'd believed in me and that she would love me no matter what, but it seemed that my mother's unconditional love might come with conditions after all. I could become whoever I wanted, so long as I became someone of whom she approved. I could do anything, so long as I didn't embarrass her. Or maybe I was reading too much into the situation. It was possible Dre had gotten into my head and I was scared for no reason. My mother deserved the benefit of the doubt, she deserved the chance to prove Dre wrong, but she could only do that if I told her, and I kept coming up with reasons not to.

"Do you think Mom wants people to believe Mindy is my girlfriend?"

"Are you and Mindy dating?" Dad asked.

"No."

"Then I doubt that's why your mom invited her."

"Are you sure?"

Dad chuckled. "I'm never sure of anything with your mom, but I think she's got more important things to worry about than the love life of her teenage son."

I might have agreed with my father before, but my mother had flat-out told me it was about the optics. "Do you think I'm weird, Dad?"

"What? Of course not."

I couldn't keep up talking and jogging at the same time, and I stopped as we passed a park and took a detour to the water fountain. I lapped up the water and splashed some on my face and neck. The sun might have been setting, but it was still brutal, and the humidity made it feel like I was breathing underwater.

"I think Mom's worried because I've never had a girlfriend," I said. "I think that's why she invited Mindy. I think she's hoping we get together, or that if we don't, the press at least thinks we're a couple."

Dad was using a nearby bench to stretch his legs. "You know I didn't have a girlfriend until I was twenty-one."

"Mom?"

Dad shook his head. "Your mom was still in the army at the time. Her name was Tori . . ." He frowned out of one side of his mouth. "Johnston, I think. We met in college; it didn't last."

"Why did you wait so long?"

"Because I wasn't ready," he said. "I was interested in *everything*—classical guitar, classical languages, computers, ancient history—but I lacked the focus to concentrate on anything. Learning took up all my time, and dating didn't cross my mind."

I'd seen pictures of my father in college, and his description of himself as a distracted dilettante didn't match the preppy young man with the easy smile and serious eyes. "Well, now I know where my ADD came from."

"Sorry about that."

"So you didn't feel weird being different?" I asked. "Weren't your friends dating?"

Dad came to stand by me and rested his hand on my shoulder. "There's nothing wrong with being different, Dean, and it doesn't make you weird."

"I don't think Mom would agree."

"Future President Janice Arnault might not agree," Dad said with a bit of cheek in his tone. "But that's because she's got to answer to voters and donors and people with agendas. Your mom, however, loves you more than anyone in the world, and that includes me."

I wanted to believe my father, but I was having a difficult time separating my parent from the politician. "Sometimes, I feel like she's already decided my entire life, and that I'm going to disappoint her if I deviate from her plan. If I don't go to college, get married, go to law school, have a couple of children, run for office, and become president by forty-five."

"Your mom's always had high hopes for you, but she primarily wants you to be happy."

"What if I want to become a teacher instead of study law?"

"She would support you."

"And if I don't want kids?"

Dad grimaced. "She's really looking forward to being called 'Granny' one day, but she would adjust."

"What if I married someone she didn't like or—"

My father cut me off. "Whatever it is, your mom will get used to it. She'll love you and support you like she always has, and so will I. And if this is really bothering you, I'll ask Nora to disinvite Mindy. We'll call it a security issue and apologize."

The offer was tempting, but I didn't want to make a fuss. "It's okay," I said. "Don't worry about it."

As sweaty as we both were, Dad hugged me tight, and I felt a little better knowing I had at least one ally. I wasn't sure if I believed my mother would be okay with my relationship with Dre, but I believed I could count on my father, and that was enough for now.

"Why don't you invite Tamal to come along too?" Dad asked. "That way it will look like you invited a couple of friends instead of a date?"

"Really?" I asked, surprised by my dad's offer.

"Sure. I'll call the Grovers and make sure it's okay if you want."

"Thanks, Dad." I wasn't sure how my mother was going to react to Dad subverting her plan, but that was his problem to deal with. I was just grateful I wouldn't have to spend my whole evening entertaining Mindy alone.

"Come on," my father said. "Race you home? Loser has to sit with Nora on the plane tomorrow."

"No way," I said. "Last time she spent the entire flight critiquing *my* debate performances."

"On three, then." Dad got ready. "One—" and then he took off sprinting toward the house. All I could do was try to catch up.

LIFE WASN'T FAIR.

My life wasn't fair.

I'd been in my room all day waiting for my parents to knock on my door and tell me they were sorry and that they weren't going to send me back to school, but they hadn't. The irony is that, before I'd met Dean, I hadn't wanted to take a leave from school. I'd wanted to stay with Mel and my friends and pretend the whole stupid election didn't exist. Now that I had Dean, I couldn't see him, and I was being sent back to school, where Mel wouldn't want to talk to me and had probably turned the others against me too.

And the worst part was that, without my phone, I had no way to let Dean know what was going on. He was probably wondering why he hadn't heard from me, inconsolable without my rambling messages to keep him entertained. The longer I went without talking to him, the more likely it was he was gonna think I hated him, and by the time I was able to tell him the truth about what was going on, it'd be too late.

I screamed into my pillow until my throat was raw, and when I sat up to breathe, my mom was standing in my doorway with her arms crossed in front of her. "By all means, mijo, give it another good scream. Get it out of your system."

I threw my pillow to the side and turned my back to her. "Leave me alone."

"So it's still like that?"

"Yes. It's still like that."

"Don't be mad at me," she said. "I'm not the one who lied to his parents, took advantage of their trust, and then was too much a fool to use cash instead of the credit card his parents gave him for emergencies. You've only got yourself to blame for this mess."

I kept my back to my mom and didn't say anything, hoping she'd leave. It's not like she was wrong. Using my credit card had been an amateur mistake, and I should've known better. But I didn't regret seeing Dean. If I had it to do over, I would've done it and not thought twice.

"Did you meet Mel in Boston?"

I shook my head. "No. Mel was probably in school. Besides, I'm not talking to her."

"Was it a boy?" Mom asked.

"No!"

"Are you sure? Eight dollars is a lot of money for one coffee."

"There's no boy."

"You think I don't remember what it's like being seventeen and feeling impatient for your life to start, but I do."

"Sure, Mom. Whatever."

Mom was so quiet for a minute that I thought I'd finally gotten rid of her, but I heard the squeak of my desk chair and knew, instead, that she was just settling in. "Your grandma *hated* my first boyfriend. I snuck out to see him, she locked me in my room. I climbed out the window, she nailed my window shut."

"Let me guess," I said. "He turned out to be a creep and you realized Grandma was just trying to protect you and you wished you'd listened to her all along."

"No, Dre. I married him."

I turned around so fast I nearly fell off the bed. "Wait, so it's okay for you to sneak around and whatever, but I'm being punished for it?"

"It wasn't okay when I did it," she said. "And it's not okay for you either. But I do understand."

"Look, I'm sorry I skipped the college tour, but Boston's only, like, thirty minutes away, and it's not like I stayed the night or anything."

"I certainly hope not."

"Besides, I'm old enough to go places on my own."

Mom nodded. "I thought you were. That's why your dad

and I allowed you to go. We trusted you to be responsible, and you weren't."

I wanted to tell my mom about Dean because I thought if I did, she would understand. I'd already known Grandma had taken a long time to warm up to Dad, so I thought she'd understand why Dean and I had snuck around. But it was too risky. She might tell Dean's mom, and I couldn't betray him like that.

"I'm sorry," I said. "But it was important to me. You know I'm telling the truth."

It felt like Mom was looking into my soul in the way that only a mother could. "I want to believe you, Dre, but I can't trust you if you keep lying to me."

"I won't lie anymore."

"We'll see."

I hung my head, trying to look contrite. "Dad's pretty pissed, isn't he?"

"I've always been a little jealous of how close you boys are," Mom said. "I'm glad, but sometimes, especially when you were younger, it was like the pair of you lived in a world I wasn't a part of."

"How come you never said anything?"

"Because how could I? I love you both, and I wasn't going to make either of you feel bad for being each other's best friend. But the bond you have with your dad means he's a lot easier for you to hurt."

"Do you think he'll get over it?"

"Eventually," she said. "Though he thinks you did it to punish him for not being around enough."

"It wasn't that."

Mom was nodding like she'd already figured that part out. "Make sure you tell him that."

"I will." I waited for my mom to say something else, but it seemed like she'd run out of things to say. "Am I still grounded?"

Mom laughed. "Oh, absolutely."

"Do I really have to go back to school?"

"We're not sure," she said. "We both think it might be for the best, but we'd have to find someone to stay with you since you obviously can't be trusted alone." The look on her face dared me to argue with her. I didn't. "So, we'll see."

"What about the debate tomorrow?"

Mom held up her hands. "You're coming to that, but you had better be on your best behavior, understand?"

"I do," I said. "I will."

"Good." Mom finally got up to leave, but she stopped at the door. "So you're really not going to tell me who the boy is?"

"There's no boy, Mom!"

"If you say so," she said. "But I'm not your grandma, Dre. Whoever this boy is, I'm sure we'll like him."

"How do you know?"

"Because if you like him enough that you'd cross state lines and risk my wrath to see him, he must be pretty special."

I wanted to tell her he was. I wanted to tell her everything. Instead, I just said, "Good to know."

DEAN

TAMAL AND MINDY hadn't stopped arguing since we'd gotten on the plane, and I was beginning to think it had been a bad idea to invite them. Judging by the look my mother had been giving the pair, I assumed she would have agreed. She had, however, taken Tamal's addition to the group in stride, though I wouldn't have wanted to be in my father's position the next time he and my mother were alone. After the plane landed and we were driven to the stadium where the debate was being held, my father found himself talking to the veterans that my mother had invited to sit with us in the front row, while my mother was huddled with Nora and her staff going over last-minute debate prep. That left Mindy, Tamal, and me alone in our greenroom.

"Dude," Tamal said. "Your girlfriend's got issues."

"She's not my girlfriend," I said at the same time as Mindy said, "Definitely not his girlfriend."

Tamal turned back to Mindy. "You really think basketball should get rid of the three-pointer?"

"That's not even close to what I said." Mindy was right when she'd said she didn't think she and Tamal would get along. Except, their arguing at least meant I didn't have to keep them entertained. "I said teams that build their entire offenses around three-point shooters make the game boring, and that they should move the line back or find some other way to fix it."

"Which is bananas!"

I tuned them out and unlocked my phone again, hoping to see a message on Promethean from Dre. I had sent him a couple of messages asking if there was a way we could meet up before or after the debate, but he hadn't replied and I was beginning to worry.

"Dean," Tamal said. "Gimme your phone."

"Why?"

"I promise I won't swipe through your pictures. Just hand it over."

"That's not . . . whatever." I handed Tamal my phone, curious what he was doing.

Tamal flipped through my apps before holding it out to show Mindy. "See, like, most of these are free apps." I didn't know when they'd moved off basketball, and I had no idea what they were discussing now.

Mindy was scowling at Tamal like she wanted to stab him repeatedly with a fork. "What's wrong with free?"

"Uh, if an app's not serving you ads and they're not selling you access, then they're just selling you."

Oh. I'd heard this particular rant from Tamal before. All about personal privacy and how we were the product and tech companies were selling all of our data. He could get pretty worked up about it. He also made a lot of excellent points.

"Dude," Tamal said, turning my phone's screen to me. "Promethean?"

"It's just—"

"Doesn't Jackson McMann own the company that created it?" Mindy asked.

Tamal nodded. "Yeah. So I wouldn't let your mom catch you using it if I were you."

"I don't really use it," I said. But, of course, Dre chose that moment to send me a message, and the notification badge bloomed at the corner of the app's icon.

"Sure." Tamal tossed me my phone.

Mindy was watching me with a secret smirk. I hadn't told her anything except that I'd kissed someone and didn't want anyone else to know, but I was beginning to regret even sharing that much with her.

I wanted to check the message immediately, but I couldn't with Tamal and Mindy watching me. Not tapping the app icon and reading Dre's message was like being covered in poison ivy and not being able to scratch.

"So are you going to debate the Rosario kid or what?" Tamal asked.

"Excuse me?"

"Didn't you see? Rosario challenged you to a debate in *Teen Vogue*."

Mindy fired off a laugh that sounded totally cracked. "You read *Teen Vogue*?"

Tamal didn't even look embarrassed. "Yeah. That a problem?"

Mindy held up her hands. "Nope."

Before they could start arguing again, I wanted to know what Tamal was talking about, so I snapped my fingers in front of his face. "Focus. What article?"

"It was some profile they did on him," Tamal said. "He had a *lot* to say about everything. He called McMann a dick, and said you'd be too scared to debate him."

My eyes must have been bulging out of my head because Tamal added, "I know, right? The balls on that kid thinking you'd be scared to go up against him."

"Are you serious?" Why hadn't Dre told me anything about it? It didn't seem like the kind of thing he would do, but maybe he'd had a reason for it. It would have been nice if he'd told me. Maybe that was what the message was in regards to. If I could only slip away to read it. Speaking of reading, while I was lost in thought, Tamal had been pulling up the article, which he began to read aloud.

"Though Dre doesn't have a background in debate, he

264

showed no hesitation when asked if he would be willing to accept one of the many invitations he's received to debate Dean Arnault at a local high school. His only fear seemed to be that Arnault wouldn't attend, and when I asked him why, he responded that Dean would be 'too scared of being shown up.'" Tamal glanced up from his phone. "You're gonna debate him, right? He should do it, right?"

When Mindy realized he was asking her, she said, "I honestly don't care."

Now I *had* to read Dre's messages.

DreOfTheDead: where u at

DreOfTheDead: need to talk to you

PrezMamasBoy: Hi, Dre.

PrezMamasBoy: I'm in the greenroom.

DreOfTheDead: can you get away???

DreOfTheDead: im in a supply closet next to the mens room

I stood so abruptly that Tamal and Mindy both turned to stare at me. "Restroom." I pressed my hand to my stomach. "We had tacos for dinner last night."

Mindy wrinkled her nose and looked away. Tamal said, "Didn't need to know that."

I left before I could embarrass myself further. The problem with Dre's directions was that the UNLV arena where the debate was being held was huge, and there were multiple men's rooms. I checked two supply closets and still hadn't found Dre, and I was getting frustrated. I turned the corner and ran straight into Jackson McMann.

As a young man, he had been slightly awkward and long-limbed, but becoming a billionaire had changed him. He was now famous for his commitment to fitness and strength training. Running into him was like running into a wall.

"Dean Arnault, right?" McMann had a soft New England accent that was difficult to place. It was noticeable but just barely.

"Mr. McMann. I'm sorry. I was looking for the restroom."

McMann pointed over my shoulder. "Seems like it's right behind you."

"Right," I said. "I mean, I *was* looking, but I found it and I went. I feel much better."

There was something about McMann's expression that made me think he knew I was lying. It was the smirk or the little crinkle around his eyes. I don't know. Either way, it was unnerving.

"You debate, isn't that right, Dean?"

"Yes, sir." Just because I couldn't stand McMann didn't mean I couldn't be polite.

"This is my first, and I'm not ashamed to admit I'm nervous. Any tips for a newbie?"

Jackson McMann was asking *me* for debate tips? Maybe if he'd been anyone else or if I hadn't watched him give an interview where he had insinuated that my mother wasn't a real soldier and had only been allowed to serve to fill a quota, I might have given him some actual advice. Being polite didn't mean I had to be helpful.

"There's no shame in admitting you're outclassed and conceding. Debate isn't for everyone."

McMann let out a belly laugh that echoed down the hall. "I'll keep that in mind."

"I should go."

McMann stepped aside so I could pass. As I was walking away, he said, "Say hi to Andre for me if you see him."

I didn't know why he would have said that, but I put it out of my mind and focused on finding Dre. It took another couple of minutes, but I finally located the right closet. Dre was waiting for me surrounded by cleaning supplies and a mop bucket. The closet smelled like bleach, but I didn't care. The second I shut the door, Dre grabbed my face and kissed me, and I sank into it without fear or shame or any thoughts at all other than that this was where I was meant to be.

DRE

I FELT LIKE I'd been drowning. Like I was a thousand feet below the surface with nothing but my last breath burning in my lungs, and I was going to die without ever tasting the sweet air again. And then I kissed Dean, and he breathed life back into me. I didn't care that we were making out in a supply closet or that there was a dirty mop touching the back of my hand or that everything smelled like ammonia. I. Was. Kissing. Dean. The whole world could vanish so long as we two remained, and I would be happy.

Dean's hands rested on my hips. He rested his forehead against mine. "Hello to you too."

I laughed. "Sorry. I was kinda suffocating."

"Hyperbole? From you? I'm shocked."

"Are you, though?"

"Not really."

"I *did* miss you."

Whatever Dean was gonna say, words seemed like a waste of time, so I pulled him into another kiss, letting go of my fear and anxiety. This was where I wanted to be. Here and nothing else.

Dean finally pulled away, but he was still smiling. "I read your interview in *Teen Vogue*. You challenged me to a debate?"

"My parents are gonna wonder where I am, and we don't have time to talk about all the dumbass things I said during that interview, but if you find a way to say yes, it might mean we can see each other again."

Dean laughed and stroked my cheek with his thumb. "I'll try. And I missed you too." He might not have been the kind of person to dramatically and boldly declare his feelings for me through an impromptu song or interpretive dance, but his emotions were so plainly etched in his eyes that he might as well have been shouting them.

My lips brushed the side of his cheek, and his eyelids fluttered. "I'm sorry I haven't been able to message you, but my parents found out about Boston—"

"What?!"

"Not about you, just that I was there. And they took away my phone. I have it back now, but I'm also kind of grounded and I can't stay because my parents are all over my ass right now, but I don't want to leave you. I just want to stay here and kiss you until your lips fall off."

Dean looked like he was trying to process everything I'd told him but was having a tough time, and I couldn't blame him. It was a lot. "I don't want you to go either, but I understand."

I kissed him again. I held on to him like we were lost at sea, even though I knew one of us was going to have to let go. "Okay," I said. "You go first and then I'll wait and follow after."

"You've been gone longer," Dean said. "So you should probably leave first."

"But I like the view when you leave."

"Dre!"

"Fine," I said. "I'll go first."

I reached for the door, and Dean stopped me and said, "Dre, there's something I have to tell you," but my phone buzzed, cutting him off.

"Shit. It's my parents asking where I am. I have to run." I kissed his cheek one last time and dashed out of the closet to get back to the greenroom before my parents sent Secret Service to find me.

As I made my way back to the greenroom, navigating the hallways, I wondered what Dean had wanted to tell me. Probably that I was the best thing to happen to him in his whole life, and he was right about that. Or maybe he'd decided to come out to his mom, which *might* have made life easier but probably wouldn't have. I didn't like hiding, but I also wasn't naive enough to believe his mom was gonna be happy her golden boy was dating a problem child. The press might get focused on me and Dean instead of on my dad's immigration reforms or Governor Arnault's views on abortion or Jackson McMann's shitty views on everything *and* his lack of actual political experience. And rather than voting for the person they thought would be the best president, people might cast their vote based on whether they thought me or Dean was cuter or whether they approved of us dating or some other nonsense.

I must've gotten turned around because this was not where my greenroom was. I was texting my mom that I was kind of lost and trying to find the room and not to worry when I spotted a sign on the wall outside a door that read "McMann." Curiosity got the better of me, and I crept to the door. His room was the same size as the one my dad had been given, but his looked like a secret hacker hideout. Every table had a laptop on it, it seemed, and there were people working, oblivious to me. No one was talking, no one was shouting into their phone the way Jose always was. It was a little freaky. I got out my phone to take a picture so I could show Dean. When I opened the camera, it was set for a selfie and I spotted McMann creeping behind me.

I shut the camera app and turned around quick, trying to look more annoyed than surprised. I'd never met him in person before and he was a lot taller than I'd expected and, okay, decently attractive for an old dude. Objectively speaking. Not that *I* thought he was attractive. He was a little too

Tech Billionaire Supervillain for my taste. Moving on. "Uh, can I help you?"

"This is actually my greenroom." McMann didn't look startled at being caught. If I had to guess, he actually looked pleased. "You're Andre Rosario, aren't you? Or do you prefer Dre?"

"I prefer old dudes to not sneak up on me, but Dre's fine."

"Jack." He held out his hand, and I let it hang there. "I liked your profile in *Teen Vogue*. You certainly have a lot to say."

Holly had included that I'd called McMann a dick. I'd expected my father to be more upset by that, but I think he would have actually laughed if he hadn't still been pissed at me about Boston. Well, that was fine if McMann knew what I thought about him. It would certainly save me having to be polite. "Yup. Just not to you. See you around."

"If you see Dean, tell him his girlfriend is looking for him."

I froze midstride and turned back to McMann. "Dean doesn't have a girlfriend."

McMann's curious expression morphed into a smug, self-satisfied smile. "I suppose she didn't explicitly say they were dating—however, he did bring her to the debate tonight, so certain assumptions could be made."

My brain was a shattered wreck, trying to piece together everything McMann was saying. It was like I'd been riding a roller coaster and the operator had slammed on the brakes while we were traveling at top speed. Was that what Dean had wanted to tell me? If Dean had a girlfriend, why the hell was he kissing *me* in the janitor's closet?

I did my best to recover, but all I could come up with was, "You really are a dick." My voice dropped an octave and all the happiness I'd felt while holding Dean had vanished.

But instead of looking offended, McMann's seemed mostly amused. "Enjoy the debate tonight, Dre."

I should have walked away. I should have walked away the moment I saw him and not engaged him at all. But I didn't because there was something about McMann that sparked an ugly, angry fire in me. The last time I'd felt that way was when Mel had found out this guy Karl she was with was dating two other girls in addition to her, and he'd tried to convince her it was her fault for not being enough to satisfy him, so I'd made up a fake set of test results showing he had super chlamydia and then left them all around school so that no girl would ever want to get with him again. He'd found me after school and given me a black eye, but it had been totally worth it.

Mouthing off to McMann didn't leave me with the same fuzzy feeling, but I couldn't stop myself.

"There's no way you're winning this election."

"There's still a month between now and Election Day," he said. "A lot of time for secrets to come out. Secrets that might tip the election one way or another." McMann clapped me on the shoulder and smirked. His eyes were cold and blue and dead. "I'm willing to bet *you* have some secrets, don't you?"

McMann brushed past me, walked into his room, and shut the door.

What had he meant about secrets, and why had he looked at me *that* way when he'd said it? There was no way he could've known about me and Dean. There wasn't even much to know yet. All he could know was what everyone else knew unless he had tiny cameras mounted on tiny drones following us everywhere we went, and that was ridiculous. The stuff of bad movies. But still, there was something in the way he said it that worried me. And what had he meant about Dean having a girlfriend? McMann didn't seem like the type of person who did anything without having a reason; I just couldn't figure his reasons out.

"Dre, there you are." My mom came around the corner and waved for me to follow her. I wanted to find Dean and tell him about McMann. I wanted to know more about his supposed girlfriend, because, yeah, even though I trusted Dean and we had potentially bigger problems, I was still a little jealous. But it's not like I could run from my mom. All I could do was wait and hope Dean and I could find a way to see each other after the debate.

DEAN

THE NOTIFICATION COUNTER on my Promethean app was growing, and I couldn't get away for five minutes to check the messages. I should have explained Mindy to Dre while we were in the closet, but I'd been so happy to see him and all I had wanted to do was kiss him that I'd let the opportunity slip away. And then I'd seen the jealous glint in his eyes when he'd spotted Mindy sitting beside me. Mindy might not have wanted any more to do with me than I did with her, but she had certainly played it up for the cameras. Or possibly just for her parents. Either way, I needed to explain the situation to Dre and reassure him that there was *nothing* going on.

Doing so, however, would require finding a way to sneak out of my parents' suite in the hotel.

"It didn't go very well, did it?" Mindy asked.

"Not unless your name is Jackson McMann," I said.

The debate had been something of a disaster, and McMann had been the clear victor. Everyone who worked for my mother was doing damage control from the hotel where we'd gone after leaving the debate. Nora was juggling multiple phones, Mom's communications director was working on a statement for her to release, Dad was fetching Mom tea and possibly something stronger if she needed it, and Mom was standing in the center of the storm, a little battered and bruised, but still in control.

None of them were paying attention to Mindy, Tamal, or me, but they were my guests, so I couldn't just leave them.

"How was that even a debate?" Tamal asked.

"It wasn't."

Mindy snorted.

"What?" I asked. "McMann didn't answer the questions. At least, not the questions that were asked."

"Just because he didn't perform the way *you* would have, doesn't mean he didn't crush it," Mindy said.

Tamal's expression was somewhere between appalled and impressed. I didn't think he liked Mindy, but he definitely respected her willingness to speak her mind. "You don't actually like the guy, do you?"

Mindy shrugged. "He's a narcissist and possibly a sociopath, but at least he's interesting. Besides, maybe it's time we elect someone who doesn't play by the rules."

Not only had McMann not played by the rules, but he had seemingly not even bothered to read them. He had laughed at them and set them on fire. "Okay," I said. "I understand you might think it's cool that he's not like other politicians—"

"Because he's not one," Mindy said.

"Right. But have you actually listened to some of his quote, unquote, *solutions*?" I gave Mindy a chance to withdraw her support for McMann, but she said nothing. "School shootings," I said. "Rosario would probably ban guns if he could, my mom has a detailed plan for better mental health training for school counselors, but McMann? He actually suggested letting the kids go *Battle Royale* on one another. How is that a solution?"

Mindy was laughing, but I didn't find it funny. "He wasn't serious."

"Sounded serious to me," Tamal said. He was only half paying attention as he traded messages with Astrid. I admit I was jealous that he could talk to her openly while I had to hide my conversations with Dre.

"He wasn't."

"Was he serious when he said the answer to climate change was to colonize the moon? Or when he said that maintaining our nuclear arsenal was a waste of money if we weren't going to use it to eliminate the competition? How about when he said the answer to our failing infrastructure was to invest in prison labor and have them rebuild our bridges and roadways?"

In the time allotted, McMann had made so many

ludicrous statements that it had been difficult to remember them all. But Mindy didn't seem bothered.

"He's pointing out how ridiculous and broken the current system is. He wouldn't actually do any of those things." Mindy seemed so certain, but I wasn't.

"Then why say them?"

Mindy rolled her eyes. "*Because* they're ridiculous. Because they make people underestimate him." She paused a moment. "Your mom and Rosario spent the entire debate ignoring McMann and tearing into each other over the same tired solutions everyone's heard before. Then McMann comes in and maybe *his* solution is totally bananas, but it's different, and maybe different is what people are hungry for."

I threw up my hands. "Sure, why not just burn everything down. That's different too."

Mindy nodded, smiling. "Now you get it."

Except I didn't get anything. McMann hadn't offered a single solution that a rational person should have thought was reasonable, but I also couldn't deny that he had beaten Rosario and my mother, though only because their own messages had been lost in the chaos.

"The two-party system is trash," Mindy said. "And America is a failed experiment. McMann was the only person on that stage tonight who didn't pretend otherwise. I think he's basically one rung above three rabid raccoons standing on each other's shoulders wearing a trench coat, but if he's willing to tear everything down, then he's got my hypothetical but useless vote."

Tamal stretched his arms over his head and yawned. "You're kinda scary," he said to Mindy.

"Thank you."

Then to me, he said, "I'm ready to crash."

I was so grateful to Tamal right then. Mindy wanted to stick around for a while, and I figured my mom wouldn't mind as long as she stayed out of the way. Tamal and I had a room down the hall.

"That Mindy's a freak," Tamal said when we were alone.

"She's definitely different."

"The way she flips from Cheery Chelsea Church girl to Princess Anarchy is creepy. Is it weird that I kind of like her? Not like I like Astrid, but like I bet she'd be cool to bowl with."

"I doubt Mindy bowls."

"Or scare children or whatever."

"I think she's only like that because of her parents," I said. "She has to act a specific way for them, and she can only be herself when she feels safe. I kind of get it."

Tamal brushed his teeth and changed into his pajamas before getting into bed. "Seems like a rough way to live. Always having to pretend. Never knowing who you can be yourself around."

"Yeah," I said. "It's not great." I grabbed clean clothes and my phone and headed for the bathroom. "I'm going to shower before bed. See you tomorrow."

"Night, dude."

I shut the bathroom door behind me, finally alone. I turned on the shower, sat on the edge of the tub, and opened my phone. Nineteen notifications. I held my thumb over the Promethean app, scared to tap it. But it wasn't a bomb. No matter what Dre said, all I had to do was tell him the truth. Explain that my mother had invited Mindy, that she'd sprung it on me, that I'd been about to tell him when he'd had to leave. Once I explained, he would understand.

Yet, I still couldn't bring myself to open the app. I knew I was being silly. This thing with Mindy was just a misunderstanding, but I was still scared. I'd known Tamal longer, but Dre was the *only* person I could fully be myself around, and I was scared of losing him. I was scared of losing more than the boy I cared about; I was scared of losing my friend.

Procrastinating wouldn't change the messages, though. It would only give Dre more time to wind himself up. So, I finally tapped the icon.

DreOfTheDead: wild debate huh

DreOfTheDead: so who was your date???

DreOfTheDead: was the guy your friend tamal you told me about

DreOfTheDead: youre not dating that girl right?

DreOfTheDead: of course youre not

DreOfTheDead: unless you are

DreOfTheDead: dont worry about me being upset

DreOfTheDead: i never expected anything from you

DreOfTheDead: okay?!?

DreOfTheDead: dean

DreOfTheDead: dean

DreOfTheDead: dean

DreOfTheDead: you already know I like you

DreOfTheDead: i like talking to you

DreOfTheDead: i like kissing you

DreOfTheDead: but i like being your friend most of all

DreOfTheDead: so whatever else we'll always be friends

DreOfTheDead: pinkie promise

DreOfTheDead: sweet dreams

Below the last message was a picture of Dre lying with his head on the pillow. His hair spread out and his eyes half-closed. Beautiful.

DreOfTheDead: ps, she was pretty but i'm prettier

DreOfTheDead: xoxo

Dre didn't hate me. My hands were trembling and my heart was racing as my anxiety turned into joy. The bathroom was filled with steam and I'd been in there so long Tamal was going to wonder what I was doing, but I had to take a moment to calm myself before I could compose a reply.

PrezMamasBoy: Hi, Dre. It's Dean.

PrezMamasBoy: Mindy doesn't hold a candle to you.

PrezMamasBoy: Also, I'm not her type.

PrezMamasBoy: My dreams will be sweet because they will be of you.

PrezMamasBoy: See you there.

PrezMamasBoy: ~Dean

DRE

DAD LOOKED LIKE a beaked goblin that had been living in the irradiated wastelands of Chernobyl. Or, at least, he was starting to. He sat quietly in the garage, in a battered leather recliner that Mel and I had stolen from the neighbor's trash in the middle of the night to use for Dreadful Dressup because my mom would've murdered me, raised me from the dead, and then murdered me again if I'd ruined any of her furniture.

I'd been itching to do *something* for Dreadful Dressup, but I needed someone to put makeup on, and without Mel my choices were limited. Dad had offered himself up without me even needing to ask. He'd been subdued since the debates, defeated in a way I hadn't seen him since he lost the Iowa caucus during the primary. That'd been a rough fight, and he'd taken the early loss pretty hard. This was different, though.

It wasn't like he was nursing his wounds; it was a bone-deep exhaustion that he couldn't seem to shake.

"Thanks for letting me stay on with the campaign." It was still a touchy subject with Dad, but Mom had convinced him to let me keep traveling with them until the election.

"You weren't thrilled about leaving school during your senior year in the first place. Why do you seem so reluctant to go back now?"

"Try not to move your lips so much when you talk." I was working on Dad's cheeks, and I didn't want him messing up the work I'd already done. Painting him as a post-apocalyptic bird goblin was *not* easy.

"Is it the same reason I'm sitting in this chair instead of Mel?"

"Yeah. We're kinda not talking."

"What did you do?"

"Me? Nothing!" Blending the face prosthesis was delicate work. I stood back to judge what I'd done so far. Not too bad.

Dad was watching me with that skeptical *Don't even think about lying to me* look that I usually attributed to Mom. "You must've done something, Dre."

I sighed. "She was pissed because I messed up some plans we'd made and she changed D and D from Sundays to Saturdays without telling me, and then she had the nerve to yell at me because I'd hung out with Dean Arnault and *didn't* think he was a monster. It's like I have no idea who she even is anymore."

Dad was quiet for a little while, and I couldn't read his

expression under all the makeup. Finally, he said, "I feel like this is my fault."

"What? No. It's Mel's fault for being such a shit."

"Dre, how can you be upset with Mel for missing you when you've spent the last few months angry with me for the same reason?"

"I . . ." I wanted to tell him it was different, but it wasn't and I knew it. I'd always known.

"You can't expect Mel to rearrange her life to suit you any more than I could expect it of you." Dad motioned for me to stop with the makeup and sit for a second. I pulled a stool over. "When I clinched the Democratic nomination, you were the first person I wanted to tell. Your mom barely tolerates all of this, and I know she thinks I'm going to lose even though she pretends otherwise and thinks I don't know.

"But I thought how great it would be to have my son by my side. Not because I hoped you'd help me appeal to younger voters or because Jose thought you'd poll well, but because I love you, Dre, and I'm proud of you, and I wanted to make you proud of me too."

It was hard taking Dad seriously when he was looking like a freaky bird goblin that'd been dunked in toxic sludge, but it was the first time in months that I wasn't angry with him. "I *am* proud of you, Dad. I always have been."

"I know," he said. "But it hurt when you didn't want to leave school, and your mom had to remind me that I had no right to be upset with you for wanting to live your life."

"Just like I can't be mad at Mel for living hers while I'm off doing my own thing?"

"Exactly."

"Even though she changed the D and D game day?"

"If you want to play on Saturdays, we'll work out how to get you there." Dad's smile slipped a notch. "Once you're done being grounded."

"Of course." I chuckled and got back to work because Dad had to be hot under all that makeup and I didn't want him suffering *too* much. "What about her shitting on me for not hating Dean, though? That's kind of messed up, right?"

"Mel has always been passionate about her beliefs. I'm surprised she hasn't protested any of *my* campaign events."

She had, but this wasn't the time to tell Dad that. "Am I wrong not holding Dean responsible for all the shit his mom believes?"

"I don't think you are."

"What if he actually *does* believe some of that stuff?" I asked. "Would I be wrong to still be friends with him?"

Dad couldn't answer right away because I was working on his lips, but when I finished, he said, "When I was your age, I read Ayn Rand. I thought her philosophy, objectivism, was the pinnacle of rational thought and political theory."

I'd never heard of her and I said so.

"Don't worry about it. Her philosophy's garbage. The point is that being young is about exploring ideas. Some of the ideas we explore turn out to be trash, and we hopefully grow out of them."

"So I'm right and Mel's wrong."

Dad held up his hands. "That's not what I said."

"Then what *are* you saying?"

"Mel's not wrong for holding people to a higher standard, and you're not wrong for giving them the benefit of the doubt. You're not always going to agree on whether someone is worthy of spending time with, and that's okay. But don't let it get in the way of your friendship."

Dad paused for a second, looking at me like he was searching for something. "I think it's fine that you and Dean have found some common ground, and I've always admired your ability to look past a person's faults. Just be certain that he deserves it."

My dad could be pretty perceptive, and my relationship with Dean was something I didn't need him thinking about too much or he might put it together that there was more between us than I was letting on. I had to change the subject. Fast.

"You're not worried about McMann winning, are you?"

"More worried than I should be."

"Why?" I asked. "He can't win, can he? I mean, even if he splits the vote, Democrats control the House, so they'd choose you as the winner, right?" I didn't live for politics the way Dean did, but that didn't mean I hadn't fallen down a few late-night clickholes trying to figure out how all this stuff worked.

287

Even under the layers of makeup, I could see Dad's worry. "Democrats barely control the House, and McMann has deep pockets. There are a lot of representatives on both sides of the aisle who owe him their careers."

"Sure, maybe he could flip a few votes, but he couldn't flip enough to win."

"Jose has been running scenarios, and there are a couple where, yes, it's possible he could win. If I lose enough votes to him to give Arnault the advantage, more might throw their support behind him just to keep her out of the White House. Whoever wins is probably going to get to nominate a couple of justices to the Supreme Court. There's a lot at stake, Dre."

Until that moment, McMann winning seemed like an impossibility. The kind of hypothetical that people talked about but that they all knew could never really happen, but now it was starting to feel like a reality, and it was kind of terrifying.

"I've been thinking of withdrawing."

I wasn't fully paying attention to my dad, so it was a couple of seconds before I processed what he'd said. My head whipped around. "Wait, what? You can't do that!"

But Dad looked resigned, like he'd already made up his mind. "If I drop out of the race now, Janice can focus her attacks on McMann without me as a distraction."

"She's just as bad as McMann!"

"Not even close, Dre," he said. "I don't agree with her on

just about anything, and she's not the leader we need right now, but Jackson McMann *cannot* be allowed to win. He would tear this country apart and destroy the relationships we have with our foreign allies. I would rather see Governor Arnault win than him."

"Then why doesn't she drop out so *you* can win?"

Dad rested his hand on my shoulder. "Because, in her heart, she's a soldier, and I don't think she's capable of surrendering."

"Sounds like you admire her."

"It's been tough being the first Mexican American to have a real shot at becoming president. It's been an uphill battle through hordes of vile racists and people who see me as nothing but the color of my skin. But Janice has also put up with her share of vitriol. The misogyny, the constant and unrelenting commentary on her appearance, the way so many people tack on 'for a woman' to the end of their compliments of her." He nodded to himself. "She's also had it rough. So, yes, I do admire her. I admire her tenacity and her strength, and you should too."

Life would've been so much easier if Dad were to drop out of the race. No more worrying about the election, no more late nights and missed dinners. I'd get my dad back and we could go to Europe after graduation like we'd planned. Everything would go back to the way it'd been. Only, nothing ever goes back to the way it was. We'd all been changed by the last few months. We were different people. I was a different person. Might as well try to unbake cookies and separate the dough into its original components.

But most of all, even though I fully believed Dad was willing to sacrifice what he wanted for the greater good, he also really wanted to be president. Not for the power, not for the glory, but so he could help people.

"You can't quit," I said.

"I haven't made any decisions yet—"

"Then don't. Stop thinking about giving up and start focusing on winning. Get out there and kick McMann's ass. Then kick Arnault's ass. Kick anyone's ass who gets in your way."

"This isn't going to get any easier, you know that, right, Dre?" I started to answer, but Dad held up his hand to let me know he wasn't finished. "I can promise you that I'll do my best to be there for you, but if I keep at this and I win, times *are* going to come when my best won't be good enough. Situations will arise when I'm going to disappoint you. When some emergency is going to pull me away from you and ruin our plans. If this is going to work, Dre, we have to be honest with each other."

The last time Dad and I'd had this talk, I hadn't thought it through, but this time I did. This time, when I answered, I was sure. "I'm not saying I'm gonna like it, and I'm not saying I'm not ever gonna be pissed about it, but I get it and I understand, and I *still* want you to keep going. I want you to *win*."

For the first time since the second debate, my dad smiled. "You really think I can?"

"Yes," I said. "And I'll be with you all the way. If you want me there."

"You know I do."

"Good," I said. "Now, let's get your beak and hooves on so we can take some pictures."

MY MOTHER WAS standing at the bottom of the stairs, holding a glass of whiskey in one hand and her tablet in the other. She loved whiskey, but only drank it on rare occasions, so either Jackson McMann and Tomás Rosario had both dropped out of the race or the world was coming to an end.

"What the hell were you thinking, Dean?"

So McMann and Rosario were still in the race.

"What do you mean?" I stood at the top of the stairs, unsure whether it was safe to come down.

My mother held up the tablet. "You allowed yourself to be goaded into debating Andre Rosario?" Her tone was acid. "Come down here. I'm not going to give myself a muscle spasm in my neck looking up at you."

Life in the days since the debate had been more interesting

than anyone had asked for. McMann was polling only a few points behind my mom and Rosario, which was unheard of for an independent, and he was taking every opportunity he could to give interviews or hold rallies. Analysts were talking about him like he could honestly win, and Mom had been doing everything she could to combat his offensive, including working with the Rosario campaign to schedule a third debate, one where she would be ready for McMann.

But Dre was the thing I looked forward to more than any other, and I was willing to do whatever it took to see him.

I descended the stairs until I was face-to-face with my mother.

"Why would you do something so foolish?"

"I let Astrid interview me for the school paper," I said. "She asked me about the challenge Andre had thrown down in *Teen Vogue* and whether I would debate him. I didn't see the harm in saying yes. I figured the Rosarios would never allow it to happen." I left out the part where I planted the suggestion that I'd be willing to do an interview with Astrid in Tamal's mind, and then let him suggest it to her like it was his idea.

"Of course they're going to let it happen! They're overjoyed because every time they trot their son out, it takes the press's attention off Rosario's ailing campaign!"

"I still don't understand why you're upset," I said. "Dre has no formal debate training whereas I'm a state-ranked debater who's been invited to numerous national debates all over the country. I'm certain I can beat him." I watched my mother's reaction closely, looking to see if my argument was working. "And it will be held at *my* school. I'll have the home field advantage."

My mother sipped her drink but kept her eyes firmly on me. "I don't like this, Dean. With McMann making a mockery of this election, I don't have time to chaperone while you play at debating with that child."

"Why do you talk about him like that?" I asked without thinking. "Maybe he's not a debater, but he's quite talented in his own right. Funny too. You might even like him if you got to know him."

"I don't know what has gotten into you, Dean, but enough is enough."

"Fine." I was trying to keep the anger out of my voice, but I feared I was failing. I just physically hurt to hear the way she spoke about Dre because, in a way, it felt like she was talking about me too. "Then I'll tell Astrid it was a mistake and we need to cancel."

"Well, you know we can't do that. How would it look if you withdrew? Like you were scared, that's how it would look."

"Yes, ma'am."

My mother pursed her lips, then let out a sigh, resigned to this. My joy at knowing I was going to see Dre was tempered by my mother's attitude. I'd won, but the cost had been high. "This is the last time you go behind my back, Dean."

"You know I would never—"

"Inviting Tamal to the debate?"

"Dad told me I could invite him."

"Yes," she said. "I've already spoken to him."

Everything I'd said was strictly true, but my mother knew there was more to it than what I'd told her. "I'm sorry, Mom. I know you were hoping I would hit it off with Mindy, but she isn't my type."

"That's fine, but when you're seventeen and you've never had a girlfriend, and then you start palling around with someone like Andre Rosario, tongues will wag, and that is the last thing I need right now."

"What if I don't *want* a girlfriend?" I asked, my tone sharp. "What if I never want one?"

My mother got a frosty gleam in her eyes. She was not used to me arguing back, and here I'd done it twice in one conversation. I had always been the dutiful son, and this wasn't how dutiful sons spoke to their mothers.

"Now you're talking nonsense, and I don't have time for your foolishness. Do your debate, and then I don't want to hear about Andre Rosario again. Understood?"

Dre had been right. This was how my mother actually felt. She wouldn't accept me for who I was. She could talk about going on *Ellen* all she wanted, but the truth was that she didn't mind queer people so long as her son wasn't one of them. The fight in me vanished. I didn't have the strength to argue with

295

her because there was no way to change my mother's mind once she'd made it up. I could be her son or I could be true to myself, but I couldn't be both.

"Yes, ma'am."

When I'd started questioning my sexuality, learning about asexuality and demisexuality and exploring who I was attracted to, I'd known that it was something my parents might not be comfortable with, but I'd remained certain that they loved me and would support me. And as I trudged back upstairs to my room, I found that my certainty had fled.

DRE

I COULDN'T STOP shaking. Why was I shaking? It was only an auditorium filled with high school students. I was a high school student. They were like me. Nothing to be scared of, except I was definitely scared.

When we found out that Dean had accepted my challenge while giving an interview to the student paper at his own school, Dad had said there was no way in hell I was going. I'd played the whole thing like the challenge had just been me shit-talking and that I didn't care one way or another. It had taken Jose and Mom teaming up on him to change his mind, with Jose saying the press couldn't hurt and Mom promising that I'd be on my best behavior. Besides, she'd argued, how much trouble could I really get into in one night in Tallahassee? Florida was more boring than Rhode Island. Finally, my dad caved, and I was allowed to go. But I had to keep my cell on so my parents could check up on me, and I had to call them from the hotel that evening so they could be sure I hadn't run off to Orlando to visit Hogwarts.

I hadn't been able to sleep the night before. In between trading messages with Dean, I'd been trying to figure out what I was going to wear. The agreement Dad's people and Governor Arnault's people had come to with the school was that press would be limited and only the students would be allowed to ask us questions, but we were still likely to make the nightly news, so I had to make my outfit count. I settled on jean shorts, because Florida, duh, and the </patriarchy> shirt Mel had given me. The palette was a little subdued, though, so I painted my nails Granapple Green.

"You're making me anxious." Dean stood beside me wearing jeans and a blazer with a shirt and tie. It was the wardrobe equivalent of a mullet. Still, he looked cute, and it was taking every ounce of willpower I had not to pinch his ass.

Mrs. Hicks, the social studies teacher who'd been showing us around—well, showing *me* around, since this was Dean's school—was giving her long-winded introduction and explaining how the debate would work. I probably should've been paying attention.

"Unlike you, I've never debated anyone before."

"You'll do fine," he said. "And I'll go easy."

"Don't you dare."

"You want me to destroy you?"

"I want you to try."

Dean grinned at me and winked, and I wanted to kiss him so damn bad. "Hey," he said, "how would you like to come over to my house after we're finished here?"

"For real?"

"I am for real," he said. He must've noticed I'd gone pale because he quickly added, "My mother is in Wisconsin and my father is in Texas, I think. Either way, they won't be home."

I wasn't sure if that made me feel better or worse. "You want to bring me to your house while your parents are away? Why, Dean Arnault, are you trying to seduce me?"

A deep blush rose in Dean's cheeks, but he quickly recovered. "I wasn't," he said, "but now I might give it a shot."

This was Dean's plan to defeat me! How was I supposed to debate him when all I could think about was being alone in his house with him? Well, I refused to let him win that easily.

Mrs. Hicks finally called us onto the stage, and as we walked out and began to head to our separate sides, I whispered, "Prepare to be humiliated."

Someone hooted Dean's name, and it was picked up by a few others before the teachers in the audience quieted them down. I didn't know how popular Dean was, but I'd assumed since we were at his school that he'd get a better reception than me. I was just grateful no one booed me or threw rotten vegetables my way.

The first couple of questions were easy. Where did we stand

on banning meat from school lunches? Were we for or against standardized testing? Should schools stop teaching old books with racist and sexist language in favor of newer books by contemporary authors? I thought I handled myself pretty damn well, but Dean was a natural, and I would've been happy to sit back and listen to him talk all day. Wouldn't have mattered what it was about. He was confident but, more importantly, he was sincere, and it made me like him that much more.

"How do we stop school shootings?"

I couldn't see who'd asked the question, but there was a layer of sadness and resignation in their voice that cut me deep. Dean got the chance to answer first, and he talked about the importance and history of the Second Amendment, and suggested the answer wasn't to regulate gun ownership but rather to better identify those who shouldn't own guns, such as people on no-fly lists and people accused of domestic violence. Mostly, he said the same things we'd all heard before. He wasn't talking about arming teachers like his mom often did, but it still didn't seem like a solution. And then it was my turn to talk. Up to that point, I'd been hiding behind the podium, leaning on it and using it like a shield. This time, I pulled the mic free and stepped out from behind it. I sat on the edge of the stage and let my legs hang over the side.

"I was in Target with my friend Mel. You might know her from Dreadful Dressup. She's the smart one; I'm the pretty one." A few people in the auditorium clapped. "Anyway, we were wandering around and there was this boy shopping with his dad. He was maybe seven or eight. Looking at toys. He grabbed a Captain Marvel action figure off the shelf, and his dad took it away and told him to pick out a real superhero. Said that dolls were for girls.

"I don't even need to tell you how many things are wrong with what that kid's father said. Though Mel took ten minutes to explain them to him, loudly, and I'm sure there's a recording of it on YouTube or something if you do need to know. She was amazing. Sadly, her words couldn't penetrate his thick skull, and his son walked away believing boys couldn't play with dolls and that girls couldn't be superheroes."

I wasn't sure where I was going with this, and I was worried I might lose everyone, but I kept talking. "Boys are taught a lot of toxic crap. Like that it's not okay to paint your nails or to care about how you look. That it's unmanly to show emotions or cry. That they should be able to handle their problems on their own and should never ask for help because it's weak.

"The problem with school shootings isn't really about guns, is it? I mean, guns are part of the problem, but take them away and shooters would just use a different weapon. We keep talking about guns because that's easy. Either we take them away so no one has them or we arm everyone. We can fight about that back and forth forever so that it looks like we're doing something when we're really not.

"The real problem is us. Boys. That we live in a world where boys get so lonely or confused or hurt that they think the only way to be seen or understood or to stop their pain is to hurt other people. That boys are taught that there's something wrong with expressing any feeling other than rage."

Someone in the back row shouted, "Ban all boys!" and a few people laughed.

I smiled, but I didn't laugh. "It'd stop the shootings, wouldn't it? But, like, these boys who do these horrible things don't appear out of nowhere. They're in our classes with us and on our football teams and we eat lunch together. But we don't see them. We don't see what they're feeling or what they're going through. Usually because they don't let us. Usually because they've been taught to *not* let us.

"The thing I like about doing monster makeup isn't making people look like monsters, it's finding the person inside the monster. Because every monster was a person first. Every school shooter was a little boy whose dad wouldn't buy him a Captain Marvel action figure. Who was taught that it's more manly to fire bullets than to shed tears.

"And I'm not saying we give boys a pass. Girls have always had it worse. Plus, there're racial issues, like how white boy shooters are *lone wolves* while brown boys are terrorists. But if we're serious about ending school shootings, then we gotta stop pretending the problem is with the guns and admit that the problem is with us.

"We have to get better at seeing the person inside the monster. And maybe if we stop filling boys' heads with so much nonsense, they won't turn into monsters at all."

302

I shrugged and got up, feeling a little embarrassed for rambling. "I don't know if that answered your question."

I turned and walked back to my podium.

Dean's voice cut through the silence that followed, and I thought he was gonna add something or rebut what I'd said—I knew he could; he was an amazing debater. But instead, he said, "I'm sorry for speaking out of turn, but I think we can all agree Dre won that round."

DRE WAS SITTING beside me in my father's car—which I hadn't strictly mentioned I was borrowing, though my father had never refused my requests before—playing with the infotainment center like he'd never seen one before. In the span of only a few minutes, he had managed to delete all of my father's preset stations and changed the navigation voiceover to a genderless British person.

And I couldn't stop smiling.

"You did great today," I said as I drove us back to my house. I'd decided to take the long way because while I was excited to be alone in my house with Dre, I was also terrified to be alone in my house with him.

"I kicked your ass."

"I wouldn't put it that way."

"Because you're a poor loser?"

I laughed out loud, which put a smile on Dre's face. "Are you sure you haven't thought about going into politics?"

The idea seemed to cause Dre to grimace in disgust. "I'm not that person," he said. "You are and my dad is, but I'm not."

"That's why you'd be good at it." When Dre gave me a confused look, I said, "I think a lot of people who are supporting McMann are doing so because he's *not* a politician. Because he's different and offers solutions no one else has."

"Okay, his solutions are bonkers, though."

I nodded. "Very much so. But yours wasn't. Everyone else sees the problem of school shootings as a gun problem, but you see it as a people problem. The solution may not be as simplistic as you made it out to be, but I think it's a great place to start."

I think I was embarrassing Dre because he turned toward the window and tried to make a joke out of it. "Copyright Andre Rosario. You know, so your mom doesn't steal my idea."

"That wouldn't work for her," I said. "It's her military background. She thinks solutions start at the top and that it's everyone's job below to carry it out."

"My dad's kind of the opposite. He worries how something will affect every single person, and he stalls out if he thinks someone's gonna be mad at him."

We pulled through the gate of my house, and I waited to make sure it closed behind us before pulling up the long driveway to the garage.

"Oh shit," Dre said. "You never told me you lived in a mansion."

Now I was the one getting embarrassed. "It's not a mansion."

"Looks like a mansion to me."

My parents had bought the house before my mother's term as governor had ended, and they planned to keep it even if my mother won the election. It wasn't nearly as big as the Florida governor's mansion, but it still had more rooms than we needed. The front was landscaped with native Florida plants to provide as much privacy as possible.

"I'm sure your house is just as big."

"It's all right. Let's see inside."

After Dre's reaction to the outside of the house, I was kind of nervous to show him the inside. I wasn't embarrassed by it, but I didn't want to look like I was bragging either. I'd always understood that my family was well-off, and that most of the money had come from my dad. Some of it he'd made, but he had also inherited quite a lot. My mother, on the other hand, had grown up in a tiny house with parents who had both worked long hours at tough jobs to provide for her and her sisters. Her parents had helped her where they could, but she'd worked hard for most of what she had, and my mom had made sure I knew where she'd come from and how hard she had worked to ensure that I had a better life than she'd had.

I led Dre into the house through the garage, showing off

the kitchen, the back patio, the sitting room, and the living room.

"You have two living rooms?"

"One's for watching TV and hanging out; the other's for when my parents have guests. They do a lot of fundraising here."

I showed Dre all around the house, avoiding my bedroom until I had run out of rooms to show him. At my door, I pushed it open and he dashed in like he was afraid I was going to change my mind and refuse him entry, but I doubted I could have refused Dre anything.

"It's so clean. And you make your bed?"

"Every day," I said. "It only takes a minute to do while I'm waiting for the shower to warm up."

Dre thumbed through the books on my shelves and examined the photos on my dresser and the awards hanging on the walls. He opened my drawers and my closet, and I let him because I had nothing to hide from him.

"I'm seriously concerned about the lack of *you* in this space."

"There is plenty of me in here."

Dre stood in the center of my room and held out his arms. "Where? I mean, who decorated this place?"

"My mom."

"See?"

"But I don't mind," I said. "It's not like I have burning opinions on bedding sets or wall colors."

"You should still be allowed to be yourself in your own

bedroom. It looks like no one even lives in here. What would happen if you left your bed unmade or didn't put your books away or bought a TV and a PlayStation?"

I shrugged. "I don't have a lot of time for video games or TV."

"That's not the point!"

"I'm sorry my bedroom doesn't meet your expectations." I stood stiffly at the door, feeling attacked. "Feel free to leave anytime."

Dre's shoulders slumped. "That's not what I meant."

"What did you mean?" I asked. "Because I'm exhausted trying to please everyone and I thought, you at least, were the one person who accepted me the way I am, which just happens to be tidy, organized, and boring."

"I'm sorry," he said. "And you're not boring." Dre walked toward me and slipped his arms around my waist. "At least, you don't bore me."

I put up a token resistance to his charm offensive, but I was beaten the moment he touched me. "Are you sure?"

"Sometimes I forget how different we are," Dre said. "I see a blank wall, and all I can think about is what colors I can paint it. You don't. And it's not a bad thing or whatever. I like your sport coats and ties and loafers, even though I'd bathe in honey and roll around in fire ants before wearing them myself, and I like that *you* like them. They're what make you so damn sexy."

"Really?"

"Those sexy, sexy argyle socks?" Dre bit his knuckle and made a sound like he was suppressing a groan. "You're lucky I didn't jump you on that stage in front of your classmates."

"Speaking of my classmates," I said. "I might have invited a couple of them over for pizza tonight."

Dre's arm around my waist loosened. "So when do I need to be gone by?"

"Gone?"

"Obviously, I can't be here when they're here."

I shook my head because he'd misunderstood me. "No, they want to meet you."

Dre's look of hurt turned to shock. "You told them about us?"

"Heavens no. But I told them that it would be rude for me to let you spend the night sulking in your hotel room, replaying in your head how badly I destroyed you during the debate, and that the gentlemanly thing to do would be to invite you for dinner. We'll have to pretend to hate each other a little."

Dre stared at me deadpan. "Won't be hard for me."

"It's only going to be Tamal and his girlfriend, Astrid, and Mindy."

"Your girlfriend?"

"Actually, I bet you and Mindy will have a lot in common." I leaned my head against Dre's. "You're not mad?"

"Why would I be mad?"

I struggled with how to put my feelings into words without offending Dre. I was good at debating because I spoke from my brain, but not so good with people sometimes because speaking from my heart didn't come as easily. But I really didn't want to keep anything from him. "The truth is, I was scared."

"Of what?"

I led Dre to the bed and sat beside him, leaving a little bit of room between us because I didn't want to get distracted. "You," I said. "Us. We talk on Promethean all the time, but we hardly get to see each other, so I feel like there's this urgency to squeeze as much into the time we have as possible. Only, I need to take this slow, and I was scared you might not understand that—"

Dre took my hand and held it, giving me those soft puppy dog eyes that melted my heart. "And you thought having your friends here would make sure I kept it in my pants."

"Something less vulgar, but yes."

"I care about you, Dean. Like, more than I thought possible. And, sure, when I see you, I want to rip your clothes off and do things to you that would give your mother a heart attack if she found out we'd done them. But I don't wanna ruin us, whatever we're becoming. So we'll take things as slow as you want. I'll court you like you're a Victorian lady and I'm the charming son of a local lord desperate to win your favor."

I laughed. "We don't need to take it quite that slow."

Dre pressed his hand to his chest. "Please, madam, cover your naked wrist before I lose all control of my senses."

"You are *so* weird."

"Good weird?"

"Definitely good weird," I said. "And, in case you were wondering, they won't be here for a couple more hours, and I would very much like to kiss you, so—"

Dre checked his watch and shrugged. "I mean, I suppose I could spare a few—"

I pulled Dre to me and kissed him. It was everything I wanted. He was everything I wanted.

DRE

I WAS IN Dean's bed with my head resting on his chest, listening to him breathe. His tie was gone and the top three buttons of his shirt were undone, and my T-shirt was somewhere on the other side of the room, flung there in the mad dash of roving hands and exploring lips. For someone who'd just said he wanted to take things slow, Dean had held nothing back. Not like we had sex or anything. All the action happened from the waist up. I mean, stuff was going on from the waist down, but it was stuff we couldn't control and did our best to ignore. Neither of us was ready to cross *that* border yet.

For the moment, I was content.

"What do you think will happen after the election?" Dean asked.

"Depends who wins."

"What do you think will happen to us?" Dean was running his fingers across my back, sending surges of electricity through me. "How will we keep seeing each other?"

I was busy enjoying the present and Dean was trying to drag us into the future. "We'll find a way."

Dean sat up on his elbow and looked down at me. "But how? If my mom wins, I'll be in DC and you'll be in Nevada—"

"Until I graduate."

"If your dad wins, you will be in DC and I'll be in Florida—"

"Until *you* graduate."

"And if McMann wins—

I clamped my hand over Dean's mouth. "Then he'll probably start a war with Russia or China or North Korea, and we'll all die in flames and it won't matter."

Dean peeled my hand off his mouth. "I'm attempting to be serious."

"I know," I said. "And I wish you'd stop."

"You don't want to plan our future?"

Our future. He'd said "our future" like he was certain we had one. I wanted us to have one, but our lives were so damned uncertain, and I thought it was better to live in the now and let the future happen when it happened.

"I do," I said. "But, like, there's so much that's out of our control. Someone's gonna win the election. It might be your mom, it might be my dad, it might be McMann, though let's hope it isn't. Either way, it'll be way harder to see each other afterward. But then we get to go to college."

"Do you know where you're going yet?"

"I know where I've applied."

"If you go to RISD and I go to Harvard, we could see each other easily," Dean said.

"I don't know if I'm gonna get into RISD. You'll probably get into Harvard, but do you even wanna go there?"

Dean looked like I'd wounded him, but I didn't know why. "Why wouldn't I? It's an amazing school."

"I'm not saying it's not, but—"

"Do you not *want* to keep seeing me after the election?" he asked abruptly.

"Of course I do."

"Then why are you acting like you don't?"

I rolled over on my back and stared at the ceiling, blowing out a sigh of frustration. "Because I'm happy *now*, Dean. I'm happy right this moment, and I want to keep being happy, but talking about the future makes me think about all the shit that could conspire to keep us apart. I also applied to School of the Art Institute of Chicago, SCAD, MassArt, and Columbia, and I bet you probably have applications at all the Ivy Leagues. We could wind up in schools that aren't a quick train ride apart."

Dean brushed a curl off my forehead. "We would still find a way to be together."

"Maybe."

"Maybe?"

"I hope so, Dean, but I don't know, and I don't want to think about it until I have to because I don't want to ruin today by worrying about tomorrow."

Dean leaned in and kissed me. "You win. Tomorrow can wait."

DEAN

IT WAS DIFFICULT to watch Dre arguing with Mindy or talking to Tamal and pretend I didn't want to slide my arm around his waist and kiss him. It was painful to watch Tamal and Astrid holding hands, and to see Dre notice them holding hands, and not be able to hold Dre's hand. I was used to being reserved, but I didn't want to be reserved when it came to Dre. No matter how much we disagreed or what we disagreed on, I still felt like we spoke a language no one else spoke. That we shared a bond no one else shared. If a time traveler had arrived from the future and told me that I was considering basing my college plans on which school would allow me to see Dre the most, I would have laughed. But that's exactly what I had been doing while I had held him in my bed. Dre might have been able to live in the moment and enjoy it without knowing what the future might hold, but doing so was more difficult for me. I couldn't predict every possible outcome, but I could do my best to make sure as many of those potential futures as possible included Dre.

"McMann's going to win," Mindy was saying. We were sitting around the patio table, eating pizza. The night was nice and cool and Tamal had been hinting he thought we should take a dip in the hot tub.

"No way!" Dre said. "He's like twenty naked mole rats in a saggy skin suit. He can't win."

Mindy rolled her eyes. "Do you really think your dad is going to fix anything? He's a politician just like the rest. Corporations control both parties. There's hardly any difference between them."

I raised my hand. "I beg to differ."

"Thank you," Dre said.

"There are plenty of differences between the parties," I went on, but Mindy cut me off before I could finish.

"On the surface," she said. "It's all on the surface. One side wants to tell women what they can and can't do with their bodies, the other side wants to tell people what they can and can't say. Both sides are trying to play the victim, but neither side is actually doing a damn thing to help anyone."

Dre snorted. "And McMann will?"

"No," Mindy said. "He'll probably blow it all up."

"And you think that's a good thing?" Astrid asked. "What about all the people who'll be hurt? I was barely old enough to remember it, but my parents lost their house the last time someone blew it all up."

"Sometimes tearing a thing down is the only way to fix it."

Astrid fixed Mindy with a contemptuous glare. "Easy for you to say. Your folks are rich."

Mindy shrugged, unfazed by the anger directed at her. "When we tear the world down, money will be meaningless."

"Mindy Maguire, teen anarchist." I shook my head and tried to diffuse the tension. "Pastor Duncan would be appalled."

Mindy rolled her eyes. "Whatever."

"Besides," Dre said. "McMann won't win."

"Exactly," I said. "My mom's going to win."

"Ha! My dad's got this."

"In his dreams."

Tamal raised his hand. "Can we talk about *anything* else?"

Astrid perked up. "Yes! I actually want to hear more about Dreadful Dressup. How did you even get into doing monster makeup?"

The attention turned to Dre, and there was a moment when it looked like he might panic, but that wasn't his style. They were as charmed by him as I was. I wondered what, if anything, would change if they knew Dre and I were together. Would they treat him differently? Would they treat *me* differently? I knew Mindy wouldn't care; I think she already liked him more than she liked me, which I had expected. It was

Tamal I was concerned about. He had never indicated that he had a problem with queer people, but I was his best friend, and I didn't want that to change.

"We had a tradition in my family that I got to pick the theme for our Halloween costumes. One year we all dressed up as warrior princesses, another year we were superheroes."

"Wait," I said. "Somewhere out there is a picture of you, your mother, and your father all wearing princess gowns?"

"And tiaras," Dre said, smiling. "Anyway. When I was nine, I decided we were going to be mermaids, but creepy, freaky mermaids. Only, my mom didn't know how to do that kind of makeup and my dad was clueless too, so I spent weeks on YouTube watching makeup tutorials, and I fell in love with it."

"Why?" Tamal asked. "I mean, it's cool, but you can do all that stuff on computers, right?"

Dre nodded, a little wistfully. "There's something special about the physical transformation. When you're standing there, half your face torn off, blood leaking out of your split lip, and you really start feeling your inner zombie, it sets you free in a way I don't think computer-generated effects will ever duplicate."

My phone vibrated, and I pulled it out while Dre continued telling the others about Dreadful Dressup. There was a message notification on Promethean, which was odd since Dre was the only person I talked to. I assumed it was a message he'd sent earlier that had been delayed, and I tapped the icon and opened the app.

Pyrogue: Hello, Dean Arnault.

I stared at the message, unsure what to do. Time seemed to stretch, and the room melted at the edges. Someone had found out who I was on Promethean. That shouldn't have been possible, but they had addressed me by name.

PrezMamasBoy: Who is this?
Pyrogue: A friend.
PrezMamasBoy: What do you want?
Pyrogue: To send you a message.
PrezMamasBoy: What message?
Pyrogue: I know.

I had received a fair amount of emails trolling me since my mother had become governor, and the number had only increased after she had become the Republican nominee for president. Usually, I deleted them and moved on with my life or forwarded them to a member of my mother's staff if I thought they warranted further scrutiny. Whoever this Pyrogue was hadn't said anything threatening yet, nothing worthy of my fear, and yet there was an icy knot in my stomach I couldn't ignore. I should have simply blocked Pyrogue, but I foolishly took the bait.

PrezMamasBoy: What, exactly, do you think you know?

Pyrogue: I know about your relationship with Andre
Rosario.

I dropped my phone. It hit the thick glass tabletop with
a clatter, calling the attention of the others down upon me.
"Shoot. Sorry." I scrambled to stand and grabbed my phone.
"I have to . . . go . . . inside for something. A drink. I need a
drink."

Dre began to stand. "I could use one too."

"No! I mean, I'll get it for you. Stay and talk. I'll only be
a minute." I rushed inside before I could make the situation
any more awkward than I already had. Instead of going to the
kitchen, I locked myself in the downstairs bathroom, where
I could read the messages without worrying about anyone
seeing them.

Pyrogue: Don't bother denying it.

Pyrogue: The truth *will* come out.

Pyrogue: Pay close attention to the news.

PrezMamasBoy: I'm sorry, but I believe you have me mis-
taken for someone else.

PrezMamasBoy: I am not now, nor have I ever been, in a
relationship with Andre Rosario.

Pyrogue didn't reply with words. They sent me two
photos. The first was me walking into the janitor's closet at

321

the second debate. The next was Dre walking out of the same closet a few minutes later. Both were time-stamped. I leaned against the sink, unable to breathe. My chest hurt and my vision was dim at the edges. I thought I was having a panic attack. Someone knew the truth about Dre and me. Someone had found out. What had Pyrogue meant about watching the news? Had they already gone to the press? If that happened, my life as I knew it was over. My parents would find out and it could hurt my mother's chances of winning the election. It would have been bad enough for her having to explain a queer child, but one who had been dating her opponent's son? This was bad, and I didn't know what to do.

I opened the door to the bathroom and ran into Tamal.

"Dude," he said. "You all right? You're looking sweaty."

I wiped the sweat off my forehead with the back of my hand. "Yeah. Fine."

"That Dre's a trip. I can see why you like him."

"Like him? Who said I like him? I don't. He's annoying and loud and I only invited him here because it was the polite thing to do."

Tamal held up his hands. "You sure you're okay?"

"Great," I said. "Everything's great. Couldn't be better."

DRE

DEAN WAS DRIVING me back to my hotel. I'd called my mom and dad and told them that Dean had invited me to hang out with his friends, and they'd told me I had to be at the hotel by nine. I could've spent all night with Dean, but I didn't want to push Mom and Dad.

"Mindy's wild," I said. "I think she and Mel would get along if they didn't murder each other first." Thinking about Mel threatened to put me in a mood, and Dean seemed like he was already in one, though I didn't know why.

"You've been quiet. Everything all right?"

"Fine," Dean said.

"Sure sounds like it."

Dean kept his eyes on the road and both hands on the wheel and he never drove over the speed limit. It was like driving with a driving instructor. But even at stoplights, he wouldn't look at me. I reached across to rest my hand on his thigh, and he flinched. He hadn't flinched when I'd touched him earlier.

"Maybe I'm being paranoid, but are you mad at me? Did I do something wrong?"

"I'm not mad at you."

"Are you just stressed out from having to pretend you didn't totally want to smother me with kisses while your friends were around?" Walking the line between friendly and *too* friendly had been difficult. I'd catch myself smiling at Dean, thinking about kissing him, and I'd have to look away and think about baseball or cat vomit or Jackson McMann so that Dean's friends didn't see right through me.

"I need to concentrate on driving."

"Then why do you keep looking at your phone every time we stop?"

"Can you just not right now?"

"Fine." I crossed my arms over my chest and turned to look out the window. I didn't care what Dean said, there was definitely something wrong, and he wouldn't tell me what it was. Maybe I should've taken him more seriously when he'd brought up college and what we were gonna do after the election. Maybe Dean, with his lists and his plans, was incapable of living in the now and not planning for the future, and he'd spent the whole night getting worked up about it. I shouldn't have blown him off like that. I should've talked it out with him and found a future where we could still be together after the election, no matter who won.

We pulled into the parking lot in front of my hotel, and I reached for the door to get out. I wasn't angry, but I was confused and I didn't know what to do if Dean was gonna shut me out.

"Did you tell anyone about us?"

"What?"

"Someone knows," Dean said. "They sent me messages saying they know about us and that we should keep our eyes on the news, and they had photos of us going into the closet at the debate."

"That's not possible," I said. And it shouldn't have been, but Dean was firing off questions and accusations faster than I could respond, and he was so angry.

"Obviously it is. Obviously someone saw us. Obviously Promethean isn't as secure as you said it was. But none of that matters because someone knows and they're going to expose us!"

I couldn't think. I needed to think. "This isn't that bad. If all they've got are those pictures, then so what? It's not like they're pics of us making out."

Dean slammed his hands on the wheel. "We don't know what else they have, Dre!"

"Then we'll deal with it," I said. "We'll tell my parents—"

"No, Dre! I don't want anyone else to know."

I bit my bottom lip and looked away from Dean. I hadn't

meant to look so guilty, but it was an instinctual reaction. And he saw it.

"Does Mel know? Did you already tell her? Dre?"

"She guessed, and I couldn't lie because she knows when I'm lying!"

"Damn it, Dre! It's probably her! You said she doesn't like me. You said she thought I owed it to the community to come out. What if she's doing this to force me?"

Mel was capable of a lot of shady shit, but there was no universe where I believed she would've outed my relationship with Dean, no matter how pissed at me she was or how much she hated Dean. "No," I said. "Mel wouldn't do that."

Tears welled in Dean's eyes. "Someone did!"

"Not Mel. We'll figure out who did it, but it wasn't Mel."

Dean was shaking his head and the tears were falling down his cheeks. "*We* won't do anything." He scrubbed his eyes with the back of his hand. "I can't, Dre. I can't do this."

I refused to believe what I was hearing. The words coming out of his mouth weren't real. Dean was just scared. He didn't mean any of it. "This is gonna be fine, Dean, I promise. We'll work it out." I tried to take his hand, but he yanked it away. "Dean?"

"We can't see each other anymore, Andre. I'm sorry. This is the way it has to be."

It wasn't *what* Dean was saying that finally broke me, it was the way he was saying it. Like I wasn't the boy he'd been kissing hours earlier, like I was nobody. "Dean . . ."

"My mother has worked too hard to get here for me to risk ruining her chance."

"What about us? What about ruining us?"

Dean looked right at me, his eyes cold and dry. "There is no us. I'm sorry." He unlocked the car doors and then turned to look straight ahead.

Everything collapsed. My life, the world, the whole fucking universe. I don't remember much about stumbling out of the car or getting into the hotel or into my room.

I don't know how long I sobbed into my pillow, but when I finally looked up, my nose was stuffed and my head hurt and I felt sick to my stomach. It was a dream, a nightmare. Dean hadn't broken up with me. He hadn't broken my heart. This was all a mistake. He was upset, but I knew if we could talk it out, I could change his mind.

I got out my phone and opened Promethean, but when I tapped on PrezMamasBoy, the app returned <User **Prez-MamasBoy** Not Found>.

DEAN

MY FATHER HAD prepared linguini with asparagus, mushrooms, and a layer of crispy Parmesan for dinner, to which my mother had invited Nora and her fiancé. It was my favorite meal that my father prepared, but that night it tasted like ash.

It had been two days since I had broken off my relationship with Dre and deleted my Promethean account, and I hadn't received any further communications from Pyrogue or anyone else. I hadn't seen anything on the news either that indicated Pyrogue had leaked what they knew to the press, though I refused to let down my guard.

Breaking up with Dre had been for the best, even if he hadn't been able to see it. The obstacles in our way were simply insurmountable. We lived too far from one another, our parents were ideological opposites, and the very act of our being together could have threatened to put a man in the White House who would, as Mindy had succinctly put it, burn the country down. I'd read numerous dire predictions about what kind of country a Jackson McMann presidency could turn the United States into, and I didn't want to live in any of them. So, yes, it was better this way.

And, yet, my favorite meal still tasted like ash.

"How are your college applications coming along, Dean?" asked Patrick. Where Nora was a fierce type-A with a wry sense of humor and the ability to get anything done, her fiancé was a soft-spoken computer analyst who worked for an insurance company.

"Nearly done. I finished Yale, UPenn, and Stanford this week. I like having options."

My mother sat at the head of the table, our stately matriarch. The debate prep for her rematch with McMann and Rosario had been consuming the majority of what little free time she had, but she managed to mask her exhaustion well. "Dean toured Harvard not so long ago."

"Do you have any idea what you might study?" Patrick asked.

"He's a born politician," Nora said.

"That he is," added my mother. "Just this week he's been invaluable. He's got a real way with people."

"And you should see him debate."

I nodded along, slowly chewing asparagus. It's not as if

anyone actually needed me to speak to be part of the conversation. My mother and Nora were doing just fine on my behalf.

"Before I forget, Dean," my mother said. "I need you to try on your tux after dinner."

"Yes, ma'am," I said. "But why?"

My mother and father shared a smile. "I thought you might like to join us at the ball Friday evening."

The ball was a fundraiser for the most important contributors to my mother's campaign. There had been no reason to assume she would want me mingling with the CEOs and conservative celebrities that had donated money to help get her elected.

"Really?" I asked. "You want me there?"

My mother nodded. "I thought you could invite Mindy."

"Though you don't have to," my father quickly added.

"Of course not. If there's another young woman you'd liked to bring who has an appropriate dress and knows how to behave, you are more than welcome to bring her."

Nora cleared her throat. "If your tux needs alterations, just let me know and I'll make sure it gets done."

"Thank you," I said. "And I don't mind taking Mindy." Which was true. I didn't have to worry that she was going to develop feelings for me that I didn't reciprocate, and if the press thought there was more between Mindy and me than there actually was, at least it was a rumor that wouldn't damage my mother's chances of winning the election.

"You've been working so hard, and I want you to know

330

how much I appreciate it," my mother said. "You're a good boy, Dean."

I should have been overjoyed that my mother wanted me at the fundraiser. I should have been honored that she thought I was responsible enough to spend time around her wealthy and famous adult friends. My mother's approval meant more to me than I wanted to admit. At least, it used to. I didn't know what it meant to me anymore.

And my dinner still tasted like ash.

"I've actually been thinking about studying education," I said. "So that I could teach."

I don't know who had been speaking or what they had been talking about, but the conversation around the table died.

"What was that, Dean?" Patrick asked.

At that moment, I could have apologized and told them it was nothing. I could have excused myself from the dinner table and gone to the bathroom to collect myself. I could have even said I'd been joking. Maybe I *should* have done any one of those things. But I didn't.

"I've been thinking I might become a teacher. Political science, maybe. Or philosophy."

Patrick was the only person at the dinner table who didn't seem a little shocked by my admission. "Would you teach college?"

"High school, I think."

"Good for you," Patrick said, and he seemed to genuinely mean it.

"An undergraduate degree in political science will still get you into law school," my mother said.

"And if I don't want to go to law school? If I want to get master's and doctorate degrees in philosophy?"

"I don't see how—"

"I'm not you, Mom."

My dad coughed. "Who's ready for dessert? I made tiramisu."

"No," my mother said. "If you were me, you'd be enlisting right after high school so that you could pay for college. You'd be fighting for any opportunity to provide a better life for you and your family. You'd appreciate all of the advantages *you* have that I did not. No, you are most certainly not me."

"Your mother and I only want what's best for you, Dean."

"What about what I want?"

Nora turned to Patrick and motioned that they should give my parents and me space, but my mother said, "No, stay. This conversation is over."

"I'm not saying I will definitely become a teacher," I said. "But I would like to know that I have the option." I wanted to know that I could be someone other than who my mother wanted me to be and that she'd still love and support me. I needed to know.

"I have no idea what's gotten into you, Dean, but this is neither the time nor the place for this." She dabbed at her mouth with her napkin and set it on the table. "Now, you are excused from dinner, and I certainly hope you will be better behaved Friday evening."

I scooted my chair back and stood. "Yes, ma'am." I looked at the others. "Sorry for the disruption."

My mother never would have been able to accept me with Dre. She wouldn't even consider the idea that I might want to do something different with my life than what she expected me to do. No matter what she said about only wanting me to be happy, she didn't believe I could be happy unless I was following the path she set out for me. And it was a path that would never include Dre or anyone like him.

I trudged up the stairs and went right to bed, not even caring that I'd missed dessert. It would have tasted like ash anyway.

DRE

I'D ONLY BEEN out of school for a few weeks, but I already felt like I didn't belong anymore. Sitting through classes, it was all I could do to keep my eyes from rolling back in my head. It was more than boredom, though. It was the feeling that I'd *already* graduated. I'd been out in the world and I'd seen what a shit show it was, and even though I was the one who'd decided to return to school, I felt like I'd outgrown it.

My parents had been too busy with the election to spend much time wondering why I wanted to go back to school, but I'd told them I was done with the election. No more school visits, no more volunteering, no more happy family photos from the campaign trail. I wanted to go back to my normal life and pretend the rest of it didn't exist.

I wasn't coping with the breakup well. If it was even a

breakup. I'm not sure if Dean was actually my boyfriend. I might've just been a detour for Dean. An experiment that he'd finished and thrown away. No matter how many times I opened Promethean, Dean's username was still not found. He had clearly deleted it, and he wasn't coming back.

"When'd you go goth?"

I was sitting alone in the art room, where I sometimes ate lunch and sketched, when Mel walked in, dropped her lunch bag on the table, and sat across from me.

"When did you even start back to school?"

"Yesterday."

Mel had dyed a strip of her hair aquamarine, and it looked good on her. But I was also still mad, so I kept the compliment to myself.

"Why didn't you tell me?"

"Because we're not friends anymore, remember?"

"Of course we are," she said. "It's not like this is the first time we've had a fight." Mel unpacked her lunch—a sandwich and some chips.

"Whatever." I honestly couldn't deal with Mel right then, even if she was doing her best to patch things up between us. "Did you tell anyone about me and Dean?"

Mel threw me one of her *Did you really just ask me that stupid question?* looks. "Who would I tell? And even if I had someone to tell, you know I wouldn't, no matter how pissed I was at you. Didn't we already go over this?" She paused for a moment and then said, "Did someone out your boyfriend?"

"He's not my boyfriend," I said. "He broke up with me." And then I lost it. Tears welled in my eyes, and I didn't want to be there anymore. I didn't want to be anywhere. But if I ran out of the room, someone might see me and people would talk, and I was so fucking over people talking about me.

And then Mel was beside me, hugging me, and I let the tears run.

"Do you want me to kill him for you? I'm always down for killing boys who break your heart."

I laughed. It was the first time I'd laughed or smiled since Dean had dropped me off. "Maybe another day."

Mel handed me a napkin and let me clean myself up before asking me what happened.

"I don't know," I said. "We went to his house and we did a lot of *stuff*."

Mel's eyebrows rose. "Stuff?"

"Above-the-waist stuff."

"Okay."

"But then after, he said he'd gotten a message on Promethean from someone who said they knew about our relationship, which shouldn't have been possible, and that he couldn't risk it and then he broke up with me. He wouldn't even discuss it. Just, one second there was an us and the next there wasn't."

Mel held my hand, managing to look both angry and sympathetic. "And that's why you thought I did it?"

"You're the only person who knew."

"I still think you're an asshole for asking," she said. "I

would never. Never. Even if you hadn't been involved."

"I know."

"You better, and I'll pretend you only asked because you were suffering from temporary amnesia caused by traumatic breakup stress."

"Sorry."

As quickly as Dean had ended our relationship, Mel and I had mended ours. The best friendships don't need grand gestures or lots of weeping and begging for forgiveness because the best friendships are never really broken, only a little bent for a time.

"If I'm not the dastardly villain, who else would've done it?"

I shook my head. I'd been asking myself the same thing, but Dean hadn't shown me the messages, so I had absolutely nothing to go on.

"And you're sure no one else knew?"

"I didn't tell anyone, and I know Dean didn't."

Mel sighed. "You probably don't wanna hear this—"

"You're probably right."

"But maybe this is for the best. If Dean was so quick to give up on you guys, maybe he wasn't as invested as you thought he was."

What Mel was saying made sense, but she was right that I didn't want to hear it. Besides, Dean might've been able to lie about his feelings, but he couldn't have faked what I felt when he touched me or when he kissed me. That was real.

"What about Jackson McMann?"

"What about him?" I asked.

Mel had her phone out and was searching for something. "I read a couple of days ago about him saying he had this huge bomb to drop, but no one paid it much attention because he also said he had a plan to create a fleet of surveillance drones that would use facial recognition technology and predictive AI over major cities to lower crime. Here!" She handed me her phone.

I scanned the article and found what Mel was talking about. It was just a line suggesting that McMann had information he was going to reveal that would shock the nation.

"I don't know," I said. "He's pulled this kind of stunt before."

"But he's got the most to gain," Mel said. "Tell me Arnault's voters wouldn't freak out if they found out about you and Dean. Hell, your dad's supporters wouldn't be too happy about it either."

Mel might've been right, but I didn't care. "We're not together anymore, so it doesn't matter."

"But if someone really does have proof you guys *were* together, they could still go public with it. Don't you think you should warn Dean?"

"Warn him about what? This isn't enough to prove anything." I handed Mel back her phone and shook my head. "Besides, Dean made his choice. I wanted to face this together. He didn't."

"So that's it?"

"Yeah," I said. "That's it."

DEAN

MINDY FLICKED AN olive that hit me in the nose. I'd expected her to wear something that looked like a prom dress, but instead she was wearing an elegant emerald-green off-the-shoulder gown, and she looked beautiful. We were the youngest people at the event by far, and most of the guests didn't seem to want to have much to do with us.

"What is your problem?" she asked.

"Nothing."

"You haven't said anything all night. Normally, I'd be okay with that, but I'm *so* bored and I need you to entertain me before I go out there and start ruining marriages for fun."

My mother had warned me before we had picked up Mindy that I needed to make certain she didn't get into any trouble. Aside from that, my mother hadn't said much else.

It was like my little scene at dinner had never happened. Under other circumstances, I would have been embarrassed by my outburst and would have welcomed my mother's situational amnesia, but I didn't want her to forget because *I* couldn't forget.

I waved Mindy off. "Do whatever you want."

"Problems with Mommy Dearest? Things were a little frosty between you two earlier."

"Aside from the fact that my mother only seems to care about me so long as I do exactly what she wants me to do? No, everything's perfect."

Though the fundraiser was being attended by the rich and famous, I felt like I was at a wedding. Tables were arranged around a dance floor, and a string quartet played covers of popular songs that I imagined Nora had selected. The food was forgettable, but there was plenty of alcohol, so no one else seemed to mind. My mother had given a rousing speech, and I'd applauded when, where, and as enthusiastically as I was expected to, but I hadn't heard a word she'd said.

"Oh." Mindy scooted a little closer to me. I'd purposely found an empty table so that I could brood without interruption. "But you've always known that about her, right?"

"I thought . . . I don't know. I thought she would support me no matter what."

"Is this about Dre? Did you tell her?"

"It's not about—" I stopped as I fully processed what Mindy had said. "How do you know about *that*?"

Mindy let out a laugh that would have drawn attention to us if any of my mother's guests had cared that we existed. "You're kidding, right? I mean, you told me there was someone, and then it was *so* obvious when I saw you together at your house. Your other friends don't know?"

"I hadn't thought they did," I said. "But now I'm not certain."

"Well, Tamal seems a little dense, so he might not have worked it out, but I thought Astrid was pretty smart. And cute."

"Don't."

Mindy held up her hands. "Just saying."

"Regardless, I didn't tell my mother because there's nothing to know. Dre and I are no longer together."

"Lovers' quarrel?"

Explaining to Mindy my sexuality and the entirety of my relationship with Dre *and* my reasons for ending it was not how I had planned to spend the evening, but that's exactly what I did.

"You didn't tell anyone, did you?"

"As much as I'd love to see McMann burn everything to the ground, I'm also not the kind of person who would do that to you. Or to anyone."

"Then it had to be Dre's friend Mel."

Mindy rolled her eyes. "This is why I'm a lesbian. Isn't it obvious? Mel wasn't responsible, and neither was I. Have you ever considered that someone hacked your phone?"

"My phone? They'd have everything. My messages, my photos."

Mindy's face lit up. "Please tell me you were trading nudes."

"No!"

"Damn. That was a scandal I could've gotten behind."

Just when I was beginning to think Mindy wasn't terrible, she reminded me why she was the worst. But while there might not have been any inappropriate pictures of me or Dre on my phone, there were some proving that we had been together. Combined with our conversations, there was enough evidence to prove we had been in a relationship. But only if my phone or Dre's had actually been hacked, which seemed improbable.

"Maybe whoever did it was just trying to scare me into admitting to the relationship because they didn't have anything concrete," I said.

"Doubtful."

"Is it? Then why warn me? And why haven't they exposed us yet? If they're going to do it, what are they waiting for?"

"The who is easy," Mindy said.

"The Rosarios?" It was a scenario I had been forced to consider. Maybe Dre hadn't known about it, maybe he had, but his parents had discovered the truth about us and had decided to use it to undermine my mother. Maybe even to blackmail her into dropping out of the race.

Mindy was shaking her head. "No way. He's not that type

of person. Doesn't have the nerve to play that dirty. Your mom would. I could totally see her outing you and then using the sympathy to drum up votes. She could support you—love the sinner—to get liberal votes, but still condemn the lifestyle—hate the sin—to hold on to the church crowd."

A few weeks ago, I never would have believed my mother capable of something like that, but now? Maybe. "You don't think she would, do you?"

"She might," Mindy said, "but I think it'd be too risky. Jackson McMann's the obvious suspect. Nothing to lose, and it doesn't matter what happens, he'll be there to take advantage of the chaos."

McMann? It seemed so unlikely, but it also felt like the kind of psychological warfare he would be into. "I still don't buy that he hacked my phone," I said. "But the photos Pyrogue sent me were from the second debate. I ran into McMann in the hall, and he could have seen me lurking around the janitor's closet. If he saw me go in and then Dre come out, he could have taken the pictures and made a wild guess that Dre and I were together." I tried to walk through it in my mind to see if it made sense, and it mostly did. "But that still doesn't explain how he found me on Promethean."

Mindy rolled her eyes. "I thought you were smart." When I didn't answer, she said, "McMann designed Promethean. It's his company."

"Would he really violate users' privacy like that?"

"You sweet, simple boy," she said. "Of course he would!"

All the pieces began to click into place. McMann saw Dre and me go into the janitor's closet, and he took the photos. Then he found my Promethean username and sent me the pictures. He wouldn't have needed to hack my phone, though it still wouldn't hurt to have Tamal take a look at it.

"As for why he's waiting," Mindy went on, "I can only guess, but if it were me, I'd use the information to mess with you and then drop the bomb when it would do the most damage."

"The third debate?"

Mindy seemed to weigh that and agreed. "Oh yeah. That would totally knock your parents off their game. They'd be all shocked, and McMann could be like, 'How can you expect either of them to run a country when they don't even know what's going on with their own children?' It's sadistic but genius."

"How can you admire that jerk when he's trying to ruin my life?" The more time that had passed since hearing from Pyrogue, the more I had begun to hope it was a hoax, but this was really happening. McMann might not have more than those two photos, but even the suggestion that Dre and I were more than friends could do some major damage. Eventually, the truth was going to come out, and there was nothing I could do to stop it. McMann was going to destroy my life, he was going to destroy my mother's political career, and he was going to destroy the country.

"You could always beat McMann to it," Mindy said. "Tell your mom before he tells the world."

"Great advice, Mindy. Remind me, how long have your parents known about your girlfriend?"

Mindy didn't snap back the way I had expected her to. "Wanna know what happens if my parents find out I'm dating a girl?"

"I—"

"There's a camp in Utah. They call it a camp, but it's basically a prison where they would use a variety of methods, including aversive conditioning, cognitive behavioral therapy, psychotropic medication, or anything else they think would stop me from being attracted to girls. At least that's what the website I found bookmarked on my dad's computer promised. And since I'm not eighteen for another two years, there's nothing I could do to fight them if they sent me . . . short of running away."

Even coming to terms with the idea that my mother might not be able to accept me for who I was meant the worst that would happen to me was having to live with her disappointment. Family gatherings might be uncomfortable, and I wouldn't be bringing potential boyfriends home for the holidays, but my parents wouldn't do something as horrible as send me to a conversion therapy camp. I had no idea any parent would go to such great lengths in order to force their children to be who they expected them to be. Maybe that was naive of me.

345

"I'm sorry."

The thundercloud that had swept across Mindy passed. "It's whatever. There are kids who have it so much worse."

"I still can't tell my parents," I said. "I'm not brave enough."

Mindy laughed derisively. "Maybe you'd be a little braver if you had someone to be brave for."

"He's gone," I said. "I hurt him, and I don't think there's anything I could do to make it up to him."

"Have you tried?"

"No."

"Then you don't know shit."

"What do I do?"

Mindy sighed and looked at me like I was the most ignorant person she had ever met. And she might not have been wrong. "Start with an apology. Go from there." She stood. "Speaking of going, I'm going to go see what kind of trouble I can cause. How many wallets do you think I can lift?"

"None would be best."

"But where's the fun in that?"

I couldn't help laughing as Mindy walked away. She was still kind of the worst, but also kind of the best. When I was alone, I pulled out my phone and set it on the table in front of me. I wasn't afraid of apologizing. I was afraid Dre wouldn't accept.

DRE

PatheticMamasBoy: Hi, Dre. It's Dean.

PatheticMamasBoy: This is my new username.

PatheticMamasBoy: I'm certain you don't want to speak to me, and you have every right to be angry. I was scared and I overreacted. I'm still scared. Terrified, actually.

PatheticMamasBoy: Mindy thinks Jackson McMann might be the one targeting us, and she believes he will leak the information to the press right before the last debate.

PatheticMamasBoy: Mindy knows, by the way. She figured it out on her own, but I'm glad she knows.

PatheticMamasBoy: I'm also glad that Mel knows. I shouldn't have been angry with you for telling her, and I shouldn't have accused her of sending me the messages.

347

I had no right to force you to keep us a secret from your best friend.

PatheticMamasBoy: I don't know what to do, Dre. Mindy thinks the only thing I *can* do is come out to my parents, but I'm afraid. You were right about my mother. I want to believe she's a good person at heart, but I'm not sure she's capable of accepting this part of me. At least not right now. Possibly not ever.

PatheticMamasBoy: The only thing that scares me more than being rejected by my mother is never seeing you again.

PatheticMamasBoy: I'm sorry. I am sorry that I broke up with you. I am sorry that I accused you of being the reason someone knows about us. I am sorry for being a spineless jellyfish and not being able to own up to who I am.

PatheticMamasBoy: I am sorry.

PatheticMamasBoy: I care deeply for you. More deeply than anyone other than my family. I thought I was confident in who I was, but you showed me what real confidence looks like. Even if you never speak to me again, you've left a mark on my soul that I am grateful for.

PatheticMamasBoy: Thank you for letting me get to know you and for helping me to know myself. You are a very special person, Andre Rosario.

PatheticMamasBoy: I suppose that's all I have to say.

PatheticMamasBoy: If you ever want to talk, this is my user-name.

PatheticMamasBoy: Okay, then.

PatheticMamasBoy: Bye.

PatheticMamasBoy: Dre? Are you there?

<Are you sure you want to block user **PatheticMamasBoy**?>

<User **PatheticMamasBoy** has been blocked. You will no longer receive messages from this user.>

DEAN

I WAS PRETTY certain I was going to vomit.

My mother was packing her suitcase, expecting she wouldn't be returning home until after the final debate. My father was sitting in a chair in the corner reading to her from the *New York Times*. From where I was standing in the hallway, I actually felt bad for what I was about to do. I was going to add a complication to their lives that they did not need at the moment. But the truth is rarely convenient, and even when telling it is the right thing to do, it still sometimes hurts.

A wave of nausea hit me, and it was so strong that I turned to run to the bathroom, but it passed. The nausea was my fear talking, and I'd let it have its say for long enough.

"Mom," I said, walking into their bedroom. "Dad."

My father looked up from the paper. "Hey, Dean. I thought you were working out with Tamal."

"I was," I said. "I did. Now I'm back."

"Good," my mother said. "We need to go over your schedule. I'd like to have you with me—"

"Can we . . . there's something I need to talk to you both about." My voice was shaky. I hadn't been this afraid to tell my parents something since fifth grade, when I had nearly failed three classes. That's when I was diagnosed with ADD, but at the time I just thought I was a failure. I hadn't failed them then any more than I was failing them now by coming out, but that didn't eliminate my fear.

My mother stopped sorting which clothes to put in her suitcase and my father set down his paper. They both gave me their full attention. "Well, Dean?" my mother said. "Spit it out. I *do* have a plane to catch."

I wished Dre were by my side for this, but he hadn't responded to any of my messages on Promethean, and I wasn't sure if he had gotten or read them. I had even sent a message to Dre's actual phone number to warn him of what I was about to do. He hadn't responded to that message either, making it clear he didn't want to speak to me. It was probably better this way. I needed to face my parents on my own. I needed to know that I could.

"I kissed Dre Rosario," I said, spitting it out without

preamble. "We were dating. It began during the security scare at the first debate, and we've been seeing each other since."

I had spent all night trying to devise the best way to come out to my parents. I was going to have to explain asexuality and demisexuality to them, and I was going to have to try to explain that I didn't think I was gay but that most of the people I had been attracted to were men, and I was going to have to tell them that I was still exploring my sexuality and that nothing was set in stone at the moment. But I feared doing so would only confuse them. To come out to them and make sure they knew this wasn't a joke or a phase or something they could control, I needed to tell them the one thing I knew with all the certainty in my soul.

"I care about Dre. I want to be with Dre."

I let *that* sink in and then I told them the rest.

My father was the first to speak. "Is Andre your boy-friend?"

"Yes," I said. "Actually, no. He was, but I broke up with him because I was scared. I've tried to apologize, and I'm hoping we can fix things, but I'm not sure if that's possible yet."

"And you're certain?"

I nodded. "About Dre? Absolutely."

My mother hadn't said a single word. She had barely even moved. She was a statue, staring at me with an unreadable expression.

"Mom?"

"No," she said.

"No?"

"I do not accept this."

Whoever said words can never hurt us had never had their mother look them in the eye and refuse to accept them. "It doesn't change who I am."

My mother threw the blouse she'd been holding into her suitcase. "I raised you better than this. At least, I thought I had."

"Jan," my father said.

"This comes from your side of the family."

"Mom," I said, but she ignored me. "Mom!"

My mother looked at me like I was a stranger. No, I'd seen her show more compassion to strangers. She looked at me like I was a problem. Something to be solved. To be fixed or cured. "You will not speak of this until after the election, not to anyone. And I absolutely forbid you to see Andre Rosario."

She shut the top of her suitcase and zipped it with so much force that I feared she was going to yank the zipper right off.

I didn't want my mother to see me cry, but I couldn't stop the tears as they welled up in my eyes. I could see my father struggling to understand what I'd told him, but at least he was trying. My mother would not even give me that much. *Maybe* if we'd had more time, she would have been able to come around, but we didn't.

"Someone already knows."

"What do you mean, Dean?" my father asked.

I told them about Promethean and the messages I'd

received from Pyrogue. "Mindy thinks McMann sent them and that he's going to expose Dre and me before the last debate."

My mother scoffed. "That girl also thinks her father doesn't know who she really spends her time with, but she's not as clever as she believes."

Dad finally stood and moved between Mom and me. "Why don't we all take a moment to cool off?"

But my mother wasn't interested in cooling off. "This is the work of the Rosarios. They used their son to get to you, and you were gullible enough to fall for his lies."

"Dre had nothing to do with it."

"You don't get to talk right now, Dean. All I expect from you is silence and compliance, do you understand?"

The "Yes, ma'am" sprang to my lips on instinct, but I bit it back at the last second because I was done being quiet. I was done doing as I was told.

"I'm sorry, Mom. I know this isn't what you wanted, and I know my timing is terrible. I never wanted to do anything to hurt you or the election, but I can't change who I am. Why can't you just accept that? Why can't you just accept me?"

Dad rested his hand on my shoulder and tried to draw me out of the room.

"I think you're a hypocrite for fighting for equality for women in the military but denying transgender soldiers the same rights to serve," I said. "And I think your plan to arm teachers to stop school shootings is going to put more people

354

in danger than it will save. I hate that you value soldiers over teachers and that you believe it's acceptable for doctors to refuse to do their jobs because of their religious beliefs.

"And I support you anyway. I accept you anyway. I love you anyway. I wish you could do the same for me."

I waited for my mother to respond. I waited for her to yell at me. I waited to see something in her eyes that showed me that what I'd said had gotten through to her. And I kept waiting until I was sure my waiting was in vain.

This time when my father tried to lead me out of the room, I let him.

DRE

MY DAD OPENED my bedroom door without knocking, walked in without asking, and sat on the end of my bed. I didn't even have the energy to be pissed about it. I didn't have the energy to do much of anything. Mel had been trying to get me to do a Dreadful Dressup shoot with her, but that required getting out of bed, and I just wasn't up for it.

"You've been secretly dating Dean Arnault?"

The words that came out of my dad's mouth couldn't have been the words I actually heard. "What?"

"That's why you went to Boston," he said. "You went to see Dean."

Shit.

"I don't know—"

"Your mom and I just got off the phone with Janice and

Doug Arnault. I think they're still trying to piece together all the information, but from what they told us, you've been seeing their son since the first debate?"

He'd done it. Dean had actually told his parents the truth. I'd gotten a text message from him a couple of hours earlier that had simply read "I'm going to tell them," but I hadn't believed he would go through with it. I wondered how they'd taken it. Was Dean okay? The news was kind of blowing my mind.

"Janice said you boys are being blackmailed? At first she accused us of doing it, but that's ludicrous. Not only would I never do that to you, but I'm not sure voters would appreciate the idea of you and Janice Arnault's son as a couple."

"We're not a couple," I said. "He broke up with me."

"You know what I mean. Are you being blackmailed?"

Finally, I could tell my dad everything. I didn't have to keep the secret anymore. I started with the lockdown and told him all the details that I knew, right up to Dean breaking my heart.

"Nobody's tried to blackmail me, and I don't think they're blackmailing Dean either. It sounded more like they're just messing with him. Mel's got this wild idea that it's McMann."

My dad stopped me there. "We can't accuse someone of wrongdoing without any evidence. Do you have evidence?"

I shook my head.

"Then for the moment, there's not much we can do on that front."

"What *are* we going to do?"

Dad's Adam's apple bobbed as he swallowed. "Janice, Doug, your mom, and I are going to hold a press conference. It will be better if we tell the media about your relationship rather than waiting for someone to leak it. We'll remind everyone that you're both minors and that you deserve your privacy and ask that you be left alone."

A press conference? My parents and Dean's parents were going to hold a press conference about my failed relationship with Dean? I didn't know whether to be terrified or humiliated. A mixture of both felt appropriate. "Why does anyone have to know anything? It's *my* life."

Dad clapped his hand on my leg. "I know, Dre. I wish you weren't caught up in this. We could involve Secret Service, try to investigate and find the person who messaged Dean about your relationship, but that would draw *more* attention to you."

"No," I said. "I don't want that."

"Neither do the Arnaults."

I bit off a caustic laugh. "I bet. How did she sound? Was she worried about Dean at all or only about how this would affect the election?"

Instead of joining my "I hate Janice Arnault" party, Dad threw me a disapproving frown. "It's tough for parents too, you know."

"What?"

"Finding out your child is going to have to travel a more difficult road than you'd planned for them. I wouldn't change

358

a single thing about you, Dre, not even your smart mouth, but that doesn't mean I don't worry about you. Just like the Arnaults worry about Dean."

"But you accepted me," I said. "I came out and you accepted it, and I never once felt like you didn't love me. How do you think that conversation went at the Arnault house? How do you think Dean's feeling right now?"

"Give them time," Dad said. "They'll come around."

"What if they don't?"

The lines around Dad's eyes and mouth deepened. I'd always known how lucky I was that my mom and dad had never tried to force me to be someone I wasn't. That they'd let me explore who I was without limits, and that I'd never felt that they wouldn't love me if the person I became didn't match up with the person they'd thought I would be.

"Janice and I have a lot of differences, but the one thing we have in common is that we both love our children more than anything in this world." Dad paused a moment, then added, "And if things do go badly for him, just know that your mom and I will do what we can to help."

I hoped Dean was okay. I was worried about him, and I was proud of him, but mostly I hoped he was okay. He hadn't wanted to tell anyone and now his mom was going to tell everyone. It didn't matter that we were only seventeen; people were going to talk about us. They'd devour the juicy drama of our lives, and there wasn't much we could do to stop it. And all I wanted to do was hold his hand and tell him we'd get through this together, but there was no "us" anymore.

"You really cared about him, didn't you, Dre?"

I nodded. "I still do."

"While I don't approve of the sneaking around, I'm glad you boys found each other, and I'm sorry that it ended."

"What do you think's gonna happen?" I asked. "After the press conference?"

"With what?"

"The election?" My phone buzzed on my nightstand, but I ignored it. Probably just Mel.

I had to change the subject so that I didn't lose myself thinking about Dean. He'd made his decision to end us because he was scared of people finding out. Now that everyone was gonna know, he might reconsider. He'd already said he was sorry. But, no. I couldn't think like that. He hadn't even given me a chance to fight for us. He'd just broken up with me and that was it. I wasn't giving him a second chance to hurt me.

"I don't know," Dad said.

"Do you think it'll help McMann?"

"People are strange, Dre. They don't always do what's in their own self-interest. They vote for the person they think is the most attractive or the person they think they'd most enjoy having a beer with, and not for the person who is the most prepared to do the job or who would keep them safe. I don't think there's any way to predict how voters are going to react."

"Did I cost you the election?"

"If you being happy is the price of losing, then I'm happy to lose."

"But I'm not happy," I said. "I miss him."

"I know you do." Dad's phone rang. His ringtone was still set to the default because he didn't know how to change it and was useless when it came to that stuff. He looked at the screen. "I have to take this."

Even though I missed Dean and was about to have my life splashed all over everywhere, I felt better now that my parents knew. I wasn't sure how I felt about *everyone* knowing, but there wasn't a whole lot I could do to stop that.

"What?!" my dad was saying into the phone, and my own phone was buzzing again. I was about to see what the hell Mel thought was so damn important when my mom showed up.

"They're all over Facebook and Twitter. They're everywhere."

"What's all over Facebook and Twitter?"

I grabbed my phone and there were a million messages from Mel, but also some from Julian and Dhonielle and Caleb asking me if I was okay and why didn't I tell them and wondering if it was even true.

I clicked on one of the links Mel had sent me and there we were. Me and Dean. Kissing. I recognized the selfie we'd taken in his bedroom right before his friends had shown up. It'd only been up for an hour and it had already been shared over fifty thousand times.

"Well," I said. "So much for the press conference."

I SPENT THE following day hiding. Wallowing would be more precise. Pictures of Dre and me and our personal conversations from Promethean had been posted and reposted all over the internet, seen and spread by millions. We had become an internet meme, the punch line of an *SNL* Weekend Update joke, and our official ship name was Drean, which sounded to me like a household cleaning product. My mother and Dre's father had canceled their planned joint press conference and had instead issued separate statements confirming that Dre and I had been in a relationship, condemning the leak of our private conversations and photos, and asking that we be left alone.

I made the unwise decision to read the comments. My relationship with Dre was "so effin' adorable!!!!" or "a perversion of God's word" or "kinda gross; that Dean guy is weird" or "unimportant . . . the election's in 3 weeks . . . don't we have better things to worry about????" Support for my mother among Republicans fell when she refused to issue a statement renouncing my new "lifestyle." I'd expected Mr. Rosario's supporters to be more open-minded, but while they weren't disgusted by Dre's sexuality, they most certainly didn't approve of him dating me. Mr. Rosario's full-throated support of his son seemed to cost him almost as much as my mother's silence regarding me had cost her.

McMann, however, surged in popularity while he fanned the flames, slyly insinuating that my relationship with Dre had been a cover that had allowed our parents to work together to undermine him. It was the most ludicrous conspiracy theory I had ever heard, and I doubted many people believed it, but some did. Enough to ensure the vote would be split.

"Dude, you reek."

I was lying in the sun on the patio when Tamal's long shadow fell across me.

"I'm wallowing," I said.

Tamal had been trying to reach me since the photos and messages had leaked, and I'd been ignoring him because I didn't want to see him. I still didn't. "Marinating is more like it."

I kept my sunglasses on, hoping Tamal would take the hint and leave, but he sat on the lounge chair beside me. "I've been calling you."

"And I haven't been answering."

"Leaving me no choice but to drop by."

"I wish you hadn't."

"Your dad called me," Tamal said.

"Whatever. Please just leave me alone."

Tamal huffed and then stood. I thought I had finally gotten through to him and that he was going to leave, but I was wrong. Tamal scooped me up like I weighed nothing. I flailed, my brain trying to catch up to what was happening, and then I was flying through the air. I was hitting the water. I was sinking to the bottom of the pool. My reflexes kicked in and I swam to the surface, gasping for breath.

"What the heck, Tamal?" I tried to climb out of the pool, but Tamal pushed me back in.

"I'm not letting you out until you quit this shit."

"Leave me *alone*!"

Tamal pushed me away from the wall again. The shock of the cold water had cleared the fog from my head, and I'd lost my sunglasses somewhere in the water. "Why didn't you tell me about you and Dre? I thought I was your best friend."

Every time I tried to swim to a place Tamal wasn't so I could climb out of the pool, he ran around to where I was and pushed me back in. The chill was starting to make me shiver.

"You are."

"Did you think I wouldn't get it? That I'd quit being your friend?"

"No."

"Then what, Dean?"

"I was scared you'd tell someone. You kind of have a big mouth."

Tamal looked like he wanted to argue the point, but instead said, "Yeah, okay. Fair point. I just hate keeping secrets, you know?"

"I know," I said. "I wanted to tell you, though. I really did."

Tamal leaned over and offered me his hand. He helped me out of the pool, and I ran to where we kept the towels so that I could try to get warm.

"So you and Dre are a thing?"

"Were."

"Why were?"

I didn't even need to ask Tamal if he had read the leaked messages because I knew he hadn't—that's the kind of friend he was—so I explained everything. The difference between telling Tamal and telling my parents was that I felt no fear with Tamal.

"Wow, you really messed up," he said when I'd finished.

"I know."

"How're you planning on fixing it?"

I shrugged because, maybe for the first time, I had no plan. I didn't know what I was supposed to do. I didn't know what came next.

"You've taken care of your phone, right?"

"Not yet," I said. "I meant to."

Tamal was staring at me like I'd grown a third eye.

"Someone leaked all your personal messages and stuff. Either your phone or Dre's was hacked." He was shaking his head. "How was that not the first thing you did? I'm surprised your mom didn't think of it."

"She's been busy," I said. "Mostly cleaning up my mess, but there's also the debate tomorrow. And I've been—"

"Wallowing."

"Yeah."

"Good thing you got me, then."

Tamal and I went inside. He hooked up my phone to his computer and ran a program that I didn't recognize. While we were waiting, he said, "You seen the newest Dreadful Dressup?"

Dre hadn't posted in a while, and I had stopped checking. "There's a new one?"

"It's awesome." While Tamal's program did its work, he pulled up Dreadful Dressup. There was a new set of photos posted this morning. Dre and Mel must have worked all night. And Tamal was correct. It was awesome.

The monster was Jackson McMann. From the front, anyway. The likeness was uncanny and a little creepy. Each subsequent photo moved around McMann until finally showing his back, which was torn open to reveal an impish, grinning, green-skinned monster in McMann's torso pulling tendons in his arms and legs to control him. The inner monster also looked a little like McMann in a strange way. It was brilliant and horrifying.

"Wow."

"Right? I bet McMann is *pissed*."

I was going through the pictures when something caught my eye. I zoomed in as best as I could on the background behind the monster's leg. It was pixelated, but I knew what it was. I recognized the "Arnault/Portman 2020" slogan on the water bottle I'd given Dre. I'd assumed he had thrown it away at the first opportunity. But he'd kept it. He still had it. That had to mean something. I wanted so badly for it to mean something.

A dialogue box popped up with an alert that the diagnostic had finished. I handed Tamal's laptop back to him.

"Bad news and bad news, Dean."

"Bad news first?"

"Your phone definitely got hacked, which isn't a surprise since this thing is older than you are. Seriously, when was the last time you updated the OS?"

I shrugged and tried to appear penitent.

"Well, whoever did it has had access to everything. Microphone, camera, pictures, GPS. They could've listened in anytime to any conversation you were near."

Hacking my cell phone explained how the leaker knew to release the photos and messages before my parents could hold their press conference. I'd blamed Dre for our problems when it had been my fault all along.

"What about Dre's phone?" I asked.

"No way to know. If he's updated his phone's OS anytime

in the last year"—Tamal glared at me—"then the exploit used to hack your phone would've been patched. I'm gonna update yours now and install some security software, but you really need to be more careful."

Knowing that I was responsible for the mess I was in woke me up. The time for self-pity was over. I needed to do something. "When you're done, will I be able to talk to Dre?"

Tamal looked uncertain. "Without knowing *how* your phone got hacked, I don't know that I'd risk it. At the very least, I wouldn't talk about anything important."

"I understand." When Tamal just looked at me, I waved at him furiously. "Hurry up!"

"Yeah," Tamal said. "I'll work on your phone while you go take a shower. You seriously reek, dude."

DRE

ONE OF THE weirdest parts of my relationship with Dean going public was that I'd never gotten to be his boyfriend out in the open. By the time the press got the news, Dean had broken up with me. The media didn't know that yet, but it was only a matter of time before they figured it out and discussed and dissected it until a juicier story fell out of the sky. No one was even wondering where the leak had come from or the impact this was having on my life or on Dean's.

All I wanted to do was talk to Dean, but he hadn't messaged me since telling me he was going to come out to his parents. The irony was that now that I wanted to talk to him, I wasn't sure if he wanted to talk to me.

To keep my thoughts from continuing to circle endlessly around Dean, I went online to moderate the Dreadful Dressup comments, which I was seriously considering shutting off until things calmed down. They were getting out of hand and were way more personal than ever before. Only a handful were even actually about the dressups. Luckily, it was easy to bulk-delete them. Still, I went through them because for every thousand comments telling me I was doomed to eternal damnation, there was one of support. One thanking me and Mel for the work we did. One saying how we'd inspired them to find and follow their own passion. One in a thousand may not seem like much, but it meant everything to me. That one was what kept me from totally falling apart.

This time when I logged in, there were more comments than I'd expected. I was starting to go through them when I noticed I'd gotten the same comment over and over from the same username. The comment? *Dre, you haven't answered my messages, but we need to talk. Please call me.* It was from a user named PatheticMamasBoy.

It was Dean, it had to be. It also could've been a trick. A trap set by a journalist who wanted to score an interview. This seemed particularly likely, especially since my parents and the Arnaults had declared we would *not,* under any circumstances, be speaking to the press. It was a risk, but one I thought might be worth taking.

But instead of immediately calling him, I stalled. I was scared of what he'd say, angry about the last thing he'd said to me, worried of what *I'd* say to him, and kind of proud of what he'd finally had the nerve to say to his parents. I checked the time stamps on the comments, and he'd been sending them every five minutes for almost two hours, which meant whatever was going on, he thought it was important. If I didn't like what he had to say, I could always hang up. I was going to do it. I was going to call Dean. Right after I cleaned my room and washed the dishes.

No. Right now.

I dialed his number.

Dean's face appeared on the screen. His hair was wet and a mess, and his face was pink. As soon as it appeared, so did his smile. God, that smile. I had no defenses against it. It hit hard, and I crumpled.

"Dean?"

"Dre! You need to check your phone. Mine was hacked. That's how they got all our texts and messages." The words flew from his mouth so quickly that they ran together.

"Way ahead of you," I said. "It was time for a new phone anyway."

Dean's lower lip quivered. "I'm so sorry, Dre. I'm sorry for accusing Mel of being the leak and I'm sorry for breaking up with you and I'm sorry for this entire mess."

I wanted to accept his apology. To tell him everything was all right and that it was water under the bridge or whatever, but I couldn't. Not yet. "You bailed on me," I said. "The first time things got tough, you broke my heart."

Those words might as well have been bullets, and I could see the moment they tore through Dean's body. His smile was gone now. "I know. I was scared, Dre. That's not an excuse. I should have trusted you."

"We should have faced it together."

"You're right," Dean said. "I told my parents about being demi. I wish we could have faced *that* together."

"Me too."

"I also told them about us."

"And then someone else told the whole world," I said with a laugh. I wanted so badly to reach through the screen and hug Dean. "How'd your mom take it?"

Dean shrugged. "About as well as you thought she would. Seems you were right about that too."

"I'm so sorry," I said. Normally, I would have taken a victory lap to celebrate being right, but there was no victory in being right about something that caused Dean pain.

"God, I miss you, Dre."

"I miss you too. So fucking much." And then I couldn't hold it back anymore. The tears welled up in my eyes, and even though I kept telling myself to be strong and not to break down, I did it anyway.

Dean said, "I hate that I caused you pain, and I swear I'll try never to do it again. Can you forgive me? Can you give me another chance?"

"I don't know, Dean." Those were the hardest words I'd ever had to say. "I was so hurt when you broke up with me—I'm still hurt—but maybe what you did was for the best. The election's coming up and our lives are so different—"

"I get it." Dean hung his head in defeat and was quiet for a second. "I saw your Jackson McMann photo shoot. It was brilliant."

"Thanks," I said. "Mel came up with the idea."

"And I saw the water bottle." He looked up at me through his soft lashes. "You kept it?"

"Kept it?" I said. "I carry that thing *everywhere*. I drink so much water I'm peeing like a hundred times a day. My mom thinks I have a UTI or something."

Dean laughed his awful, wonderful laugh, and I cracked a smile, forgetting for a moment all the pain, all the trouble being in a relationship with Dean had caused. And I remembered how being with Dean made me feel like there was nowhere else I wanted to be, and no one else I wanted to be with.

"Fuck it," I said. "I don't care who wins the election or who lives where or how many cable news shows know how I feel about you. I don't want to be without you for another second."

"Really?"

"Yes."

Tears rolled down Dean's cheeks, cutting tracks through his beautiful smile. "You are, quite possibly, the most amazing human being I have ever met."

"Possibly?"

"Don't forget," he said. "I have also met Ellen."

Technology was amazing because it meant I could sit

and talk to this amazing boy even though we were miles and worlds apart, but the things I felt for him were too big for words, and the technology didn't exist yet that would let me reach through the phone to show him how I felt. All I could do was smile and laugh and bask in the glow of being part of Dean's life again.

I could've stared at his face until my battery died, but there were other things we had to deal with. "So what do we do now?"

"I think Jackson McMann is Pyrogue."

"Mel thinks it's McMann too," I said. "I told my dad, but he won't do anything about it."

Dean nodded. "Neither will my mother." A shadow crawled across his face. "She'd prefer to forget the whole thing ever happened."

It was difficult for me to hate anyone, but I kind of hated Dean's mom right then. I was sure he'd tell me everything she'd said in his own time, but I didn't need to know the details to see how much her reaction to the truth was affecting him. "Dean . . ."

"It's fine," he said. "Let's focus on McMann. I have an idea about that." The dark clouds parted, and he was my Dean again. "Do you think your father would allow you to invite Mel to the debate? I know it's short notice."

"I can swing it."

"Good. We *must* expose McMann. But in order to do so, we need his phone or computer so that we can prove he sent the messages as Pyrogue or that he was the one who leaked our pictures and messages."

"Agreed," I said. "How?"

Slowly but surely Dean's smile returned, creeping up like the dawning sun, just as beautiful and just as bright. "Do you still have Promethean on your phone?"

DEAN

EVERYTHING NEEDED TO be perfect. My mother wouldn't accept anything less. No distractions, no mistakes. Not tonight.

The third debate was being held at the University of Washington in Seattle as a concession to McMann. Not that the city had rolled out the red carpet for him. My father had agreed that I could bring Tamal and Mindy as my guests, and all my mother had to say on the matter, though not directly to me, was that she hoped they would keep me away from "the Rosarios' child." She couldn't even call Dre by his name. He was just "the son" or "that troublemaker" or, when she saw him in pictures, "him," spoken with the same loathing that befouled her words when she mentioned McMann.

My mother's instructions, delivered through one of her

aides, were that I was to remain in the greenroom at all times. Unfortunately, I was going to have to disobey her wishes in order to do what I had to do.

"I need to use the restroom." Mindy, who was wearing a sweet blue dress that made her look like a doll, which really conflicted with the Mindy that I knew privately, rose from the chair she had been sitting in, and left without waiting for a reply.

"That girl weirds me out," Tamal said. "One day I'm going to read a story about how she wound up a serial killer."

"Or the CEO of a wildly successful company."

"Same skill set."

"Either way, I'm glad she's on our team."

Tamal leaned toward me. "Do you think this will work?"

I chuckled. "Probably not. Are you having second thoughts? I would understand if you wanted to back out."

"You're my best friend, Dean. You don't bail on best friends."

"Not even when it means committing a felony?"

Tamal waved that off like it meant nothing. "Your mom will pardon me after she wins the election."

"*If* she wins."

"You're right," Tamal said. "I should suck up to Dre just to make sure I've got all my bases covered."

My phone vibrated. I picked it up and checked the screen. "Shoot. Mindy forgot her purse." Mindy's silver clutch was wedged between the cushions in the chair she had been sitting in. "I'm just going to run it to her."

Tamal pulled his laptop out of his backpack. "Fine. Whatever. I'll just be here playing games."

When I neared the door, one of my mom's aides stopped me. He was a younger guy who looked like he took his job way too seriously. "Sorry, Dean. I can't let you leave."

I held up the purse. "Mindy forgot her purse."

The guy shook his head. "Then she can come back and get it herself."

I lowered my voice. "She kind of needs something that's in here. Something personal." I let his mind fill in the blanks. I didn't exactly lie. There really was something personal in Mindy's purse that she needed. If this guy thought that thing was a tampon, I was fine with that, though I would never understand why they made some men so squeamish.

The guy grimaced. "Go. But be quick."

"Understood."

Navigating the stadium at the University of Washington was easier than the one at UNLV had been, and I didn't get lost once. I did, however, have to make a detour when I nearly ran into my mother, father, and Nora. I didn't know where they were going, but I was grateful they hadn't seen me. That would have ruined everything.

My destination was exactly where the map I had downloaded online had said it would be, and I stood outside in the hall trying to slow my hummingbird heart. It beat with fear and anticipation. It beat for the person on the other side of the door.

I opened the door and walked in.

DRE

"DO I LOOK okay?" I asked Mel. "Because I feel like an investment banker."

Mel and I were sitting in an empty office that looked like it belonged to someone who did payroll or another type of administrative job. It wasn't a big office, but it was large enough for us to work.

"For the millionth time, you look fine."

"Okay, but I don't want to look fine. I want to look appropriately professional but with style. I want to look—"

The door opened. Mel and I both turned toward it, the lie we'd prepared on our lips in case it wasn't someone we were expecting. Thankfully, we didn't need the lie.

Dean walked in, shutting the door behind him, and then just stood there wearing an expression that was equal parts bashful and nauseated. He looked ridiculously handsome in his gray suit, with his hair parted perfectly.

"Hey," he said.

"Hey."

"I like your suspenders."

"I like your tie," I said. "It's giving me corporate tyrant ruling over an evil empire vibes."

Mel threw up her hands. "For fuck's sake, just hurry up and kiss so we can stay on schedule."

Dean rushed to me, and I threw my arms around him and I was kissing him again and then I was punching him in the arm for breaking up with me in the first place, followed by more kissing.

"I'm so sorry." Dean held my face in his hands and kissed my forehead.

"I get it," I said. "I should've been more understanding of what you were going through."

Mel cleared her throat, and I stood aside and motioned at her. "Dean, I'd like you to meet my best friend, Mel."

Dean offered her his hand because of course he did. I was surprised when Mel shook it. "Your mom's agenda is the worst. If she wins, I will use my friendship with Dre to protest her at every opportunity. Also, if you hurt Dre again, I will make your life miserable."

"My life was pretty miserable without him," Dean said.

Mel leaned in, still holding his hand, and lowered her voice. "You have no idea what real misery is."

Dean looked a little shaken. "Is she serious?"

Mel drew her finger slowly across her throat while grinning. She was enjoying herself entirely too much.

"All right, Mel, you can finish threatening my boyfriend with unending torment later," I said, prying them apart. "Should we get started?"

"I'm ready," Dean said, keeping one eye on Mel.

"Sure, whatever," Mel said. "But I feel like I should say, again, that this is bonkers and we should find another way. *Any* other way."

I'd already tried convincing Mel this plan was our only option, so I just shrugged. Dean still had some fight in him to spare, though.

"If we don't stop McMann now, we won't get another chance." Dean looked determined but less optimistic than I was expecting. "Heck, the election is in a couple of weeks. We may already be too late. But we still have to try."

Mel wrinkled her nose. "Yeah, okay. No more speeches from you. Get in the chair, we don't have a lot of time."

DEAN

I DIDN'T KNOW what the future held for Dre and me, but I wanted to explore it with him. I wanted to explore who I was and who he was and who we could be together. As I walked out of that room, leaving Mel and Dre behind, I was sure of nothing but that.

I wheeled a mop bucket in front of me, limping slightly as I made my way down the hall. Gray hair tied off in a ponytail hung down my back, and my suit was covered by a pair of dingy overalls. No one paid attention to me. Those who saw me moved out of my way as if I were surrounded by a repulsor field.

This time, as I approached the door, my heart was beating normally. I wasn't scared. Seeing Dre and not knowing if he could forgive me, facing my mother and telling her I wasn't the son she expected me to be, those situations were scary. This was a breeze.

McMann's name was on a sign taped to the side of the door of his greenroom. I passed by, looking for him, but he wasn't inside, so I moved out of the way to wait. I sent the message: **I am in position.**

I didn't have to wait long before Jackson McMann came striding down the hall with his shoulders back and his head held high, flanked by a stylish young woman who I assumed was his assistant. McMann looked victorious. Like someone who believed he had already won.

"Mr. McMann!" A short man in a clean-cut blue suit made his way toward McMann with his hand extended. "Might I have a moment of your time?"

McMann brushed the man aside as if he wasn't there, as if he was hardly a human being at all, and walked into his greenroom.

"Asshole," the man muttered after him, and left the way he had come.

With McMann finally where I needed him, I pushed my mop bucket toward the open door and walked inside.

"Are you here to fix the toilet?" McMann's assistant asked, and I nodded. "It *should* have been fixed before we arrived. Mr. McMann was very clear regarding his requirements for a private restroom."

"I'm on it."

In fact, Dre was the one who had clogged that particular

toilet. I had overheard my mother complaining about McMann's ridiculous demands to my father and knew he would be given a greenroom with a private restroom. I didn't know how Dre had gotten in, but he had sworn he could do it, and he had.

McMann's greenroom looked similar to the way Dre had described it from the previous debate. More like a computer lab than a place to relax. Men and women were working on their laptops, sitting wherever they could find space, and McMann himself was seated in front of a computer, typing furiously, oblivious to what was happening around him. This was nothing like my mother's campaign, all noise and controlled chaos. McMann was known for his need for quiet, and there was something strangely lonely about watching him sit in a room surrounded by people that didn't speak to one another.

Inside the restroom, I spent a minute working on the toilet even though I had no idea how Dre had clogged it. Nor was I sure I wanted to know. My only job now was to kill time until the next phase of the plan, which was scheduled to begin any minute.

"You asshole!" Dre's voice carried through the room. "I know you leaked the photos of me and Dean and all our messages."

I crept to the door and peeked into the room to watch.

Jackson McMann looked up from his laptop and smiled. "Andre Rosario? Is that you? Why don't you come in?"

Dre looked so dashing in his suit and his bow tie, but

I couldn't think about that at the moment. I needed to be ready.

"Victoria," McMann said. "I need the room. Andre and I have some things to discuss in private."

The assistant, Victoria, herded everyone out of the room, and shut the door behind her. This was *not* part of the plan. But I was still in the restroom, and I wasn't going to let anything happen to Dre.

"Why'd you do it?" Dre asked. I couldn't tell whether the bravado in his voice was genuine or not, but it sure sounded real.

McMann stood and motioned toward the couches. "Sit, Andre. Would you care for an espresso? Some water, perhaps? No? Then why don't we chat for a moment. And Dean, you can come out too. I think you should also be involved in this conversation."

DRE

DEAN SLUNK OUT of the toilet looking utterly defeated while McMann watched, wearing a smug smile I wanted to smack off his face.

"Did you really think that Scooby-Doo shit was going to work?"

"I'm sorry," Dean said to me.

I leaned against him and rubbed the back of his hand with mine. "It's not your fault."

"Your phones, please." McMann held out a black bag. There was nothing we could do but drop our phones in. After we did, McMann sealed the bag shut. "This bag will prevent any signals from getting in or out, allowing us to speak privately."

"I've got nothing to say to you," I said. "Well, okay, that's not true. I've got a lot to say, but—"

"Enough." McMann wore a toothy grin and looked so damned proud of himself. He was only missing a mustache to twirl. "Your ridiculous plan was doomed from the start."

"We almost had you," I said, trying to sound more confident than I felt.

"Did you?" McMann reached into his pocket and pulled out *his* phone. "I still have this. That *man* in the hallway? Your friend. Mindy Maguire, right? She was supposed to lift my phone from my pocket and return it to your greenroom, where your other friend, the one with the foreign name, was going to attempt to hack it and expose me to the world. Isn't that right?"

Dean pulled off the gray wig, dropped it to the ground beside him, and unzipped his coveralls. With the makeup Mel had used to age him, he really did look like an investment banker now. Fine, yes, I was a little turned on.

"We're so screwed," I said.

"You can't do anything to us," Dean said to McMann. "Tamal and Mindy know where we are. If we don't return soon, they *will* tell my parents."

"And I can't wait for that to happen," McMann said. "I can see the headlines now. Children of presidential hopefuls attempt theft of Jackson McMann's property. Foiled by their own hubris." He tossed the phone onto the desk beside him.

"Don't you feel even a little bad about screwing with our lives? How big a dick do you have to be to leak the private pics and conversations of a couple of teens in love to the press?"

Dean's head spun toward me so fast it just about twisted off. "Wait, we're in love?"

I hadn't thought about the words as I'd been saying them, but as soon as I realized what I'd said, my mouth went dry and I briefly forgot about McMann. "I mean, I don't know. It's probably too soon for that."

"Probably," Dean said.

"But if I was starting to fall, would that be so bad?"

"Who will catch us if we're both falling?"

McMann snapped his fingers in the air. The crack forced me back to the present, where we were being held captive by a megalomaniacal dickhead.

"What?" I said. "We're kind of having a moment here."

McMann was sneering and, honestly, it was killing the vibe in the room. "I don't care about either of you *or* your ill-fated relationship. It was simply a means to an end. Imagine my surprise when I caught Andre trying to take a picture of my room during the debate and saw that he was a Promethean user.

"I was hoping to find information I could use against your father, Andre, but I found your conversations with Dean instead."

My mouth fell open. "You didn't need to hack my phone because you had access to my Promethean account!"

Dean shook his head. "But I thought it was supposed to be secure. Encrypted so that no one but the sender and recipient could access the messages."

"How did you even figure out my username?"

McMann shrugged while wearing an evil grin. He looked like a supervillain in that moment, and he probably would've thought that was a compliment. "I cross-referenced every Promethean username in our database against your known social media accounts until I found a match. You also used DreOfTheDead when you linked your Nintendo account."

"Betrayed by my Switch!"

"And with Dean's username, I was able to use an exploit in that pitifully old phone he carries around that allowed me to gain access to his call logs, GPS, camera, microphone. I knew everywhere he had been."

I smacked my forehead. "That's how you knew what we were gonna do."

Dean was looking a little pale. "Tamal patched my phone. He said it was secure again."

McMann was watching us with a bored expression, like we weren't even worthy of his contempt. We were roaches and he was just squashing us under his shoe. "But you planned this ridiculous caper within Promethean. You practically called me up and told me everything you were going to do."

"You don't have access to only *our* Promethean accounts," Dean said. "You have the ability to access any user's messages, don't you?"

"Data is king," McMann said. "I don't sit around reading the inane conversations of average users. The majority of people are boring. Instead, algorithms mine the data for keywords that give me insight into the hearts and minds of the masses. I know what they're talking about, what they're afraid of, what will drive them to the voting booth to cast their ballots for me."

I could feel Dean shaking beside me, though I couldn't tell whether he was trembling with fear or rage. I was leaning hard on my anger because it was the only thing keeping me from collapsing.

"Do you even wanna be president?" I asked.

McMann laughed. "Not particularly. But it's great for my stock prices. And as president, it will be easier to get legislation passed that's favorable to me. Cheaper too."

"All of this is so that you can get richer?" I asked.

"Money is how we keep score."

I looked at Dean. He didn't seem to have anything else to say, and I couldn't stand to look at McMann for one minute longer without the risk of puking.

"What now?" I asked.

McMann seemed to consider our situation for a moment. "We have two choices. The first is that I call Secret Service, tell them that I caught you attempting to break into my room, and we cause a scene involving your parents. The debates would likely be canceled, which would be a shame."

390

"What is the second option?" Dean asked. How he was managing to keep his voice so steady was a mystery to me.

"You leave with your tails tucked between your legs, keeping all of this to yourselves, I win the debate, then the election, and you boys go on with your lives."

I raised my hand and said, "Is there a third choice?"

"No."

Dean took my hand and pulled me toward the door. "We should go, Dre."

"Are we really gonna let him get away with this shit?"

Dean's shoulders slumped. "He already has."

"Correct," McMann said. He tossed Dean the bag with our phones in it. "You should leave now. I have a debate to prepare for." He sat back down in front of his laptop as if his dismissal had caused us to cease to exist.

Dean opened the door, letting McMann's assistant back in, and we left.

DEAN

DRE AND I returned to our respective greenrooms and waited to be led to our seats where we would watch the debate. Mindy, Tamal, and I didn't talk much, and I didn't see my mother until our escort told us it was time.

"Dean." My mother pulled me aside in the hallway and told Nora to give us a moment.

"Mom."

My mother pursed her lips and stared hard at me, her face an unreadable mask. I didn't know what to expect from her, and I was pretty certain nothing she could do would have shocked me. "You couldn't have found a nice Republican boy to date? I've heard gossip the junior senator from Georgia's got a son who might be your type."

"Would it have mattered?" I asked.

"I *do* love you, Dean."

"All of me or only the pieces your voters approve of?"

She looked like she was trying hard to blink back tears. Her lips moved as if she was going to say something, but before she could, Nora popped in and told us it was time.

Our escort herded us to another spot to wait, where we were joined by the Rosarios and Mel. There was a palpable tension between my mother and Dre's father, but I didn't see the point in pretending any longer. I made my way to Dre and took his hand, daring anyone to stop me.

Jackson McMann was the last to arrive, wearing that self-congratulatory smirk he wore in every photo. He had such a punchable face.

I squeezed Dre's hand. He looked at me questioningly, and I nodded.

Dre cleared his throat to get everyone's attention. "Mr. McMann?" he said. "There actually *is* a third option, and we choose that."

"Excuse me?" he said. Confusion was not a look that suited him well. And as much as I detested McMann's smug face, I didn't want to miss his reaction to any of what was coming.

Dre's father was looking at him. "What are you talking about, Dre?"

I waited for Dre to catch my eye before taking over. "As we speak, a story is spreading across social media about how Jackson McMann used a back door within Promethean, the program that he helped create, to spy on Dre and me for the purpose of stealing and leaking our private photographs and conversations. In addition, he used the same back door to data mine the accounts of *all* Promethean users in order to influence the election."

Nora was first to her phone, followed quickly by Jose. My parents and Dre's parents both still looked perplexed. But it was the look on McMann's face that made it all worthwhile. The smirk was gone, replaced by the shock of someone who had believed he was untouchable. If I'd had a camera out, I would have captured the moment he realized we had beaten him. As it was, his expression will live in my memory forever.

"It's all lies," McMann said. "Unsubstantiated lies, and no one will believe you."

Dre shrugged. "They don't have to believe us. It's your voice doing the explaining."

Dre's mother grabbed the back of his collar and yanked him around to face her. "Andre Santiago Rosario! What did you do?"

"Yes, Dean," my mother said. "Explain yourself immediately."

I felt bad that I'd kept this from her, and I was relieved to finally stop keeping secrets. "Dre and I attempted to tell you that McMann was responsible for the leak, but you wouldn't act without proof, so we devised a plan to prove it ourselves. Tamal discovered that the Promethean app was what had given McMann access to hack my phone, and we used that knowledge against McMann. Even after we had secured our phones, we knew he could still access our conversations on Promethean. In fact, we were counting on it."

McMann looked truly confused at this point, and I almost felt bad for him, but not really.

"That Scooby-Doo shit?" Dre said. "All an act. We played you. You thought Mindy was trying to lift your phone and that you were so clever preventing it, but she wasn't taking anything. She was leaving a wireless mic behind."

Mindy curtsied and then gave McMann the finger. "You've still got my vote, though."

"You also believed we wanted your phone so that we could hack it," I said.

Tamal chuckled. "Like I need the physical device to do that. All your computers are connected to the Wi-Fi." He looked at my mother. "Governor Arnault, would you be interested in a spreadsheet of all the senators Mr. McMann believes owe him favors?"

"I don't think that will be necessary, Tamal, but thank you anyway."

Tamal offered up a shrug. "If you want to take a peek at it, I dumped all his files to LeakBarrel, so you or the FBI or whoever can sort through them."

McMann was stuttering, fumbling for the words to deny our accusations, but the proof was already out there.

"You were so confident you had us that all we needed to do was stand there and allow you to incriminate yourself. It was far easier than I expected." I stood in front of McMann, unable to hold back my triumphant smile. "Would you like to withdraw from the race now or wait until after the debate?"

McMann's skin had gone pale, and his assistant was trying to show him something on her tablet. But he kept looking from me to Dre, his brain attempting to understand the full scope of his loss and to work out where everything had gone so wrong. After a tense moment, he shoved past us and took off down the hall.

"Love wins, asshole!" Dre called after McMann as he fled.

I CANNOT TELL a lie. Watching Jackson McMann run away after we dropped the truth on him was one of my favorite things ever. I don't know how many laws we broke, hacking his computer and recording him without his permission, but either my dad or my boyfriend's mom was definitely gonna be president, so I figured we'd get through this without a felony record.

When they tried to show us to our seats, Dean made some noise until we were seated together. I guess now that our relationship was out in the open, he wasn't willing to go back to hiding, and I was *not* complaining.

The debate started late because while the news of McMann's shenanigans was all over social media, it hadn't yet trickled down to the folks in the audience or to the moderators. An effort was made to find McMann, but he'd cleaned out his greenroom and fled like the criminal he was.

It felt weird sitting there hoping my dad obliterated my boyfriend's mom in the debate, but that was the world we were living in. It wasn't personal. I might not ever like Janice Arnault, and she was probably never gonna like me, but we had to find a way to respect each other while Dean and I were together, which I hoped would be for a long, long time.

After the introductions, the moderators dove right into it. Unlike the previous debates, these questions had all been sourced from the audience and social media.

"This question is from Candyce in Tazewell, Tennessee. She wants to know: How do you feel about your sons dating?"

Dean squeezed my hand. We were sitting right there. Did they really have to bring up our relationship?

"Mr. Rosario, you're first."

My dad caught my eye, saw me sitting with Dean, and he smiled. "I feel pretty great about it," he said. The audience laughed, and I began to relax a little.

"Someone tried to use my son's happiness as a weapon to divide us. Happiness isn't a weapon. Love isn't a weapon. When two people find each other the way my son and Governor Arnault's son have found each other, we should celebrate them, not use their joy to tear each other down.

"The person responsible for trying to divide us chose not

to appear on this stage tonight, but I want him to know that he didn't win. He failed in his attempt to divide us. In fact, if anything, he brought Janice and me closer together, and we've discovered that we have a lot to discuss. Such as how we're going to punish our sons for lying to us and sneaking around." He paused, looking directly at me, which earned him another round of laughter.

"I may not always agree with the choices my son makes, but I will always love him and I will always support him. Unconditionally."

Dad smiled at Governor Arnault as he finished speaking. Fine, whatever, I teared up. It was sweet. And embarrassing.

I felt Dean's tension radiating off him as his mother stepped forward to answer. I didn't know if they had patched up their relationship, but I hoped she didn't say anything to hurt him or I'd have to go all angry boyfriend on her, and I was pretty sure Secret Service would not appreciate it.

"You know?" she said. "I'm not thrilled with it." I was ready to leap out of my seat and go after her, and there was no one who could've stopped me.

"From the moment Dean was born, I started thinking about his future. I wanted him to have an easier path through life than I did. I wanted him to have everything his heart desired and to not have to fight each and every day for it. I believe that's every parent's hope for their child's future.

"When Dean told me about his relationship with Mr.

Rosario, I knew that this was going to make his life more difficult. I knew that he was going to have to fight for his happiness. And I couldn't help feeling like I had failed him as a mother. I thought I could fix it by forcing him back on the path that I had envisioned for him. But there comes a time when a parent has to allow their child to make their own choices, even when we may not agree with the choices they're making.

"If this relationship is what Dean wants, then he is going to have to fight for it. And I want him to know that while it may take me some time to understand these changes and to come around, I will always fight for him and I will always fight beside him, and I will never, ever stop loving him."

A hush had fallen over the audience, and there wasn't a dry eye in the place. Even my dad was dabbing tears from the corners of his eyes with a tissue.

"So, no, I'm not thrilled," Governor Arnault said, "but that's because I happen to think my son is just about perfect and that there's not a person alive who's good enough for him. Though I suppose I'm going to have to give young Mr. Rosario a chance." She pointed right at me. "Don't mess it up, son."

That got the audience laughing again, but she was serious, and I was seriously scared. When I glanced over, Dean was smiling.

"Tomás was right. Love shouldn't divide us. In fact, when we are divided, love is the bridge that keeps us connected.

And I will always love my son."

Thankfully, I wasn't going to have to take down Dean's mom on live television. What she'd said was actually pretty sweet. I still wasn't going to vote for her, though.

"Now," Governor Arnault said, "seeing as our sons aren't running for president, why don't we talk about some real issues?"

DEAN

MY TRAIN WAS late getting into the station. If my anxiety could have sped things up, we would have made the trip in no time, but all it did was make the minutes pass more slowly.

I pulled up the news to pass the time. Another story about Jackson McMann. This time he was being indicted for tax fraud. He was already dealing with multiple civil suits filed against him by his investors, criminal trials for a slew of charges related to his use of Promethean to spy on users, and, to top it off, his wife was divorcing him. I tried to find it in me to have a little compassion for the man, but it was difficult.

My phone vibrated. It was the group chat I was in on Promethean, which was now owned by a nonprofit organization that actually cared about security and had eliminated the code that had given McMann backdoor access.

HotTamale: we're still playing that D&D thing next weekend, right? I got the best character.

Meltdown: yes, but I need your characters soon!!!

MindysGayAF: chaotic evil's the bad one, right?

Meltdown: you can't play chaotic evil, Mindy!

MindysGayAF: try and stop me.

Meltdown: dre!

Meltdown: please explain to these people how this game works???

HotTamale: dean, whatre you gonna play?

PrezMamasBoy: I was thinking I might play a cleric. Thoughts?

HotTamale: i figured you for a paladin.

HotTamale: they're the ones that are all good and shit right?

DreOfTheDead: dean cant play a cleric

Meltdown: ???

PrezMamasBoy: Then what should I play, Dre?

DreOfTheDead: a thief obviously

DreOfTheDead: cause youve already stolen my heart

MindysGayAF: i'm not playing anymore

Meltdown: BOOOOOOOO

HotTamale: take it private you guys

My train finally arrived in Penn Station. I desperately wanted to shove my way past the people in front of me, but I remained patient. It was a skill being Dre's boyfriend had helped me hone.

Staying together hadn't been easy. After the election, we both still had to finish our senior year of high school and then graduate. We were able to spend a little time together, but I spent a few weeks volunteering in the Urubamba area of Peru, working to provide clean sources of water, and Dre went traveling through Europe. We both had our choice of colleges, and while it had been tempting to choose schools that were geographically near one another, we made a pact not to base our decisions on that. I chose Harvard and Dre chose Columbia. We weren't able to see each other every day or even every weekend, but we made time when we could and we made it work.

Our parents had all come to accept that this was the new normal, though my mother was still shamelessly trying to set me up with that Republican senator's son. I doubted our families would ever sit in the White House together sharing a holiday meal, but anything was possible.

Finally, I got off the train at Penn Station and made my way in, keeping an eye out for Dre. We hadn't seen each other for three weeks, and it had felt like forever.

"Nice socks," said a voice behind me.

I pulled up my pants to reveal my bright yellow socks covered in pink hearts. "Thank you. My boyfriend gave them to me."

"Boyfriend? Shucks. The sixes are always taken."

I slapped Dre's arm. "Kiss me before I kill you."

And he did. Dre kissed me and everything fell into place. I

forgot about missing him and how much I hated being apart. I lived in that kiss, ignoring the people watching us. There was always someone watching and taking pictures and trying to write stories about us. I no longer cared.

"Miss me?" Dre asked.

"A little."

Dre rolled his eyes. "All right. I've got the whole weekend planned—"

"Is your roommate going to be there this time? It's weird when he watches us make out."

Dre shook his head. "We've got the place to ourselves."

"Perfect," I said. "I do have homework to do, though, so we have to make time for that."

"Only you would bring homework to do on our romantic weekend."

"Homework is sexy. Philosophy homework is sexiest of all."

Dre laughed because what else was he going to do?

"And we've got the Drag Queens Read event on Sunday morning. Are you sure you want to do this? Your mom is definitely going to see the pictures."

I hadn't told my mother I'd agreed to let Dre dress me in drag so that I could read stories to kids, and I wasn't sure how she was going to react, but I was living my best life and she would just have to deal with it.

"I've been thinking of names."

Dre took my hand and led me toward the doors. "I'm scared," he said. "Let's hear 'em."

"Juno Edid."

"I don't get it."

"Like Betty Don't?" he said. "Betty Don't. Juno Edid. It sounds better when you say it out loud."

"No it doesn't. Next."

"Dinah Meetya?"

"It's fine. You don't need a name."

"Augusta Wind."

"How much worse is it gonna get?"

"Dixie—"

"Nope!"

"I love you, Dre."

Dre leaned his head against my shoulder as we walked, and I had never felt so happy. "I love you too, Dean. You're still not using any of those names."

ACKNOWLEDGMENTS

Writing *The State of Us* has been an absolute joy in every way, but bringing Dean and Dre's story to life wouldn't have been possible without the help of some amazing people.

I want to thank Dave Linker for trusting me with this story, and for his steady guidance throughout. Carolina Ortiz for her exceptional insight and always thoughtful questions. Jessica Berg for pulling everything together and Jen Strada for her copyediting wizardry (and for loving em dashes as much as I do). I also want to thank Corina Lupp, who designed the cover, and Mia Nolting, who provided the illustrations, for creating a cover that is nothing less than a celebration of love.

This is my first book with HarperTeen, and I know that there are a thousand people behind the scenes I haven't had the pleasure of meeting yet who have been and will be absolutely instrumental to *The State of Us*. I hope that I'll get to continue working with you all so that I can one day thank you in person. Until then, thank you for all your hard work. It means the world to me.

As always, I owe endless gratitude to Katie Shea Boutillier, who steers the ship and keeps me from foundering. I also owe many thanks to the entire team at Donald Maass, which has been with me through nine books now, and remains the solid foundation upon which I am able to build my career.

I wouldn't be able to write a single word without the tireless support of my family. They may not always understand what I'm talking about, but they always listen.

In addition to being my first book for HarperTeen, *The State of Us* is also the first book I wrote in full in Seattle, and I want to give a shout-out to the outstanding team at Third Place Books, especially Avery Peregrine, for making me feel so welcome in a new city.

I owe any success I've had to the teachers and librarians whose love and support has sometimes been the only thing that kept me going. The work they do so often goes unrecognized, but I want them to know that we see them and appreciate all that they do.

And, finally, thank you, readers. Dean and Dre exist because of you.